She stared back at him, her big brown eyes filled with defiance, her hair down around her shoulders, her legs visible beneath her tussled skirts.

She was small and shapely, the perfect pocket Venus, exactly the kind of woman he found most attractive.

He'd played his part, but his threats failed to work.

He'd torn her clothing. He'd touched her soft, warm skin. He'd breathed in her scent and memorized her curves, all the while his wits forming images of hot desire.

He hadn't wanted to stop. Antoinette Dupre, voluptuous, her skin creamy all over, her long brown hair a veil about her, her eyes heavy-lidded and her coral lips parted.

She was perfect and he wanted her . . .

SARA BENNETT

HER SECRET LOVER

AVON
An Imprint of HarperCollinsPublishers

This is a work of fiction. Names, characters, places, and incidents are drawn from the author's imagination or are used fictitiously and are not to be construed as real. Any resemblance to actual events, locales, organizations, or persons, living or dead, is entirely coincidental.

AVON BOOKS
An Imprint of HarperCollins*Publishers*
10 East 53rd Street
New York, New York 10022-5299

Copyright © 2008 by Sara Bennett
ISBN 978-0-06-133689-8
www.avonromance.com

First Avon Books paperback printing: November 2008

Avon Trademark Reg. U.S. Pat. Off. and in Other Countries, Marca Registrada, Hecho en U.S.A.
HarperCollins® is a registered trademark of HarperCollins Publishers.

Printed in the U.S.A.

10 9 8 7 6 5 4 3 2 1

This book is for May Chen, my editor at Avon, for her enthusiasm and cheerfulness, and always with the right word to say when I need it. Thank you!

HER SECRET
LOVER

Chapter 1

June 1851
The road to Wexmoor Manor, Devon

Antoinette Dupre closed her eyes behind her spectacles, shielding them from the flickering light as the sun dipped lower through the trees. Not far to go now. Lord Rudyard Appleby's manor was isolated, well off the main highway, which was one reason she was riding in a coach instead of traveling by steam train.

The other reason was that she was a prisoner.

She didn't want to go but she had no choice; she was completely in the power of Lord Appleby. And the most frustrating thing about that was she'd finally discovered a way to destroy him once and for all, but before she could put her plan into practice, he had sent her away into deepest Devon, to his house, Wexmoor Manor.

She put a hand to her bodice, feeling the reassuring crackle of paper. The letter was still there, safe. Her ticket to freedom, and more importantly, the freedom of her younger sister, Cecilia.

Thinking of Cecilia made her smile despite her dire situation. Her sister, three years younger than Antoinette, would think this a great adventure—traveling alone in a coach to an unknown destination—but then Cecilia, tall and fair and vivacious, was very different from Antoinette. Antoinette, small in stature, with glossy brown hair and brown eyes, was by nature serious and rather bossy and took her responsibilities to heart. Always as neat as a pin, still she struggled with a figure that was definitely more hourglass-shaped—dumpy if you were being unkind—than the fashionable ideal of slender and willowy. She did have one weakness, a compulsion she couldn't seem to resist and which she blamed on her ancestress, a mistress of King Charles II. Fine undergarments. Silk and lace and satin, frilly and feminine. Sometimes she wondered what it would be like, to hold a man in thrall, to give yourself over entirely to the sensual side. But, as it seemed unlikely Antoinette would ever know the answers to those questions, she contented herself with indulging in her secret wicked pleasure.

She took off her spectacles and pressed her fingers to her eyes.

The worst of it was she had no one to talk to, no one to trust. Cecilia was safely tucked away in Surrey with her governess, Miss Bridewell, and other than those two, Antoinette had no one else she dared unburden herself to. These past few weeks in London she'd been watched continually by Lord Appleby's servants, and she didn't expect

Wexmoor Manor to be any different—worse, because at least in London she'd been able to go about, even attending the opening of the Great Exhibition, and enjoying the new sights and sounds.

But that was before she'd understood Lord Appleby's true intention in inviting her to his Mayfair house.

Suddenly the coach lurched. Antoinette dropped her spectacles. Outside there was a popping noise, followed by shouts from the coachman and his boy. She leaned forward to grasp the window frame, just as a galloping horse drew alongside the coach. The rider wore black, everything black, including a black mask covering the upper half of his face. He kept pace with the coach, and although her poor eyesight made him appear blurry, there was something almost mesmerizing about him. And then he leaned down and stared at her through the dusty glass.

And smiled the smile of a dangerous predator spying his prey.

He was there for only a heartbeat, and then he'd spurred his horse on, but it was long enough. Antoinette felt as if his regard had burned itself into her skin. As if he had left a brand upon her.

Confused, startled, her heart thudding, she pressed herself back into the soft leather of the seat. She told herself that this was England in the reign of Queen Victoria, and highwaymen belonged to an earlier and more lawless age. Or was this isolated corner of Devon yet to catch up with the more civilized parts of the country?

But if she was imagining things, then so was the coachman. Antoinette clung to the strap, bracing herself against the wildly rocking vehicle as the driver attempted to outrun the highwayman. Her straw bonnet slipped off as they tipped dangerously around a corner, and there was a loud bang as the coachman's boy fired his blunderbuss. Antoinette squeaked, trying to see beyond the window, but it was all a blur of trees and earth and sky. And then the coach began to slow until eventually it shuddered to a halt.

Antoinette sat a moment and caught her breath, wishing she could loosen her stays beneath the tight-fitting bodice of her tan taffeta and emerald green velvet traveling dress. Her hair, a moment ago neatly pinned and parted, was hanging down, hampering her movements, and her skirts and petticoats were tossed and tangled, displaying far too much silk-stockinged leg above her lace-up boots.

What now? she asked herself. Was she to cower inside and await her fate? Practical, sensible Antoinette had never cowered in her life. Bad enough that she'd been sent into the country to a place she didn't know by Lord Appleby, a man she detested, but to be trapped inside her coach by an anachronism? No, she wouldn't have it.

Antoinette released the catch on the window and after a brief struggle forced it down.

Cold, moist air wafted in, and with it the pungent sting of gunpowder. Undeterred, Antoinette stuck her head out of the coach. The scene before her was chaotic. The coachman and his boy were on the ground, hands in the air, and the masked man on the horse was pointing a brace of pistols at them. "Be silent," she heard him order in a gruff voice as the coachman began to argue.

Antoinette's mind worked furiously. Was he after her money and her valuables? She'd brought so little with her. Most of her luggage was still in London, and her scant pieces of jewelry were locked in Lord Appleby's safe.

The two men had turned their backs to the highwayman, and—she peered hard with her naked eyes, trying to make out the scene—he began to tie their hands. This was ridiculous. Antoinette turned away, searching for her spectacles, telling herself that if she could see him properly she would feel braver. She did not for a moment imagine she might be physically unsafe, or in any danger of being molested.

Unlike Cecilia, Antoinette was not the sort of woman men glanced at twice. Well, not usually. There *was* the time when Mr. Morrissey developed a strange obsession with her, and began to write very bad poetry in her honor, but everyone knew he was a little odd, and besides, he soon forgot her when the vicar's lovely wife arrived in the village . . .

The coach door was flung open. Her thoughts froze; Antoinette gasped. He was leaning in, looking at her, and despite the lack of clarity in her vision—or perhaps because of it—he was even bigger than she'd thought. He cut out the light and filled the door space, his hands gripping the frame, a pistol dangling casually from his fingers.

What did you say to a highwayman? For some reason the proper form of address escaped her.

"Give it to me," he said in a deep voice.

"Give it . . . ?" she echoed in a whisper.

His tipped his head, and she knew he was taking in her disarray. She sat up straighter, brushing down her skirts and pushing back a long strand of hair. When she looked at him again he was smiling, but it wasn't the sort of smile a gentleman would give a lady.

"I know you have it," he said in that same deep, slightly husky voice. "The letter. Give it to me."

Shock froze her. *He knew!* She only just prevented herself from reaching up and clutching the letter against her skin in its hiding place inside her bodice.

"Who—who sent you?" she demanded shakily.

"Who do you think?" he mocked.

Lord Appleby. She hadn't been so clever after all. He knew she had in her possession the letter that could destroy him, and he'd sent this man after her to fetch it back. What better way to dispose of the evidence and her chance to use it than to stage a robbery? Oh, he was very clever.

But she couldn't allow this to happen. It was Cecilia's future that was at stake, as much as her own.

The big man was climbing into the coach, and his broad shoulders blocked out the light. There was something very menacing about him, she thought, as she blinked up at him, her mind racing as fast as her heart, searching for a way out. He slipped the pistol into his belt and drew off his gloves, slowly, while she watched. When he was finished he casually reached forward and put a hand on her knee.

His skin was hot, his bare fingers thick and blunt. It was his touch as much as the unexpectedness of it that shocked her. She jumped back, pressing herself into the farthest corner.

His masked face loomed closer, and she could see the glitter of his pale eyes through the slits. His mouth was no longer smiling now but held in a straight line, grim and determined.

"Give me the letter. Don't make me search every inch of you, because I will. *Every inch.*"

The threat was no idle one, and Antoinette knew the sensible thing to do would be to hand over the letter. But she didn't feel sensible. She was desperate and frightened, and the letter represented her one last chance of escape. Lord Appleby had already destroyed her reputation and ruined her good character. What did it matter what this man did to her?

He was watching her closely, trying to read her thoughts. She tipped up her chin and stared back at him. "I don't believe that even a man as low as you would molest a lady who had done you no harm," she said, with barely a tremor in her voice.

He gave a soft, breathy laugh. "Wouldn't I, my little brown sparrow?" He flicked at a fold of her tan skirt. "Believe me, Miss Dupre, I would do anything to get that letter back."

He knew her name!

If she had been in any doubt before, then she was no longer. Lord Appleby was behind this. Strangely, with cold, hard certainty came a reduction in her fear. Antoinette knew she could not allow him to take the letter, not willingly anyway, and whatever he did to her, she would have to bear in brave silence.

Antoinette shook her head, her refusal in her expression and the stubborn jut of her chin.

He didn't try to talk her out of her stance; perhaps he knew it would do no good. Instead he lurched across the space toward her, grasping her arms, his big body heavy as he pressed upon her smaller form. She struggled with him frantically. Her straw bonnet, still dangling around her neck by its ribbons, was crushed between them.

He gripped at the cloth of her bodice.

She felt him tense and tug. Violently. There was a ripping sound. Shocked, she stared down. The tan taffeta with green velvet trimmings was hanging open. Her peach silk chemise, also torn, gaped open, too, disclosing the crisp lace of her corset, while over the top spilled a great deal of her bosom.

"There," he said breathlessly. "I warned you."

The letter! Where was it? Antoinette dared not look. Perhaps it had fallen down into the folds of her skirt, or behind the cushions of the seat. He must not find it. Nothing else mattered . . . *nothing* . . .

"Do your worst," she heard herself say. "Search every inch of me, if you must. I will never give up the letter."

He gritted his jaw and she tensed, preparing herself for what he'd do next. Then he reached out both hands and planted them full on her breasts.

She gave a little scream.

Hastily he withdrew. "Tell me and I'll leave you be."

She said in a shaky voice, "I'm not afraid of you."

His mouth curled. "Liar."

He lifted his hands, watching her, and moved forward. She held her breath, every sense alert, every nerve tingling with what was about to come. As his hands closed over her tender flesh once more, she made a sound in her throat. He groaned, softly.

Cautiously she flicked him a look from beneath her lashes. He looked disconcerted, as if he'd surprised himself. Then his broad chest rose and fell heavily, and his pale gaze lifted to hers from behind the black mask. He looked younger than she'd imagined him to be, only a couple of years above her twenty. She saw something that caught and held her; he seemed familiar in a way that she knew was impossible and yet was undeniable.

And in that moment a dangerous spark began to burn between them.

Color tinted her skin. Warmth curled in her belly and climbed higher, suffusing her breasts where his palms rested, making her flesh tingle.

There was a delicious sense of delight about his touch, a wicked wantonness, that was entirely new to Antoinette. The fact that no respectable young lady would allow such a thing to happen, and certainly not enjoy it, didn't matter at all—she had long ago decided she was out of step with the rest of society. Somewhere within the turmoil of sensations a cool voice—the voice of her wicked ancestress—said: *So this is what it feels like.*

"Tell me." His voice was strained, deeper than ever. "Don't push me, sparrow. I really am capable of anything."

She shook her head.

He cursed. "Where is it?" he said, his jaw bunched tight. His hands tightened on her breasts, as if he couldn't help it, and then slid down over her ribs to the narrow band of her waist, feeling for anything hidden beneath her clothing. For a moment he was distracted by the remains of her chemise, the silken peach cloth and fine French lace. He flicked at it with a fingertip.

"A plain brown sparrow on the outside, and a bird of paradise underneath," he murmured. "No lady wears undergarments like this, Miss Dupre. You give yourself away." He leaned closer. "Do you wear perfume, too?" His nose was all but buried in her bosom; Antoinette felt his warm breath on her skin. "The scent of woman," he mumbled. "I wonder what else I will find?"

Antoinette felt as if she should say something courageous but she'd run out of words. Instead she turned her face away, refusing to answer him or look at him. She heard that breathy laughter. And then his hands lifting her skirts.

Such intimacy from a stranger was unthinkable in a world where no woman even dared to show her bare arms in public during the day. As Antoinette held herself tense, waiting for what would come next, she felt his hand brush lightly over her uncovered knee.

"Silk stockings," he murmured. "Very fine. Now these were made to be seen."

"You are insolent," she managed with a dry throat. Her gloved fingers clenched.

He cupped her thigh, ran his hand along it, as if searching for the letter hidden in her drawers. He did the same with her other leg. "Very nice," he said. "Does Lord Appleby buy you these pretty things to wear? Does it give him pleasure to unwrap you, slowly, like a bonbon, and find your soft center?"

Antoinette swallowed. His large hands were at her hips, and she noticed they made her troublesome curves appear less dumpy, while at the same time his touch was sending a maelstrom of conflicting sensations through her. One of them was certainly pleasure, but heightened beyond anything she'd felt before. It worried her . . . frightened her. She had to force herself to be still when she wanted to jump up and run. But was she running from him, or herself?

He made a sound of approval, as if her shape pleased him. Those pale eyes were glittering. He drew his hands downward and his fingers accidentally brushed her most intimate place; or was it on purpose? Antoinette squeaked and jammed her legs together, trapping his hand like a vise. He looked surprised, and then he stared down at his hand, hidden in the folds of cloth, cozy between her thighs, and grinned.

"Go away," she gasped, self-preservation finally tipping the balance on her need to be courageous. Reaching to pull the rags of her bodice about her, she said, "You've searched me and found nothing, now leave me alone."

"I can search you again." There was a hopeful note in his voice.

Antoinette fixed her brown eyes on the pale gleam behind his mask. Was he teasing? Her voice came out louder than she meant: "No!"

He sat back. His hair was wheat fair, with a curl that made it seem to dance around his head in the fading sunlight streaming in the open coach door. When she found herself wondering what it would feel like to run her fingers through it, Antoinette knew she must get him out of her coach.

"Please go . . ."

His smile hardened and his gaze dropped to her thighs. "You are holding me captive, Miss Dupre, and while I am enjoying it very much, it is making it difficult for me to go anywhere."

His hand was still held in that intimate embrace. Antoinette opened her legs and wriggled away from him, pushing down her skirts. "How dare you?" she managed, her voice trembling as much as her hands.

"How *dare* I?" he repeated, and there was something in his voice that warned her to be careful. "Oh, I dare, little sparrow. I am a man who dares anything."

"A man who manhandles helpless women!" she said shrilly, her composure cracking.

He laughed and said, "There's nothing helpless about you. Perhaps the truth is you are enjoying yourself a little too much, Miss Dupre."

The blood rushed to her head—she had to stop him. Antoinette flung herself at him.

He caught her wrists, easily restraining her. Her hair whipped about as she pushed forward again. He grunted and wrapped his strong arms around her, holding her tightly against him, her face buried so deeply into his chest that she could hardly breathe. But still she wriggled and struggled, fighting him and railing against the entire situation she found herself in.

He was too strong. The muscles in his shoulders and arms bunched, and she knew with frustration that he was holding back so as not to hurt her. That was when she gave up.

"Hush, sparrow."

His voice was a deep rumble as he slipped his arm around her waist, supporting her, while he stroked her untidy hair from her face, and then smoothed her damp cheeks with the back of his hand. Until then she didn't realize she was crying. Shattered, feeling like the only survivor of some dreadful shipwreck, she lifted her heavy lids and looked up.

He was bent over her, and now he groaned. She felt his mouth on hers, warm and passionate, exploring her lips and molding them to his, tasting her own salty tears. This forbidden desire had struck like lightning, and sensible, practical Antoinette didn't know how to halt it. Worse, she didn't want to.

She heard him sigh. "You are wasted on Lord Appleby."

The coach door closed, softly, and when she dared to look again the highwayman was gone.

Trembling, frantic, she began to search about for the letter. She found it tucked behind her, crumpled but safe. She clutched it to her, relieved beyond words.

Does that mean he'll come looking for it again?

The voice—her ancestress's voice—made her start guiltily, because instead of being afraid at the prospect of another run-in with the highwayman, she was looking forward to it.

Chapter 2

She was still sitting there, stunned, when the coachman reached her, rubbing his freed hands, worry in his eyes as he took in her disheveled state.

"Are ye all right, me lady?"

Antoinette looked up at him. She hadn't thought of this man as her friend, not after he had caught her trying to sneak out of the second-from-last coaching inn and unceremoniously bundled her back into the coach. "Don't even think of running off, me lady," he'd warned her. "I have orders to shoot, and so I will."

"You'd shoot me?" she'd said in angry surprise.

"Aye." His eyes had narrowed, he had bared his teeth, and she had believed him.

Now, far from being a monster, he looked tired and shaken.

"Me lady?"

"I believe I am in one piece, thank you." If the highwayman expected her to faint or have a fit of hysterics, then he was mistaken; she was made of sterner stuff.

She'd had to be.

Her parents had died when she was barely five and Cecilia just turned two, leaving them to the guardianship of their uncle Jerome, a dreamy, otherworldly man. They had loved him dearly, but he had never been much of a guardian when it came to practical matters. As she grew older Antoinette had taken over the reins of their household and their lives, and so it had been until six months ago when their uncle died and Lord Appleby stepped into their midst.

At first Antoinette quite liked him. Appleby was a self-made man and proud of it, and she found his conversation interesting, although sometimes overly concerned with himself. His manufacturing company was involved in the building of the Paxton-designed Great Exhibition building, and when it opened on May 1 she had hoped to visit London and wander through the many rooms of displays from all corners of the world.

Her uncle Jerome claimed Lord Appleby as an old friend, but Antoinette wondered if they were really little more than acquaintances. They seemed to have met at one of the London clubs, and then Appleby arrived to visit when Uncle Jerome was in his last illness. After that he seemed to be always there, and after Uncle Jerome died, he came to call upon Antoinette and Cecilia, offering in some measure to take the place of their relative.

Cecilia, always eager to believe the best of people, insisted Lord Appleby was just being kind, but Antoinette was more cautious. Money, especially a fortune as large as the Dupre girls' fortune, could cause people to do wicked things. But, as Cecilia pointed out, Lord Appleby, with his London house and country properties and manufacturing business, was already a wealthy and influential man. His latest venture, supplying the cast-iron components for the Great Exhibition building, had made him a household name. Why would he want their money?

When he invited Antoinette to come to London and be his guest at the opening of the Great Exhibition, she'd agreed. As well as the pleasure she expected from attending such an event, she thought it would be a good chance to get to know Lord Appleby better.

And now she knew him better.

Dusk was on the verge of night as the coach began to slow. Antoinette huddled within her fur-lined cloak, fetched from her luggage by the coachman, and peered through the window. She could see a long driveway down into a valley, and there, at the bottom, soft lights shining from many windows. Wexmoor Manor appeared to be a stone building of three stories, old and a little forbidding.

She was here at last.

As they drew closer, servants came out onto the cobbled forecourt and stood silhouetted against the flare of torches. No London gaslights here. The coachman jumped down from his seat and opened the door for her, and as she stepped down, he touched the brim of his hat. In the flickering light he seemed almost shamefaced, as if the holdup had been his fault.

"I hope you'll put what happened out of your mind, me lady," he said quietly. "It were just some lad on a prank, I reckon. Best forgotten."

Amazed, Antoinette blinked at him behind her spectacles. "You could have been shot!"

"Oh well, I weren't, so no harm done," was his answer to that, and he shuffled his feet.

But of course! Antoinette realized with a sense of betrayal. The coachman was in on the plot. Lord Appleby would not have risked his man getting shot. The whole thing was staged for her benefit. Probably the servants at Wexmoor Manor were aware of it, too. Well, she would know the answer soon enough.

"Miss Dupre?"

Antoinette turned to face the figure at the open door, silhouetted against the light; a big woman with a cloud of white hair. "I'm Mrs. Wonicot, the cook and housekeeper here at the manor. Do come inside." Her voice was authoritative as she led the way.

Flaring candles did little to relieve the effect of dark wood paneling and gloomy Jacobean furnishings. A moth fluttered about a vase of sweet roses, the spent petals scattered on the polished floor. Antoinette breathed in a combination of flowers, wood polish and . . . mutton stew. Her stomach rumbled.

"Miss Dupre? This is Wonicot, my husband."

Mrs. Wonicot was trying to capture her attention. She was a big, motherly-looking woman, but there was something cold and suspicious in her eyes, and her mouth had such a disapproving look that Antoinette knew she could expect no welcome here. Her husband, a small man with a balding head, murmured a greeting without looking up from his boots.

"We didn't know you was coming until yesterday. Lord Appleby's letter didn't reach us till then." Mrs. Wonicot's voice was growing chillier by the minute, as if the tardiness of the post was Antoinette's fault. "We've done our best to prepare, of course, but we're a long way from London here. I hope you're not expecting all the comforts you're used to, miss."

"I'm sure there will be no need to—"

"Sally . . ." Wonicot interrupted, and touched his wife's arm in what could have been a comforting gesture or one of warning. He colored when he saw Antoinette watching and went back to staring at his boots.

"We're only poor ignorant country folk here," Mrs. Wonicot finished triumphantly.

Antoinette drew her cloak around her and decided that she was too tired to be bothered with haughty housekeepers. Tomorrow, maybe, they might be able to find some common ground.

"My room . . . ?" she hinted, watching a couple of burly servants carrying her luggage up the oak staircase. There was a small landing at the top, and candlelight illuminated a portrait, a man wearing dark clothing and white lace, glaring down at her.

Lord Appleby's ancestors? But surely not. He was a self-made man and the first of his family to have more than two farthings to jingle together in his pocket, as he was so fond of telling anyone who would listen.

"Your room's up here. This way." Sally Wonicot waddled ahead, puffing as she mounted the stairs, head held high. Wonicot remained in the hall, but as Antoinette followed the housekeeper, she was certain she felt his eyes lift from his boots and fasten on her back.

She was deep in enemy territory here. She could trust no one.

An ache gripped her heart. She missed her home in Surrey. She missed her sister and Miss Bridewell, far more of a friend and confidante than a mere governess. It was Miss Bridewell who had sent her the letter, after discovering Lord Appleby's dark secret. It was Miss Bridewell who had warned her of the dangers of her situation, making Antoinette aware that it was unlikely Lord Appleby would accept the loss of her fortune without a fight. *Tread carefully*, she had written. *Trust no one.*

How right she had been! "This is it." Mrs. Wonicot's sour tones interrupted Antoinette's thoughts as she opened the door at the end of a short passage.

The bedchamber was clean, with a faint trace of lemon polish. The reflected gleam on old wooden surfaces and the scent of newly washed draperies spoke of much effort to ready the room in time. An old four-poster bed with time-dulled red velvet curtains stood in pride of place.

"King Charles slept in that bed when he was at war with Parliament," Mrs. Wonicot offered, noting Antoinette's interest. "Him that had his head chopped off."

The grate was empty and cold, but the evening was mild enough not to require a fire. Candles flickered in a draft from the window, and Mrs. Wonicot hurried to shut the casement, muttering about the dangers of the night air.

"Oh please don't, I enjoy the night air." Antoinette spoke before she could stop herself.

Mrs. Wonicot turned and gave her a disapproving stare. "Be it on your own head then," she warned. "I won't take responsibility if you sicken and die while you're here."

"I'm sure no one would expect you to," Antoinette assured her, and removed her cloak, turning to lay it over a chair. From behind her came a gasp. She looked over her shoulder. Mrs. Wonicot was staring at her, mouth open, hand pressed to her generous bosom.

"Your clothes! Goodness gracious me, child, whatever happened?"

Her tone was so different from the earlier chilly one that for a moment Antoinette was too surprised to answer her. She'd completely forgotten the state of her dress, but now she looked down at the torn bodice ruefully. "We were held up along the road by a highwayman."

The woman swallowed, shook her head. "You must be mistaken."

Angrily Antoinette asserted, "I assure you I am not! A man in a mask held us up at pistol point and demanded . . . Well, he was searching for . . . for jewelry. He tore my clothing and—and man-handled me." She felt her face color.

Mrs. Wonicot appeared to be genuinely shocked, but a moment later her expression hardened and she pursed her lips. "I'm sure it was nothing of the kind," she said firmly, as if daring Antoinette to argue with her. "Just a lad having a lark, that'll be what it was, Miss Dupre. You're not used to our country ways."

"Are these country ways?" Antoinette retorted angrily, gesturing at her torn clothing. "This was no lark, Mrs. Wonicot."

"If you say so." She seemed determined not to believe Antoinette.

"I want it reported to the local magistrate."

The woman's eyes widened, and now there was fear in them as well as defiance. "Whatever for? You're not hurt, are you?"

There was something very wrong about this conversation, Antoinette decided. Mrs. Wonicot was trying to put her off, and the only reason she would do that was if she knew exactly who had held up the coach and was protecting him. Antoinette smelled a conspiracy. As if the housekeeper realized she'd blundered, she turned away, hastily making for the door and murmuring about sending up a supper tray.

A moment later Antoinette was alone.

The room was very quiet. Antoinette wished Mrs. Wonicot hadn't told her about King Charles sleeping here, because now she felt as if he were watching her, with or without his head. But of course he wasn't, and even if he was, Antoinette knew she had more to fear from the living than from ghosts.

She went to the window and stared out into the darkness. Lord Appleby's London house was in Mayfair, where she had truly felt at the heart of a big and bustling city. London never slept. Now all she could hear were the country noises; the murmur of farm animals and the hoot of owls, punctuated by the rustle of the garden.

Was Cecilia looking out over the park back at their home in Surrey? Antoinette prayed she was safe, and that Lord Appleby was too busy in London to think of her.

She remembered the threatening note in his voice when she refused to marry him and hand over her fortune.

"You know, if anything were to happen to you, dear Antoinette, your sister would be the sole heir to your family fortune. I'm sure she wouldn't turn me down. A little persuasion, a reminder of what can happen to young women who are too independent, and she'd soon agree to be my bride. What do you think?"

Antoinette shivered. Appleby was wrong. Cecilia would fight him, just as she had, and that was what had worried her ever since she'd read Miss Bridewell's letter. She knew now what His Lordship did to women who stood up to him.

There was a flickering light through the trees. Thick woods, like a dark bulwark, sheltered the house to the north, and the light seemed to come from within those woods. Was it another house? A neighbor or a tenant? Then she heard the scrape of boots on the cobbles below, and looking down at the forecourt saw the dull glow of a lantern, swinging in the hand of someone walking toward the woods.

For some reason she thought she recognized Wonicot, perhaps the gleam of light on his bald head. Whoever it was, he was certainly in no hurry. Antoinette wondered if he was heading toward the village for his nightly ale, with the added bonus of an hour or two away from Mrs. Wonicot.

She yawned. She was tired; the journey had been an eventful one. She needed to sleep so that she could be alert tomorrow and ready for anything Lord Appleby's servants might have in store for her. Antoinette removed the precious letter from inside her stays and slipped it under her pillow. Tomorrow she must find somewhere safer to hide it.

Until she escaped and made her way back to London.

Chapter 3

Gabriel tore off his mask and threw it into the corner. Frustration and anger, mostly with himself, made him want to smash something. Or someone. Lord Rudyard Appleby would do. How he would love to have Appleby before him now, his prisoner, in chains and groveling for forgiveness.

It was a nice image, but Gabriel doubted Appleby was the kind to grovel. He probably thought he'd done nothing wrong in stealing Gabriel's rightful inheritance. He probably thought himself clever because he'd made Wexmoor Manor his, and left Gabriel with a hole in his heart.

He sank down in the chair in front of the fire and rested his head in his hands. A clock ticked on the kitchen dresser. The cottage was still furnished with his aunt Priscilla's belongings, although she had been dead for many years now. When she'd lived here, and Gabriel was a boy, he'd been fascinated by her. She knew about herbs and incantations, and he was certain she was a witch. Sometimes the girls from the village came and had their fortunes told, although his grandfather didn't encourage it.

"What about my fortune?" Gabriel asked her one day, when he was watching her crush some pungent herb with her mortar and pestle.

She'd looked at him, her pale blue eyes—so like Gabriel's—seeing inside his skull. And then she smiled. "Your fortune? I don't know about that, but I can see your fate. A bird, that's your fate, my boy. A little brown sparrow will be your fate."

Gabriel groaned into his hands and shook himself like a dog.

Was his aunt's prediction finally coming true?

No, it was coincidence, that was all. Antoinette Dupre reminding him of a brown sparrow meant nothing, just another problem to bedevil him. Why did nothing go as planned? The holding up of the coach certainly hadn't. Although the coachman and his boy had played their parts well, and Antoinette Dupre had been there, just as he'd been told she would be, he hadn't been able to get the letter from her.

He knew she had it. A few crumpled pages, written in his mother's sloping hand, the key to regaining his inheritance. All he had to do was take it—by force if necessary. And he'd been prepared to use force, right up until the moment he flung open the coach door.

She'd stared back at him, her big brown eyes filled with a steady defiance, her hair down around her shoulders, her legs visible beneath her tousled skirts. She was small and shapely, the perfect pocket Venus, exactly the type of woman he found most attractive. And his wits went wandering.

Somehow he'd played his part, but the threats he offered in such a menacing voice failed to work. Lord Appleby, he thought, must have promised her a great deal to keep the letter safe. And what better hiding place was there than snug and cozy against his mistress's bosom?

He'd torn her clothing. He'd touched her soft, warm skin. He'd breathed in her scent and memorized her curves, all the while his wits forming images of hot desire. And still no letter.

Gabriel rubbed his hands over his eyes again and sighed.

He hadn't wanted to stop. Antoinette Dupre, voluptuous, her skin creamy all over, her long brown hair a veil about her, her eyes heavy-lidded and her coral lips parted. She was perfect and he wanted her.

Gabriel shifted uncomfortably, his body responding to his thoughts. Pointless pain, he told himself. The woman was Appleby's mistress— he'd seen her in the man's arms with his own eyes. It followed that she was his possession, loyal to him. So how could it be that when he'd flung open the coach door and seen her, knowing all he knew, he'd momentarily forgotten where and what and why he was there?

Instead he'd thought about her and Appleby, and a hot wave of jealousy had washed over him, scalding him, urging him on. *Take her from him,* said the deceptively reasonable voice in his head. *Appleby's mistress for your inheritance; that's fair.*

Was that why he'd kissed her? Even now he remembered the feel of her lips and the sweet promise of her mouth.

His holdup plan was risky, Gabriel knew that, but he felt he had no choice. Once Appleby's powerful friends tracked him down and found him, he'd have to leave the country. He had his escape already organized, but once he was over the channel he'd no longer be able to fight for his inheritance. Appleby would have won and he'd be reading English newspapers in a foreign land and dreaming of home.

"Curse it, no!"

He'd die before it came to that.

He *must* find that letter. The mistress had it and he would find it, even if he had to strip her completely bare to do so.

She deserved to be punished for what she was, grasping and manipulative, out for all she could get. Why else would a woman like her align herself to a bastard like Appleby? Gabriel would take what he wanted from her, and when he had the letter, and his fill of her lush body, he'd vanish like a shadow in the moonlight.

"Master?"

Gabriel jumped up and spun toward the door. It was Wonicot, his sparse hair windblown from the walk through the woods to the cottage, his chest heaving. Sometimes he forgot the servants weren't as young as they used to be; they were so much a part of Wexmoor Manor. Just as he was.

"Wonicot," he said. "What is the matter?"

The old man was carrying a basket, and whatever was in it smelled delicious.

"Sally sent me," he said, setting the basket down on the table. "Me legs aren't what they were, master; forgive me for taking so long."

Gabriel watched him for a moment, but the old servant seemed to be studiously avoiding his eyes. "Have you seen her?" he said sharply.

"Her?"

"You know who I mean. Miss Dupre. Lord Appleby's mistress."

"Yes, sir, she's in her chamber. Says she's tired out, but I reckon Sally's welcome didn't encourage her to stay downstairs any longer." He looked up, his eyes curious. "You didn't hurt her, did you, master?"

"I was looking for the letter," Gabriel said, but even to himself it sounded like an excuse. "She refused to hand it over."

"I see, master," Wonicot replied levelly. "That would account for it then."

Gabriel picked up a slice of bread and dipped it into the bowl of mutton stew.

"Sally said to tell you that Lord Appleby sent down his man o' business last week," Wonicot went on, producing a bottle of claret from the basket, with a glass—one of his grandfather's good ones.

"Did he now?" growled Gabriel.

"Told us he was intending to sell. Saw no reason to hang on to it, he said, a poorly place like this. Needs too much money to put it right, he said. Might be best all round if it were pulled down and leveled."

Although Gabriel didn't reply—he didn't trust himself to—the older man seemed to sense his feelings. "No need to worry yourself, sir," he soothed. "You'll find a way to get the manor back again, and then everything will be right as rain. Your grandfather used to say that things had a way of sorting themselves out for the best."

"You have more confidence in me than I have in myself, Wonicot. I can't even frighten a weak and feeble woman into giving me the letter."

"That's 'cause you're a gentleman, master," Wonicot explained. "You've been brought up to be kind to women, so it goes against your grain to frighten them. And I wouldn't call Miss Dupre weak and feeble. She's got a look in her eye, that one."

Gabriel grinned.

Pleased to see his spirits recovered, Wonicot fussed about the table, pouring the claret.

"Sally wants to know if you'll be coming over to the manor for breakfast in the morning, Master Gabriel?"

"Tell her I will. I wouldn't miss her cooking for anything."

"She'll be pleased. Although . . . are you sure Miss Dupre won't recognize you, master?"

"I'm sure, Wonicot. I'm looking forward to 'meeting' her." He chuckled.

Wonicot appeared doubtful but he didn't argue. "Very good, master."

"And remember who I am, for God's sake. No 'master' in front of the minx."

"As you say, ma—" He stopped himself.

Gabriel watched him totter to the door. Appleby was going to sell his birthright, his inheritance, his life. As long as he could remember, he'd seen himself as the master of Wexmoor Manor, carrying on the long tradition of Langleys who had resided here. The monetary worth of the place was immaterial—Gabriel wasn't a poor man—but in other ways it was priceless. But it wasn't just he who would be affected; there was Wonicot and his wife and all the others who depended upon Gabriel for home and hearth.

Just as Wonicot opened the door to leave, someone else came rushing in. They collided.

"Gabriel—" the name burst out of her before she realized it was Wonicot she'd sent reeling back. She stopped, embarrassed. Young, slim, and pretty, Mary Cooper had light hair and a sweet smile, and she'd been in love with Gabriel ever since he could remember. He had a fair idea what she was doing here and he wished she wasn't.

Wonicot was frowning at her, blocking her way into the cottage. "What are ye doing here, Mary Cooper?" he scolded. "This is no place for a girl alone."

"I was finished," she retorted sulkily, "and Mrs. Wonicot herself said I could go."

"Go to bed, I'd reckon, not out into the night."

"I wanted to see master," she said, with a shy glance at Gabriel.

Thank God Wonicot was here, he told himself. Times had changed. Gabriel remembered how, when he was many years younger, he'd thought no girl could be lovelier than Mary Cooper. They had kissed and cuddled and whispered sweet nothings, but fortunately his grandfather had seen what was happening and informed Gabriel in no uncertain terms that he would not countenance his grandson ruining the servants. Later, when he went to school and to London, he'd met and kissed many other women, and his childish infatuation was forgotten. But Mary had never forgotten; she still loved him.

He supposed it was flattering to be the subject of such single-minded and unswerving affection. Gabriel tried to be kind and patient, but sometimes he wished she'd find someone else to lavish her affection on.

"Mary," he said with a smile, "I thank you for thinking of me, but Wonicot is right. You must go back and—"

"I'm to be her maid, you know," Mary interrupted, with a little bob of a curtsy and a giggle.

"Miss Dupre's maid?" Gabriel said, raising his eyebrows.

"Aye, *her*." Her expression became earnest. "I'll unpack her luggage, and I'll search every inch of it for you, master. If that letter is there, then you can be sure I'll find it."

"Thank you, Mary, I'm grateful, but you must be—"

"I'd do anything for you, Master Gabriel." And she gave him a look so piercing as to be unnerving in its intensity.

Seeing Gabriel's discomfort, Wonicot clicked his tongue and, taking the girl's arm, turned her about. "Good night, master," he said firmly, and closed the door behind them. Gabriel could hear their footsteps receding, and Mary's high voice as she made her protests, and then there was silence again. Not even the wind was stirring the trees in the wood tonight.

Gabriel sank down in his chair and turned his claret to reflect the candlelight. Mary might search Antoinette Dupre's baggage, but Gabriel knew she would find nothing. What he was seeking was kept closer to her person. Warm against her skin. And he was going to find it, yes he was, even if he had to seduce her.

He smiled and raised his glass in a toast. "To seduction," he said, "and the luscious Miss Antoinette Dupre."

Chapter 4

His hand on her shoulder was warm, heavy with promise, as he smiled into her face. "Antoinette," he murmured in his deep, husky voice, "I knew the moment I saw you that you were the one for me."

"How could you know?" she whispered. "No one can know for sure."

"Because you make my heart sing, little sparrow."

In the dream it sounded wonderful, but as Antoinette began to wake she was thinking such words coming from the highwayman's mouth were very unlikely and a little odd. She never expected to make any man's heart sing.

Antoinette was the sort of woman who would run a household capably and well, keep within her budget, and organize her servants so that nothing ever went amiss. People respected her and were a little intimidated by her. Her husband, if she ever married, would appreciate her for those qualities, knowing that she would make his life comfortable and easy. But no, she could not imagine herself being the subject of any heart singing.

She blinked and opened her eyes, and gave a gasp.

Someone was peering down at her, and for a moment her dream and the face became confused. A heartbeat later she realized it wasn't the man in the mask hanging over her but a pretty young woman in a mobcap that barely restrained her blond ringlets. The expression in her dark eyes was so intent it sent a chill through Antoinette.

When she saw Antoinette was awake, the girl's expression changed in an instant. "Forgive me, miss," she said, apologetic. "Mrs. Wonicot sent me up to ask if you was ready for your breakfast tray, but you was sleeping so deep I couldn't wake you."

"I had an eventful journey."

With a smothered yawn Antoinette sat up. The chilly morning light was gleaming through a chink in the drapes, but today there was a welcoming fire burning in the hearth. Antoinette watched the flames dancing, the tension leaving her. Until she remembered where she was: Wexmoor Manor, Lord Appleby's isolated property, and deep in enemy territory.

"What is your name?"

"Mary Cooper, miss," the servant introduced herself. "I'm to help you dress and look after your clothes, and I'm a fair needlewoman. I don't do hair, though Mrs. Wonicot says she can do your hair, if you'd like."

"I can manage my own hair, thank you," Antoinette said pleasantly, hiding a shudder at the thought of Mrs. Wonicot tugging at her locks. "Besides, I thought Mrs. Wonicot was the cook and housekeeper?"

"Well, she used to be some sort of lady's maid in London," Mary Cooper replied disingenuously. "She can name you all the great folk, and all the scandals. Then she decided to turn her back on that, marry Mr. Wonicot, and live at Wexmoor Manor."

So all the talk about the lack of polish here at the manor was nonsense. Mrs. Wonicot was playing games, and Antoinette was more than ever determined not to trust her.

"Will you have your breakfast tray now, miss?"

"No. I think I'll come down, thank you, Mary."

"Oh." The girl looked startled. She chewed her lip. "I don't know what Mrs. Wonicot will say to that, miss. She was certain you'd want a tray."

Antoinette gave her a conspiratorial smile. "Let's surprise her then, shall we?"

"Very well, miss." She went to leave, only to hesitate by the pile of luggage. "I'll unpack these for you. Shake the creases out. Do you want me to find something for you to wear now, before I go?"

"No, Mary, thank you. I'll manage for now."

Mary had picked up the tan dress Antoinette had tossed over a chair back the night before, and now she stared wide-eyed at the torn bodice. "My goodness, whatever happened here, miss!"

Antoinette climbed out of bed. There was warm

water waiting, thanks to Mary, and soft towels and a scented ball of soap. "I was held up on the journey here, Mary. A ruffian tried to rob me."

"Oh, miss." Her eyes were perfectly round.

"I don't know if even your expertise as a needlewoman would be enough to mend that. It is only fit for a rag now."

Mary glanced up at her, and there was something in her face, a flash of emotion that Antoinette could not place before she dropped her gaze once more. "I'll see what I can do anyway, miss."

Antoinette was glad when the maid was gone, carrying the torn dress in her arms, and she could consider her plans for the day. She drew the drapes back and looked out at the first day of her captivity in Devon. The untidy remains of what had once been a formal garden lay beyond the cobbled courtyard, and to one side a rather amazing overgrown hedge. Or was it a maze? Wexmoor Manor must once have been quite something.

A pity she didn't intend to be here long enough to appreciate it.

In order to escape Antoinette knew she needed to know as much as she could about Wexmoor Manor and the people who lived here. Of course they mustn't know her plans; she'd have to lull them into believing she was content to remain here. But Antoinette had no intention of staying. She needed to get back to London and put an end to Lord Appleby's evil plot.

The letter was safe for now, but all depended upon her putting the information to use. If she lost it . . . if it was stolen . . . Antoinette knew that must not happen.

Dressed in a dark green morning dress, with a scarlet shawl about her shoulders and her spectacles firmly in place, Antoinette made her way downstairs. The hall was even gloomier than last night—no sunlight penetrated here, and without the glow of the candles it felt depressing. She hesitated, wondering which room was set aside for breakfast, and then she heard voices drifting along the passageway from the back of the house, where no doubt the servants had their quarters.

Antoinette was used to running her own house and going wherever she pleased in it, but she was well aware Mrs. Wonicot would not appreciate her poking her nose into the areas of Wexmoor Manor where she reigned supreme. Still, she'd determined she would not be intimidated by the Wonicots. With quick, purposeful steps, she set off to seek out her enemies.

Gabriel cut up his sausage with his knife and fork, nodding a compliment at Mrs. Wonicot as he chewed. "Delicious," he said. "You are a fine cook, Sally."

She blushed with pleasure, disguising it by fussing about the stove, shifting pans and pots. "That madam upstairs doesn't think so," she said darkly. "Hardly ate a thing on the supper tray I sent up last night."

"That's 'cause you scared the poor girl half to death," her husband interrupted.

"I doubt anything could scare that one," Sally retorted. "She's far too sure of herself. Cunning, that's her. You can see it in her eyes. Well, she'd have to be, wouldn't she? To catch and hold on to a slippery character like Lord Appleby."

"She didn't want a breakfast tray, neither," Mary chimed in from her perch on the stool by the end of the big kitchen table. "After Mrs. Wonicot offered an' all! Insulting, I call it. Instead she said she'd come downstairs."

Mrs. Wonicot sniffed. "If she thinks she's going to sit in state in the breakfast room, all by herself, then she can wait until I'm ready."

Mary, enjoying herself, held up the torn dress with a little smirk at Gabriel. "She says this is only fit for the ragbag now, master. I reckon I could have it for myself. The cloth is very fine, don't you think? Although brown is such a dreary color."

Gabriel swallowed his sausage. "Brown can be rather becoming," he replied at last, thoughtfully, remembering Antoinette Dupre's dishabille, her brown hair tangled about her, her brown eyes wide. She'd been like a trapped animal, something half wild and desperate hiding behind the veneer of a lady. He'd wanted to kiss her, to taste her. To tame her.

He still did.

"She don't seem like the sort to be Lord Appleby's mistress," Mary's voice interrupted his thoughts. "Nor anyone's mistress, come to that. She looks like a governess."

"But that's a front, don't you see?" Sally Wonicot said with relish. "Underneath all that she's a clever little minx who knows just what to do to make a man her slave."

Gabriel's imagination took flight. He'd enjoy finding out just what clever little tricks Antoinette Dupre did know. He wanted to delve behind her bland exterior and find the wildness hiding inside. Anyone who wore such finely made and exquisite undergarments was not the epitome of a conventional woman, that was for certain.

The door opened.

The woman he'd just been fantasizing about stepped into the kitchen as if she had every right to be there.

Surprise sent Gabriel hunching forward in his chair, and he put a hand up to his face for good measure. Wonicot stumbled to his feet, moving to block his master from the newcomer's gaze, while Sally put her hands on her hips and glared.

"The breakfast room is through the door opposite the stairs," she said frostily.

"Oh? I thought I'd save you the bother and come and join you," Antoinette said with a meaningless smile. She came farther into the room, her wide green skirts sweeping the floor. The sunlight shone through the windows high on the back wall, while the door was open into the kitchen garden, and bright light and herbal smells filled the large, friendly kitchen. Antoinette looked about her and gave a little nod, as if the room met with her approval.

Gabriel watched her sauntering about from the

corner of his eye—the gentle sway of her hips, the way the light gleamed on her neatly pinned hair, the elegant curve of her throat, and the swell of her breasts beneath the tight-fitting green bodice and scarlet shawl. He gritted his teeth, remembering perfectly what she looked like without her clothes.

Wonicot shuffled his feet anxiously and cast Gabriel a quick glance over his shoulder. Gabriel thought he was worrying unnecessarily. He was dressed as a groom, the cap on his head hiding his hair and with a few swatches of coarse black horse hair attached to it for good measure, and the hunch of his shoulders disguising his normally straight posture. Antoinette would look at him and see a groom. But just in case, he'd found himself an extremely smelly jacket—Mrs. Wonicot had insisted he leave it outside—that would drive away even the most tenacious ladies.

He took another sideways glance at her and noticed something he hadn't before.

She wore spectacles. Small, round, with metal frames, they made her brown eyes seem larger than ever. The fact that she hadn't been wearing them when he came upon her inside the coach made Gabriel even more confident he would remain unrecognized.

"I did not realize you once held a position in London," Antoinette said, meeting Mrs. Wonicot's displeasure head-on, "although I can tell an expert hand has been at work about Wexmoor Manor."

There was a silence. Gabriel watched Sally curiously, seeing the struggle going on inside her not to start liking someone she was determined to *dis*like. "I do my best," she said at last, grudgingly accepting the compliment.

"Then I hope Lord Appleby appreciates you."

Wrong thing to say, Gabriel thought, hiding his grin behind his hand.

Sally puffed herself up. "I'd prefer not to discuss Lord Appleby with you, miss. Mr. Wonicot?"

Her husband didn't like being pushed to the forefront, but he took a breath and did his duty. "Oh aye, Lord Appleby is a very busy man," he muttered. "Very busy."

Sally gave him a narrow look; clearly this wasn't what she'd wanted from him.

"I'm sure he is," Antoinette said, "but then so are you. I don't need to stay here if you feel the work is too much for you."

"You are a guest in his house," Mrs. Wonicot retorted, "and you will stay here as long as he wishes it."

"I thought I might travel to the nearest large town," Antoinette countered airily. "I need some bits and pieces."

Sally smiled as she declined the request. "Oh, I don't think so, miss. We haven't time to take you, and I'm sure His Lordship wouldn't want his 'guest' gallivanting all about the countryside."

Antoinette didn't reply, but she must have understood by now, if she hadn't already, that these were no friends of hers. She was Lord Appleby's mistress, sent out of the way when a scandal

threatened to upset His Lordship's business dealings and incur the disapproval of the queen. She
had the letter, and they were unlikely to let her
out of their sight until they parted her from it.

"At home I am quite used to riding about on my
own." Her voice was cool and confident, but the
impression was spoiled by her spectacles slipping
down her straight little nose. Gabriel had never expected to find those round glasses so appealing.

"But you're not home now, are you, Miss
Dupre?"

"What of the garden? I will walk about that."

Mrs. Wonicot was ready for her. "You can if you
wish, but I'd stay away from the maze."

"The maze?"

"Aye," Wonicot piped up, " 'tis the oldest maze
in the county."

Mrs. Wonicot gave him a look. "What Wonicot
means to say is that the maze is not safe. If you
were to go inside it, then it's quite possible no one
would ever find you again."

They all waited, hoping she'd argue some more
so that they could continue to squash flat her pretensions. Instead she shrugged and looked away,
her straight and unflinching gaze settling on Gabriel. Still hunched over his plate, he picked up a
whole sausage with his fingers and crammed it
into his mouth. Her own mouth, lush and soft and
the color of peach flesh, hardened in distaste.

"This is Coombe," Sally explained. "He's a
groom and a gardener, and anything else needs
doing outside. We usually feed him in here, out

of the way. He doesn't like people much. Do you, Coombe?"

Gabriel grunted, and crammed more sausage into his mouth, wiping his greasy hands on his shirt.

Antoinette's face was a picture of revulsion. He almost laughed. "Perhaps it would be better if I went to the breakfast room after all, Mrs. Wonicot," she said, heading for the door. "I can see I am in the way here."

It closed behind her.

Just in time.

Sally burst into snorts of laughter, joined by her husband and Mary. "Did you see her face?" Mary gasped. "I thought she were going to faint! That's the last time she'll come in here."

Gabriel swallowed his mouthful and washed it down with a swig of ale from the mug in front of him. Unlike Mary, he wasn't so sure Antoinette Dupre would be put off so easily. As Sally Wonicot had already discovered, she was a clever little minx.

She would need careful watching.

Gabriel smiled, silently volunteering for the task.

Chapter 5

I t was nighttime, and the house that had seemed so still was now suddenly alive with unseen dangers. The darkness around her could easily hide the watching eyes of strangers, and every creak was a footstep. Antoinette closed her eyes and forced herself to be calm. She was alone, everyone else was in bed, there was nothing to be afraid of. That was why she had waited to leave her chamber until after the long case clock on the landing struck midnight—to be certain she would not be seen.

"We keep country hours," Mrs. Wonicot had announced in that bullying voice when she finished serving supper in the dining room downstairs, as if daring Antoinette to disagree with her. Which meant, Antoinette assumed, that the servants were about to retire and she should, too.

Antoinette, used to friendly chatter and smiling faces and a house full of warmth, was already feeling isolated by life at Wexmoor Manor. Now she faced the prospect of a long evening sitting silently in her room. She hadn't even packed a book to read, and she was certain any letters she might write would be pocketed by the servants or sent on to Lord Appleby.

"Is there a library?" she asked, reluctantly rising to her feet.

A tight-lipped Mrs. Wonicot showed her the library, but stood waiting while Antoinette chose a book. She took her time perusing the titles, expecting Mrs. Wonicot to go away. The collection was a jumble of classics and educational tomes. One volume, bound in tooled leather with gold leaf, purported to be the *History of the Langleys of Devon.* There were books about British birds and plants, about traveling to exotic locations, and on the higher shelves—placed out of reach of young hands—a number of somewhat dubious titles. Antoinette was just stretching for a book called *Nights in the Sultan's Harem* when Mrs. Wonicot's voice made her start. The cook was still there.

"Sir John was very fond of his books."

Surprised, Antoinette looked up, and saw a tear in Mrs. Wonicot's eye. "Sir John?"

"He spent hours in his library. Forgot to eat some days, bless him."

"Who was Sir John? Did he live here?"

Mrs. Wonicot seemed to catch herself, metaphorically closing the door on her innermost thoughts, her expression once more forbidding. "Have you finished now, Miss Dupre? I have to be up early in the morning and I need my sleep."

"Yes, thank you, I'm finished."

But what Mrs. Wonicot didn't know was that

Antoinette had filed the library away for later reference.

Now here she was, back again, alone in the darkness. Even the oil lamp up on the landing did little more than dribble a faint line of light over the first few treads of the staircase. The silence was eerie. But, she reminded herself, she had no choice. The safety of the letter was paramount.

She was certain that Mary Cooper, the maid who unpacked her luggage, had used the opportunity to go through her personal belongings. Of course, unpacking required a certain amount of handling of one's private items, Antoinette knew that, but there were things there was no need to rummage through—such as her writing case—and Antoinette was sure its contents had been searched. The ribbons that held the case together were tied differently and the papers were not quite as neat as usual.

It was possible Mary was simply nosy, but Antoinette believed the explanation was more sinister than that.

The sooner she hid the letter, the safer she would feel. As her insurance for the future, it was her most important possession.

The leathery smell of the library was strangely comforting, and she wondered again who Sir John might have been. One of Mrs. Wonicot's previous employers? Maybe she had a soft spot for him? Had he broken her heart when he refused a second helping of her jam roly-poly pudding, forcing her to flee to Devon and marry Wonicot?

Antoinette giggled at her own silliness and then put a hand to her lips, startled at how loud the sound was in the silent house. Sober now, she ran her hands along the shelves and found the position she'd memorized earlier, then drew out her chosen book. It took a moment to slip the letter between the pages and return the book to its spot. Antoinette straightened the spines, covering any sign that they had been disturbed. Now the only thing to do was to pull a book at random that she could use as an excuse, in case she was seen.

With a satisfied little smile, Antoinette closed the library door softly behind her. There! It was done! It was as she turned that she sensed a change in the atmosphere. As if . . . she was no longer alone.

Her eyes scanned the shadows, trying to pierce their secrets. Was . . . was there someone near the parlor door? Her heart beat harder. She would have waited until daylight to come down here, but all day long she had been followed about, first by Wonicot and then by the groom with the revolting table manners. Whenever she went outside the house, either one or the other of them would be nearby, pretending to be busy with some job but in reality keeping watch on her. And when she went back inside the house, there were Mary and Mrs. Wonicot, popping up unexpectedly, peering over her shoulder. Antoinette was constantly, frustratingly aware of being observed. Spied on.

She'd actually been relieved, when she crept out of her bedchamber after midnight, that no one was sleeping across the threshold. Apparently Lord Appleby's spies needed their rest as much as she—or maybe they didn't expect her to be brave enough to venture out onto the gloomy landing and down into the darkness of the hall.

The shadowy figure by the door hadn't moved. Antoinette seemed to recall noticing some sort of bureau there when she passed by during the day. That must be it. She was simply imagining things. Boldly she took a step toward the staircase, reaching out for the newel post.

A strong arm came around her waist, another closed over her mouth, stifling her scream. She dropped the book. The next thing she knew she was lifted bodily and carried backward. A door opened and closed, and any light from the lamp went with it.

Darkness so thick it seemed to press against her eyes, enveloping her face, making it hard to breathe—or was that his hand? His chest was a hard wall against her back and his arms like iron bands restraining her. The backs of her thighs, in her thin nightdress, were resting against the front of his, and she felt the muscles in them shift and tighten as he stepped backward against the wall.

For a moment, all she could think was that he was so big, so strong, and she felt so small. She would never escape him.

But she wasn't a child. She was a woman with a great deal to live for, and a heartbeat later she was fighting her captor, twisting and turning in his arms, and clawing at his gloved hand as she struggled to scream.

His whisper brushed her ear. "Be still and I will let you go, little sparrow."

Her highwayman!

Her shocked stillness was more to do with the realization of who he was than obedience to his order. But he didn't know that. He took his hand away, slowly, ending with a fingertip caress. As he loosened his hold on her waist, she slid down his body until her bare feet rested upon the toes of his boots, but he didn't release her completely.

"What are you doing here?" She turned her head up toward him, her voice sharp as she struggled to regain her calm.

"I've always wanted to see a rich man's house," he said.

"You're trespassing on another man's property." She felt him shake in laughter.

Suddenly he stepped away from her, leaving her cold and alone. She swayed, disoriented, and reached to steady herself against the wall. She saw now that it wasn't completely dark; there was a faint light coming through the drapes, enough to show her the shape of the furnishings. She recognized her surroundings now; they were in the parlor.

"I wanted to see you again."

His voice was to her left and she turned toward it, every sense focusing on him. She could make out his moving form, large and tall. There was a clink of crystal as a stopper was removed from a decanter, and then the gurgle of liquid being poured into a glass. He was helping himself to Lord Appleby's brandy. Well, what did she expect? Loyalty to his employer? He was an arrogant thief.

"Why did you want to see me again?" she said, more as a distraction than because she wanted to know. Now she'd had time to reconstruct the layout of the room in her mind's eye, and she realized the door was close by. With luck she could escape and give the alarm.

But it was too late. He moved back beside her, standing so close that the warmth of his body made her skin prickle. He reached out, and she felt him touch her hair where it lay loose about her shoulders. He caught up a handful of the soft strands and tugged her closer, not cruelly but hard enough so that she didn't fight him.

"Let me go," she said icily.

"Why? Aren't you curious? I'm much younger than Lord Appleby. You might enjoy having a younger man in your bed for a change."

Antoinette's first impulse was to deny it. The world might believe her to be Lord Appleby's mistress, but she knew the truth. But this was Appleby's man, and she needed to use caution in her dealings with him. She contented herself with "If I wanted another man I wouldn't choose a penniless thief who molests women."

He ignored her; his voice dropped seductively. "A woman like you deserves the best."

"And you are the best?" she mocked.

"Oh yes. I am."

His arrogance knew no bounds. Her heart was beating very hard now, but luckily he couldn't know that, or see her face. "I suggest you go back to wherever you came from, and I will pretend this never happened."

"Come with me. I have my Black Bess outside. Ride with me and the wind."

"So now you are Dick Turpin?"

"Don't you find Dick romantic, little sparrow? I thought all the ladies swooned at the thought of that dashing rogue."

"I am not like all the ladies," she retorted.

"So if Dick Turpin doesn't please you, what does? What do you long for when you are lying awake in the night and there is no one there to see those longings in your face? Who does your body ache for?" He was closer now, his voice soft and insidious, as if he wanted to get inside her head. She turned and took a sideways step toward the door, meaning to escape him, but he came up behind her and his arm slid over her shoulder, diagonally across her chest, and he held her captive again.

Once more the heat of his body was pressed against hers. She could feel him, every inch of him, from his heavy arm squashing her breasts to his long legs nudging hers through the thin stuff of her nightgown.

"I want you," he groaned, and she felt something substantial prod her lower back.

Was that . . . ? Could that be . . . ? She froze. Antoinette might be a spinster and an innocent, but she thought she knew what *that* was. Her breath caught in her throat; she tried to find her voice and protest, but only a squeak came out. He brushed the pulse in her throat with his fingers, pausing briefly, before running his hand downward over the bodice of her nightgown.

Antoinette knew he was searching her again, looking for the letter. But that didn't explain the evidence of his passion, still hard against her. Perhaps he couldn't help that. Perhaps it was an automatic reaction? She knew so little about men and their ways.

The two top buttons of her nightdress were undone. He slipped his hand inside and cupped her breast, caressing her in a way that seemed to imply he meant business.

"Let me show you what you're missing," he rasped.

Later she knew this was when she should have stopped him. A scream, a slap, anything to drive him away. That she didn't was a confusing mystery. Instead she heard herself say, "You know nothing about me."

Her voice was husky, barely audible. His touch was doing things to her, surprising things. Her breast seemed to swell, her nipple to harden and ache, and even stranger, there seemed to be a connection between her breast and the intimate place between her thighs, because the more he caressed her, the more that place throbbed and burned.

"I know your skin is like silk," he answered her statement. "I know the swell of your breast." His fingers slid down farther, moving from one breast to the other. Suddenly he sat down in an armchair, taking her with him, and she found herself planted on his lap.

She knew she had to stop him. Her lips formed the words, but as he gently tugged on her nipple with his fingers, she found herself groaning instead, her throat aching. Something inside her was building, and although it was new and frightening, still she wanted to know what it was and how it would end. She wanted to experience this feeling.

"I am no man's plaything," she said, when she'd caught her breath.

"Who said I was playing?" he murmured. And yet that was exactly what he was doing, teasing her, taking away her ability to think. He turned her, placing her sideways across his knees, and bent his head, and she felt his mouth, hot and wet, close over the thin cloth of her nightgown and the breast beneath. Her nipple ached unbearably, and yet the heat of his mouth didn't seem to soothe it. She twisted, gasping.

Again she opened her mouth to tell him to stop, but he was sucking on her nipple again, tugging the turgid flesh, and the aching tension between her legs began to grow in intensity. She arched her back, her fingers tangled in his hair. He cupped her other breast in his hand, stroking and squeezing. Her muscles trembled weakly, her breathing was little more than gasps. Something was happening to her, as if she were aboard a runaway horse with no way to . . . to . . .

"Stop!"

Finally she got the word out, but it was too late. Muscles she didn't know she had were contracting, clenching, and a great sunburst of pleasure exploded inside her.

When she came back to her body again, it was with a wonderful sense of languor, as if all the strength had been siphoned from her. He was kissing her neck, his lips moving slowly to the line of her jaw, tickling and soothing at the same time.

"You're wonderfully sensitive, sparrow," he said. "Or I'm bloody good at lovemaking. Let's try again." He brushed his fingers over her breast once more, then blew warm breath on the damp cloth. She shivered violently.

Oh, he was dangerous. *This* was dangerous.

Antoinette knew for the sake of her safety and sanity, she must escape him.

She twisted out of his grip and stood up on shaky legs. Her solution was to drive him, and the danger he represented, away from her. Far away. Eager words tumbled over themselves.

"I have Lord Appleby, one of the richest men in England, and he gives me everything I want. Why would I want anything to do with you?"

She saw the gleam of his eyes as he looked up at her, the hiss of exhaling breath. Too late Antoinette realized that instead of driving him away, she had thrown him a challenge.

* * *

Gabriel knew that what she was saying might well be true, but he didn't believe her. Even if she refused to accept it yet, he knew the truth. He could give her the sort of pleasure Appleby, with all his wealth, was incapable of giving her. He'd just proven it.

He pulled her back into his arms. She was trembling with anger and passion, and the ache in his groin redoubled. The only way to relieve himself of the pain was to bury himself deep inside her, and he wasn't going to do that tonight, but that didn't mean he couldn't show her what she was missing.

Gabriel's mouth closed on hers in a deep kiss. He felt her stiffen, as if she was intending to resist, and then almost immediately she melted against him, her arms encircling his neck and drawing him down.

She made his head swim. What had begun as a plan to seduce her and steal the letter from her was no longer so clear-cut. He wanted her. The seduction had taken on a life and importance all its own.

And he knew now that she wanted him. He'd brought her to her peak simply by touching her and kissing her breasts. Her soft lips clung and she made a little sound, half moan and half purr.

Perhaps he could take her now, he thought dizzily, his need making away with his wits. Why not? A woman like this wouldn't expect to be wooed or courted. She was Appleby's mistress, and had probably lived a life less than respectable. She wouldn't expect gentle treatment.

He lifted her, drawing her thighs around his hips, feeling his hardness pressing against the place he was dying to get inside. He cupped her bottom, arching against her, his body rigid with pleasure.

But he'd misjudged her.

The flat of her hand struck his cheek, hard enough to sting, and then she was pummeling him with her closed fists, struggling in his arms. He let her go, and as soon as her feet touched the floor she was gone. The door opened and she was running across the hall and up the stairs. Briefly her scantily clad body was silhouetted against the lamp before she vanished toward her room.

Chapter 6

Weakly, his legs barely holding him up, Gabriel leaned against the doorjamb. He could still feel her clasped in his arms, the intimate heat of her so close to where he most wanted it. He'd never desired a woman this much. Did she feel the same? God, Gabriel hoped so, because he didn't want to be in this on his own. The woman was a witch, with the ability to drive him to madness with a single glance.

He turned back into the parlor and poured himself another drink. His mood changed, the complications of his situation becoming clear. Anyone who would give herself to a man like Rudyard Appleby, he reminded himself, must be beyond contempt. His lip curled. *Contempt*, that was what he should feel for her. Did the fact that he'd kissed her and fallen under her spell even for a moment make him contemptible, too?

There was a history of male Langleys making fools of themselves over unsuitable women. One of Gabriel's ancestors had brought home a bride, a king's castoff, another man's mistress, and suffered for it. Such women must have an irresistible allure for Langley heirs, Gabriel thought, and he was simply following family tradition.

The thing was, he didn't trust himself.

Ever since he'd learned that Lord Appleby had stolen Wexmoor Manor, Gabriel had felt as if the brake that had always ensured a measure of restraint, even in his most hotheaded moments, was finally gone. He became reckless and frustrated, and he wanted to get to Appleby. Antoinette Dupre just happened to be standing in his way.

He took another mouthful of brandy and sat down in the chair where a moment ago he'd brought Appleby's mistress to a spectacular climax. Had Appleby ever achieved that? Simply by caressing her breasts? From her reaction he didn't think so.

Gabriel closed his eyes. *Appleby*. His thoughts began to slip backward to when he'd first learned the truth, and he found himself reliving probably the worst night of his life.

Gabriel's world came crashing down on the evening he visited his father in the Albion Hotel in Bond Street. Sir Adam Langley had arrived from the country and sent for his son, and Gabriel, expecting a fatherly chat and the usual warnings about changing his carefree bachelor ways, turned up without the slightest inkling that this was the point when life as he knew it as a wealthy young gentleman was about to come to an abrupt end.

"But Wexmoor Manor is mine! You know it

was always meant to be mine. My grandfather . . . your father promised it to me. I spent most of my childhood there. I grew up there. He only left it to you because when he died I was not yet twenty-one, but it was always meant to be held in trust for me."

"You're not the only one to be disappointed," Sir Adam spoke in a sharp voice, sounding unlike himself. An invalid for many years, he looked even frailer than usual, and his hands were shaking as he reached for the glass of peppermint tonic, placed at his side.

"Disappointed!" Gabriel repeated furiously. "Surely that's an understatement? Wexmoor Manor is mine. I refuse to give it up to anyone, especially a man I don't even know!"

Sir Adam drank slowly, as if he was biding his time. Some of the tonic spilled onto his fashionable waistcoat, but he didn't seem to notice as he finally set the glass down. Gabriel and his father had never been close; he'd been far closer to his grandfather, Sir John, and it was from him that Gabriel had learned his love of the manor. Sir Adam preferred his Somerset property, inherited from his maternal side.

Occasionally Gabriel had wondered why his father and he were near-strangers, but many of his peers had similar lives, and he'd put it down to being sent away to school at eight years old. But now here was his father looking at him not with indifference but with actual distaste and dislike.

It struck him to the heart.

"This isn't just about you. I have lost my share of Aphrodite's Club as well," Sir Adam said irritably.

"Aphrodite's Club?" Gabriel frowned. "But what about Marietta? You promised her your share of the club, you and Aphrodite."

"Don't you think I know that?"

"I'm trying to understand. I'm certain I can—"

"What? Fix everything?" Adam's eyes were blazing, his fingers white on the arms of his chair. "You're as arrogant as Appleby, but then that's hardly surprising."

He stopped, his chest swiftly rising and falling, and suddenly he appeared guilty, as if he'd said too much. He looked away, fiddling with the signet ring on his little finger.

"I need to rest. We will speak tomorrow."

"No, Father, we will speak now." Gabriel refused to leave. "Explain to me how such a thing could happen? How you could lose Wexmoor Manor and Aphrodite's Club as if they were mere buttons from your waistcoat? This man who now owns them—Lord Appleby? Does he have some hold over you?"

Sir Adam managed a humorless laugh. "If only you knew."

"Father—"

"Frankly I'm surprised you're acting like this. Since you reached your majority you've shown no signs of settling down at Wexmoor Manor. The house and grounds are in a mess, and I can't manage them *and* the Somerset house. My father expected you to take up the reins when you turned twenty-one, and that was four years ago. He saw you as the bright hope, said you'd go far. Farther than me, anyway."

There was something in his voice. Gabriel recognized it, could hardly believe it. "You were jealous. Because my grandfather was closer to me than you."

The truth made for an uncomfortable silence. "It was my own fault," Adam admitted dully. "I pushed you away. I was never able to put the doubts from my mind."

"Doubts? What doubts?"

"Gabriel, enough."

"No, I want to know. If you're doubting my attachment for Wexmoor Manor, then you're wrong. I have plans to restore the manor to its glory days. Grandfather left me some shares in the Great Northern Railway, and I've been busy reinvesting the profits, building up enough money to do what I promised him I would before he died. I'm just about ready to start; if I'd known there was a time limit . . . In God's name, don't tell me you've taken away my future before I've even had a chance to live it!"

"I'm sorry," his father said, uncomfortable, "but I can't. Appleby gets what he wants. Just leave it, Gabriel, for God's sake. You will have the baronetcy when I die. You will be Sir Gabriel Langley, isn't that enough?"

But it wasn't enough, not nearly. Gabriel wanted to shout it out, but he didn't trust himself. He was furious. He wanted to shake the truth out of his father, but he knew it would do no good. Adam had a stubborn streak a mile wide, and for some reason, he'd decided not to explain his actions to his only son.

Gabriel turned and strode from the room. Outside, his mother waited, her face sickly white. "I'm so sorry, Gabriel," she whispered, tears in her eyes.

"This man, this Appleby . . . ?"

"This is my fault."

Gabriel saw the pain. He didn't understand it, but he knew something was very, very wrong, and if Sir Adam wouldn't tell him what it was, then his mother must. But still her next words were completely unexpected, and they shocked him.

"Before I married your father I was another man's mistress."

He swallowed down the lump in his throat. He didn't, he realized, think any the worse of her because of what she'd just revealed; it wasn't that. He was shocked because it had never occurred to him that his sweet and gentle mother had such a risqué past.

"Why?" he rasped.

"I was foolish enough to believe the promises made to me. I ran off with him and then I was trapped, ruined, with no way of going back. Your father knew, of course. He accepted matters. Besides, we were in love, deeply in love. So I left this man and married your father. I did not see him again until just recently."

She'd been avoiding his gaze, but now Gabriel took her hands gently in his and squeezed them, forcing her to look up at him.

"Mama, none of this matters. In our family a scandal is as normal as breathing."

She smiled in acknowledgment, but he could see it was an effort. "Oh, Gabriel, if only that was all it was. A scandal."

"Tell me," he insisted.

She met his intent blue gaze, so like his father's. "When the news came out about the Great Exhibition, I saw Lord Appleby's name in the newspapers, and I wrote to him. I . . . I had fond feelings for him, once. I told him I was pleased he was such a success, and I spoke a little of my own life." She swallowed. "I was relieved, you see, that he had found happiness in his life and business. I'd always felt guilty for abandoning him."

"Appleby was the man you . . . ?"

"Yes. I was his mistress. Do you begin to get an inkling now, Gabriel? Are you sure you want to know more? There is much worse to come."

"Tell me."

"After I left Appleby and married your father, I discovered I was with child."

The words fell like stones into the well of his heart, but this time she didn't pause to allow him time to recover.

"I wasn't certain who the father was but we— your father and I—decided it didn't matter. You would be his child no matter what. When you were born I was sure you were Adam's son—in many ways you are very like him—but Adam couldn't accept the truth after all. He's always found it difficult."

"He thinks I am Appleby's son." He could see the truth in her eyes.

"No! Not really. But he has doubts." She sighed. "I should never have written to him. It appears that he made inquiries into our lives and now believes you are his, and he is threatening Adam with disclosure."

"I can't imagine my father being worried about that."

"He isn't. Not for himself. It is me, Gabriel. He says he doesn't want me to be exposed before the censorious eyes of society. No one knows about my past, you see. We've always kept it a secret. It would be . . . difficult. I would imagine the ladies of the parish would refuse to speak to me." She tried to laugh, but it sounded more like a sob.

His mother was always busy in the village where she lived; she was a part of the community, a well-loved part. What would a scandal like this do to her?

"Why would Appleby want to hurt you, Mama?" he said gently.

"Because I dared to love another man better than he, and I left him to marry that man and live happily ever after. That is what he cannot forgive, Gabriel."

"So this is all about hurt pride and revenge?" Gabriel muttered.

"I think so. He wants us to suffer. You, especially, because you should have been his son. He is childless, did you know? All his pride in his achievements will come to nothing when he is dead—he has no one to pass it on to."

His mother, still beautiful, managed a shaky smile. "Can you forgive me, Gabriel?"

He wrapped her in his arms, feeling her fragility, suddenly afraid of what was happening to them. No matter what she said, he knew she couldn't survive being ostracized by her friends and neighbors. It would break her gentle heart. Fury swept through him in a hot, scalding wave, taking with it any consideration of caution.

"I'm so sorry about Wexmoor Manor," she murmured into his chest. "I know you love it."

"No doubt that was why Appleby demanded it, to cause us all the most pain and suffering." He set her at arm's length, pinning her with his intent gaze. "Tell me, Mama, where does Lord Appleby live?"

"Gabriel . . ."

"Where?"

She told him, caught between loyalty to her husband and worry for her son, and fearing for them both. Gabriel gave her another quick hug of appreciation and made for the stairs, causing a maid to jump to one side as he hurried down them. And then he was throwing open the door to the street and slamming it shut behind him.

He'd walked straight out into a soaking rainstorm.

As he stood, drenched, staring up at the gray

sky, he felt as if his whole world was disintegrating around him. His father believed he wasn't his father, his mother insisted he was, and Appleby was punishing him either way. Well, he wasn't taking it lying down. He'd force His Lordship to return his house and land, and at this moment—he clenched his fists—he was quite capable of violence.

Gabriel set off in the direction of the Mayfair home of Lord Rudyard Appleby, a man he'd never heard of until a few moments ago. A man who might possibly be his father.

He knew the sensible thing to do would be to turn around and go back to his home until he cooled down. But he wasn't feeling sensible; he kept walking. By the time he reached the prestigious Mayfair address, the rain had slowed to a miserable drizzle. He stood, staring up at the house, his clothes soaked and heavy, his fair hair plastered to his head while trickles of water ran down his face and into his eyes. In contrast to his personal hell, bright light spilled from the windows and the open door, and the happy chatter of voices flowed out into the evening.

Lord Appleby was holding a party for his fashionable friends. Well, he thought darkly, let them enjoy themselves while they might. He would have it out with him.

As he crossed the threshold a liveried footman blocked his path, but one glance at Gabriel's expression sent the young man backing up. Satisfied, Gabriel strode on, his sodden shoes leaving wet patches on the priceless rugs, through dazzling halls and rooms heavy with the scent of flowers and expensive perfume. The brilliance of gaslight was everywhere, replacing the now outdated candles and lamps, as if Lord Appleby was determined to show everyone he was a modern and progressive man.

One room held a large model of the Great Exhibition building, nicknamed the Crystal Palace because it was built of glass and metal. He paused to stare, and then he remembered what his mother had said, and realized that he'd heard of Lord Appleby after all. He was one of the manufacturers who'd won a contract to help construct the already famous building.

"Sir? I must ask you to leave."

He turned. Another footman, this one older and more officious-looking, his mouth pursed, his censorious gaze taking in the state of Gabriel's clothes. There was a knot of startled-looking guests hovering in a doorway behind him.

"I want to see Lord Appleby," Gabriel said.

The footman gaped at him. "I'm sorry, sir, but that is quite impossible."

Impatiently Gabriel pushed past him and into the stunned group, grasping the arm of an elderly gentleman with a red-veined face. "Tell me where I can find Lord Appleby," he demanded, in a way that made it clear his patience was ending. The old gentleman pointed a shaky finger diagonally across the room, toward a closed door.

As Gabriel walked toward it, leaving muddy

tracks on the fine Turkish carpet, he heard a low hum of disapproval and didn't care. The servant was hurrying behind him, bleating something about "not yet!" but no one could stop him from flinging open the door.

The scene inside was not what he'd expected.

They were clasped in each other's arms. The man, his dark hair turning to gray, his stocky body made elegant by perfectly fitting evening wear. The woman, half turned away, dressed in white. She was bowed backward in the clasp of his arms, her throat arched, curls of her glossy brown hair tangled with pearls. From this angle there was something very erotic in the creamy line of her throat and the swell of her breasts above the low, beaded bodice.

Just for a moment Gabriel forgot why he was there.

And then he heard the shocked silence behind him turn into a roar of excited chatter. Too late the couple realized they were being observed. The woman gasped and pushed her companion away. With her back still turned, she ran from her ruin, exiting through a farther door.

The man didn't run. He smoothed his cravat, a little smile playing about his lips, as if he wasn't in the least sorry. His gaze, so dark as to be almost black, passed over the shocked faces to the footman. He raised an eyebrow.

Was this his father? Was there some resemblance?

"I'm sorry, sir," the servant gabbled, "I was

waiting until the signal, but this gentleman burst in before I could—"

Appleby held up a hand to stop him. His gaze fixed on Gabriel. "Do you want something?" he demanded in a voice that still held more than a hint of Northern England.

Gabriel stepped inside the room and slammed the door behind him. Lord Appleby looked faintly alarmed.

"You aren't one of my guests," Appleby said, frowning now. "I'll ask you again: What do you want?"

"I want to know why you've stolen my inheritance."

Lord Appleby's alarm turned to surprise, and then amusement. Somehow that was more shocking to Gabriel than downright anger. Appleby reached for a box on a small table and found a cigar inside, lighting it. "Gabriel, I presume."

"Yes." Gabriel towered over Appleby, but it didn't feel like an advantage.

Appleby watched him, eyes narrowed through the smoke. "You don't resemble me, boy, although you've a look of my mother's family."

Gabriel held his temper with difficulty.

"Sir Adam cast you out without a penny, has he?" Appleby continued, still smiling. "Never mind. You can get a job, a real job. I have plenty of mills you can graft in." His black gaze slid over Gabriel with scorn. "That's real work."

"I don't need a lecture, just give me back what belongs to me."

Appleby took a puff on his cigar. "No."

"You have no right—"

"And you do? Because of an accident of birth? No, you can't have your inheritance back. I have plans for it. Now you've had your answer, get out of my house before I throw you out."

"I'm not your son."

"No? If you're not you should be. Your mother was a good bedmate, always ready to give as good as she got. I'd be very surprised if I didn't impregnate her."

Gabriel hit him, plumb on the nose.

After that everything turned to madness. Appleby started roaring, calling for his servants, blood spilling onto his expensive clothes. Again the door was flung open, the guests crowding in behind the officious footman. And Gabriel took off.

"Come back, you damned pup!" Appleby shouted. "I'll ruin you. You can be sure of that. I'll see you ruined!"

Gabriel supposed he was already ruined. A man like Appleby would have powerful friends, and he'd use them. As he ran into the rain outside he wondered where he could go. Not to his father, that was certain, and he no longer had the manor house in Devon.

But there was one place he'd always felt welcome, despite the identity of the woman who owned it and the relationship she'd once had with Sir Adam. And, he remembered belatedly, she had also lost something she loved. Besides, when he was a callow seventeen-year-old, in the throes of his first love, she had offered him good advice. Advice for which he was still grateful.

Gabriel set off for London's most infamous brothel: Aphrodite's Club.

The chiming of a clock brought him back from the past. Gabriel was sitting in the darkness, staring at nothing, but in his mind the image of Appleby and the woman in his arms lingered.

He hadn't realized it at the time but now he did. That sweet curve of throat and bosom, the dancing brown curls—they belonged to Antoinette Dupre. Any doubts he might have had that she was Appleby's mistress evaporated.

Chapter 7

Antoinette propped her chin on her hand and stared into the night, her long hair tumbling over her back and shoulders, her bare feet curling on the threadbare carpet. Her body was alive and on fire, full of sensations she'd never imagined, let alone experienced before. The stranger had done this to her, and she didn't know whether to give herself over to it wholeheartedly, or fight like hell.

It didn't help that she was alone and confused. Without Cecilia and her household around her—the only family she had—she felt truly abandoned.

And of course that was what Lord Appleby wanted.

To bring her to her knees. To tear her reputation to shreds so that he could do as he liked and no one would believe a word against him. That was why he had lured her to London, to his Mayfair house, to ask her to marry him, and, when she refused, to arrange to have them seen together in a position so compromising, it was impossible to dispute it.

She still shuddered at the memory.

The heavy weight of his fingers on her shoulders, his wet mouth on her throat, as he bent her backward over his arm. Unable to move, she'd been his prisoner. At first her mind was frozen, too shocked to know what was happening. And then the door opened, and the guests crowded toward her, their faces . . . The memory made her queasy. Running away was her only option. Even if she'd been brave enough to stay, they would never have believed her.

After a sleepless night she had been ready to confront him.

"Never mind," he'd replied mildly, "you'll enjoy being my wife, Antoinette. I am very generous to those who please me well."

The look in his eyes, the curl of his mouth . . . Antoinette was sickened by what he was suggesting. Not that she was a prude, she had never been that, but this man had stolen her reputation and was set on taking her fortune. And now it seemed he wanted her body, too, if she let him.

"It's my money you covet, isn't it? That's why you want to force me to marry you."

" 'Force' is such an ugly word, Antoinette, but, yes, you *will* marry me. If you don't, I'll turn my attentions to your sister."

Her heart gave a hard thud. "I will never allow you to harm Cecilia!"

"How can you stop me?" His eyes narrowed. "Who will believe you over me? I dine with lords and ladies and members of Parliament; Her Majesty the Queen asks my advice on Northern England, as if it's a foreign country. Your struggles are pointless."

Antoinette wondered how she could have believed him to be a kindly man. Of course, he had invited her to London to attend the opening of the Great Exhibition, and she had enjoyed it very much, and it was only when she began to notice she was attracting smiling looks and overheard comments of her soon-to-be-announced nuptials with Lord Appleby that she realized what was happening.

Surprised, she'd tried to refute the rumors, but no one seemed to believe her. And then he did ask her to marry him. She refused, as gently as she could, explaining that she had no plans to marry yet. "My sister needs me," she'd said. "And strange as it sounds I have always held the hope that if I ever marry it will be for love."

Whatever he thought of her naïveté, he appeared to accept her decision, which was the only reason she'd reluctantly agreed to stay on in London to help him host his soiree. And all the time he'd been planning to set her up in a compromising position. To ruin her reputation and force her to marry him whether she wanted to or not.

"I think you're despicable. Whatever you do or say, I will never give you what you want."

He yawned at her brave words. "You may as well; everyone believes you already have."

"I know the truth."

Suddenly he seemed to tire of the argument. "You will do as I say," he said harshly.

"I won't."

He smiled, but there was something so calculating in it that she was chilled to the marrow. "Let me put it this way, Antoinette. Imagine you were to meet with an unfortunate accident. Cecilia would be your heir, the Dupre fortune would be hers. I'm quite sure the poor girl would be overcome with grief, and so grateful for my help and support. Who could blame her if affection soon turned to love and wedding bells rang?"

Sickened, furious, and frightened, nevertheless Antoinette kept her back straight and her chin up. If her voice shook then, she hoped he would think it was due to rage.

"Why are you doing this?"

Appleby stood up and moved to the sideboard with its array of breakfast dishes. He lifted a cover and greedily eyed the contents of the silver plate. "I need money, Antoinette. I am on the verge of an abyss. If my manufacturing business is to remain soluble, I need funds. The contract for the Great Exhibition and the new customers who will be coming to me must believe I am perfectly sound. Appearance, you see, is everything. If I can hold on, then the future will be bright, but if it is discovered I am nearly bankrupt, then I am finished." He helped himself to sausage and bacon. "You see I am doing you the honor of being frank."

"So you want to steal my fortune for your own benefit?"

"I have far greater need of it than you. Men rule the world, Antoinette. Women are there for our pleasure and to give us children, nothing more."

And with that he sat down and began to eat.

But he knew her too well, she realized. He knew she would do anything, bear anything, for the sake of her younger sister. And now she was a prisoner in his Mayfair house, with no way of convincing those surrounding her of the truth.

Even the highwayman believed Lord Appleby's lies; he'd said as much. He'd treated her like a woman who knew the ways of men, and still she'd fallen under his spell.

Antoinette hugged her arms around herself. Why did she find him so attractive? Why did the feel of his body against hers, the brush of his fingers, the taste of his lips, make her want to surrender? Was it some sort of chemical reaction? Yes, that must be it; there was a scientific reason for what she was feeling. She must look at it coolly and calmly and see it for what it was. The man was not a magician; he could not control her against her will. She would find out who he was and expose him to a magistrate. What was the punishment for holding up a coach and molesting its occupant? Transportation to New South Wales, probably, if not worse.

Antoinette put a fingertip to her lips, feeling their softness, remembering the way he had kissed her. It was a shame, really. She would have liked to experience more of his kisses.

If circumstances had been different.

* * *

Gabriel woke, bleary-eyed, to someone shaking him. For a moment he didn't know where he was, but then he became aware of Mary Cooper's soft, urgent voice, and groaned. It felt as if he'd only just gotten to sleep. If he wasn't dreaming of Appleby's sneering face, he was slowly undressing Antoinette Dupre, and he was wrung out.

"Master Gabriel? You must wake up!"

He rubbed his hands over his face and tried to gather his wandering wits. "What is it, Mary?"

"Oh, thank goodness! Master, she's gone to the magistrate's house! Mr. Wonicot says you must stop her."

Gabriel wished he hadn't brought the brandy back with him last night. He sat up. And instantly regretted it. Trying not to stagger, he swung himself to his feet and made his way carefully to the washbasin and splashed cold water onto his face until his head began to clear.

"Explain yourself," he ordered.

Mary, who had been waiting impatiently, rushed into speech. "Miss Dupre was asking who the magistrate was and where he lived. She went on and on. Mrs. Wonicot tried to put her off but she wouldn't be put off. 'You haven't answered my question,' she kept saying, all hoity-toity like. I don't think someone like her has the right to be so bossy, master, not when she's no better than she should be."

Gabriel was sorry he'd missed the scene Mary was describing. He found the thought of Antoinette being bossy strangely exciting.

"Master?"

Mary was watching him with narrowed eyes, and Gabriel realized he was smiling to himself. He wiped the smile from his face, assuming a serious demeanor. "Yes, yes, I heard you. Go on. What happened when Sally told her where to find Sir James Trevalen?"

"Well, master, there and then she ordered Mr. Wonicot to saddle a horse! Of course he said that saddling horses was Coombe's job, so she straightaway told him to fetch Coombe to do it. Well, he told her that he didn't know where Coombe was. And do you know what she did then?"

Clearly he was meant to guess, but Gabriel had lost what patience he had. Mary must have seen the glint in his eyes because she hastily answered her own question.

"She saddled the horse herself! That tells you she's no lady, don't it, Master Gabriel?"

"So where is she now . . . ?"

"She set off to visit Sir James. We all tried to talk her into waiting for you . . . eh, for Coombe, to ride with her. To make it proper, like. But she wouldn't listen to a word we said. She's gone to tell Sir James all about the highwayman and have you . . . *him* arrested and locked up. Oh, master, what will you do?"

Her pretty, worried face might have stirred him once to gentlemanly concern, with a good dose of lust. It occurred to him that he felt neither. These days he was more interested in pocket Venuses with glossy brown curls and eyes that gazed into his with a mixture of curiosity and courage. Who would have thought it? He still didn't understand it himself.

But now was no time to dwell on the peculiarities of his attraction for Antoinette Dupre.

"So she's ridden off alone?" he said.

"Aye, master." Mary waited breathlessly for his instructions, eyes bright.

"Then she's either very brave or very foolish. Sir James is a friend of my father; he won't take her side against me. And he despises Lord Appleby as much as we do. As long as his position isn't compromised and he's forced to act, then I am safe."

He looked around for a towel, and Mary handed him one. He dried his face and hands.

"When did she set out?"

"Not long since." Mary seemed deflated, as if he hadn't done as she'd expected. "You could still ride after her and stop her," she added hopefully.

Gabriel shook his head. "No point," he said. Let her go off to Sir James and exhaust herself running around in a fruitless effort to have him arrested. It would avail her of nothing. Then, tonight, when she slept restlessly in her bed, she would receive another visit from her highwayman. If Miss Dupre thought she was getting rid of him that easily, then she was very much mistaken, and he would enjoy telling her so.

"You're smiling again," Mary said suspiciously. "What is there to smile about, master?"

"Nothing at all, Mary, except that the sun is

shining and I am home at Wexmoor Manor, where I belong."

She looked even more confused, but he didn't bother to enlighten her. He was already thinking of later.

Chapter 8

The ride from Wexmoor Manor had brought a flush to her cheeks and a sparkle to her eyes. Antoinette was used to riding every morning at home, and she had missed the exercise while in London. Not that she was a brilliant horse-woman—Cecilia was far better—but she enjoyed being outdoors, and the time allowed her to gather her thoughts and consider what needed doing in the hours to come.

On the ride this morning she'd considered what she should say to Sir James Trevalen and how she was going to put her case. She was not foolish enough to think he would believe her when he knew nothing of her—she was certainly hoping he knew nothing of her ruined reputation, and she wasn't going to mention it. But surely part of his responsibility as magistrate was to look into her allegations? And that might be enough to frighten off the highwayman . . . and Lord Appleby.

All she needed was a little time, enough to get away from here and back to London and use the information in the letter, and this might be the way to achieve it.

Sir James Trevalen's house was smaller than Wexmoor Manor but of a similar age. Of weather-worn gray stone and lichen-tinted slate, it loomed over her as she drew up her horse at the front door, the facade only slightly softened by some carefully trimmed ivy.

"Do you have an appointment with Sir James?" The servant who opened the door looked inclined to deny her entry, but Antoinette wasn't having it.

"No, I don't, but he will still see me." Antoinette, used to being obeyed, stepped boldly forward.

Chastened, the servant showed her into a sitting room while the master of the house was fetched.

A large mirror hung on the wall, reflecting her image. She noted the neat, plum-colored riding outfit, her hair smoothly coiled at her nape, and her eyes bright behind her spectacles. Her skin was flushed from the ride. She looked passable, she told herself critically, for a woman who'd barely slept. But it was as she lay tossing and turning in her bed that she'd come to her decision; that the only way to rid herself of the dangerous presence of the highwayman was to have him arrested.

And he *was* a danger to her. Because of whom he worked for and the hidden letter, yes, but there was more to it than that. He made her feel vulnerable in a way she'd never felt before. While he was nearby there was a very real chance she might forget the danger she was in and that he represented. That instead she would begin to remember the touch of his mouth on hers and the husky sound of his voice. She would lose her focus in the throes of more of the exquisite pleasure he'd given her last night when she'd completely lost control.

Losing control was new for Antoinette.

"Miss Dupre?"

Sir James Trevalen was a slight, middle-aged man with a face darkened by living under a sun in far hotter climes. His quizzical gray eyes fixed on hers, and his smile was so kind that Antoinette felt the sudden urge to trust him. It was because she was alone and friendless, she knew that, but the need to spill everything to him was almost irresistible.

She did resist it.

Appearances, as she had discovered to her cost, could be deceptive, and the world outside her previously insular world was often a dangerous place.

"Sir James. Thank you so much for seeing me. I'm sorry to interrupt your—"

He waved away her apology. "I always have time for those who require my help and advice. I take it that is why you are here? You have a problem you wish to lay before me?"

"I do. But I'm not sure how to tell my story without shocking you, Sir James."

His eyebrows rose and his smile vanished. "You must feel free to unburden yourself within these walls; I am not in the habit of repeating confidences. And I assure you I am not easily shocked."

"Thank you, Sir James."

"Please, do sit down, Miss Dupre, and tell me all about it."

Antoinette perched on the edge of the chair and realized her knees were shaking, but her voice was firm and steady as she told her story. "I arrived at Lord Appleby's house, Wexmoor Manor, two nights ago. The reasons for my visit are immaterial . . ." She went on, briefly detailing the journey, until she came to the holdup. Of this she made a great deal while telling him nothing of her understanding of the reasons that it happened. By the time she finished she had turned the highwayman into a ravening monster, half man and half beast.

Sir James, who was watching her intently throughout her story, now spoke quietly. "What you tell me is shocking indeed. I am sorry to hear you have been so mistreated, and I will do my very best to discover the perpetrator of this crime."

There was a genuineness about Sir James that gave her a sense of confidence he would carry out his promise. "If you do find him . . . what will happen to him?" she said reluctantly.

"He will be arrested and brought before me. I have no doubt he will be jailed for his crime, perhaps even hanged. What you have told me is very serious, Miss Dupre. Such a man cannot be allowed to run amok in my district attacking defenseless women."

Hanged! Antoinette had known it might be so, but for some reason, hearing the word spoken aloud made it all the more real. She remembered the firm touch of his lips on hers, the intent look in his eyes when he trapped her in the coach, as if she was so much more than he'd imagined. And then the way he'd comforted her and wiped away her tears, his big hands so gentle.

"I wasn't completely defenseless," she heard herself say. "That is, I—I fought him and drove him off." She stumbled on. "And it isn't as if I have never been kissed before! Well, not like that perhaps . . ." Her thoughts slid back to the touch of his mouth, and suddenly she didn't know if she could do this. It was one thing to drive her enemy away, to give herself time to escape, but to send a man to his death . . . No, it was too much of a burden on her conscience.

Abruptly Antoinette stood up, Sir James following more slowly. He looked thoughtful, his gaze fixed on her face, as if he found her an interesting study.

"Miss Dupre, I can see the memory has upset you," he said. "Perhaps you wish to partake of some refreshment before you go?"

"No, thank you, Sir James. I should get back." If she stayed she might end up telling him the whole story was a lie, even the bits that were true. As it was she blurted out, "The servants at Wexmoor Manor think it was all a harmless prank and I am taking it far too seriously."

"Ah." Sir James tapped his cheek. "Perhaps they

know who it is, Miss Dupre, and wish to protect him. Have you thought of that?"

"I've thought of nothing else."

"I'd advise you to leave this matter in my hands, Miss Dupre. I will get to the bottom of it. For now you must put it from your mind and enjoy your visit to our part of Devon. Will you promise to do that?"

He was very gallant; Antoinette found his manner comforting. "I will, sir. It is only . . . whatever this man has done, I would not like to think that I will be the cause of his death."

Sir James nodded seriously. "I see you are a compassionate woman, Miss Dupre, but you have done all you can. I am taking charge, and I will see that whatever must be done will be done. Believe me, I am a fair man. Do not trouble yourself any further, please."

Antoinette agreed that she would try, but still she left wondering if she'd behaved too rashly. Rashness was an unfamiliar trait in Antoinette's character; usually she was a woman who considered her every action coolly and calmly and at length. But the highwayman had rattled her; he had shaken her from her cozy world, and she'd yet to find safe ground.

As she stepped outside a familiar voice called, "Miss!" Antoinette looked up in surprise. It was Wonicot, mounted on a horse and holding hers, and looking very uncomfortable indeed. "You shouldn't be out on your own, Miss Dupre," he said by way of explanation.

"Are you my bodyguard, Wonicot?" she inquired, as they set off for Wexmoor Manor. She should be cross with him for spying on her, but he so obviously didn't want to be there that she didn't have the heart.

"Just obeying orders," he muttered.

Whose orders? Antoinette asked herself. Mrs. Wonicot's, Lord Appleby's, or the highwayman's?

"Sir James believed me when I told him I was held up by a highwayman," she said with a sideways glance.

Wonicot nearly lost his balance, clinging to the horse's mane to stop himself from falling. "You shouldn't have told him," he said at last. " 'Tisn't nothing to do with him. 'Tisn't his business."

"He's the magistrate; of course it is his business." They rode on a moment. "Did you know, Wonicot, that a man can be hanged for a crime like that?"

He paled. "Hanged? Oh, surely not, miss. No, he wouldn't do that. Not to his—" But whatever Wonicot was going to say he thought better of it and shook his head. "You shouldn't have done it," was all he said.

Antoinette had much to think about as they clip-clopped along the road. One thing she decided upon: Sir James was right, the matter was out of her hands now. Anyway, it wasn't as if it was her fault he'd chosen to rob the coach, was it?

Determined, she switched her thoughts to her return to London and saving herself and Cecilia. And she would save them, and see Appleby punished. Afterward, life could return to normal. She could go back to being the chatelaine of her home and living her own life. To being herself. Antoinette was used to a life in which each day was planned, each week had its allotted tasks, each year its predestined cycles. There was something very comforting in having your life managed so completely.

But instead of comforting her, she found that this vision of her future had the effect of depressing her. It occurred to her that she was enjoying her current predicament. The sense of uncertainty and giddy, dangerous excitement as she was pursued by a stranger who did such wicked, pleasurable things to her. She gave a little shiver. All these years she'd been mistaken in her own character. She wasn't the cool and levelheaded young woman she'd imagined; someone very different lurked beneath the smooth surface. Someone who was insisting that now it was *her* turn. And now that she'd been set free, it was going to be very difficult to send her back.

Antoinette was still deep in thought as she rode into the stable yard. Wonicot had dropped behind her and was no longer in sight, as she slid down onto the brick surface. She gave her mare a pat on the nose, telling her that she was a beautiful girl and promising more rides in the future. It was only when she heard someone clear his throat behind her that she realized she wasn't entirely alone.

It was Coombe. He was lurking in the shadows

by the stable door, a cap pulled low on his head and his coarse black hair sticking out from beneath it in tufts. His sleeves were rolled up over grubby but muscular forearms, and there was a neckerchief tied around his throat.

"Take your horse for you, miss?" He spoke in an accent so thick it was almost incomprehensible.

"Thank you." She led the mare toward Coombe. "She's a lovely animal," she said, smiling politely, and hoping he didn't notice her nose twitching.

Coombe didn't feel the need to be polite. He took the reins from her and slouched toward the stable doors, his heavy boots ringing out on the bricks. After a moment of indecision, Antoinette decided to follow him. Maybe Coombe on his own would turn out to be a fountain of information.

It was gloomy inside the stable building and she stopped, taking a moment for her eyes to adjust. Coombe was already busy removing the mare's saddle, his head bent over his work, moving swiftly for such a big man. At the sound of her approaching steps he looked up, and although she couldn't see more than shadows, she sensed he wasn't pleased to see her. His surliness made her even more wary, and she decided that was another reason not to get too close to him. But if there was a chance Coombe could help her out of her predicament, then she must try to win him over to her side.

"Have you worked here long, Coombe?" she began in what she hoped was a nonthreatening voice.

He grunted, not even bothering to glance at her.

"Have you *lived* here long?" Antoinette was patient.

Another grunt, this time followed by a shrug.

"Tell me, Coombe, do you enjoy working for Lord Appleby?"

He froze, and then he spat on the straw. Well, that was plain enough, wasn't it? Perhaps she'd found an ally in this most unlikely of places.

"Is Lord Appleby a frequent visitor to Wexmoor Manor?"

He held up one finger at her, his face too deep in the shadow of his cap for her to read his expression, before returning to his work.

"Only once?" Antoinette said in amazement. "I thought . . . I presumed he'd owned the manor for a great many years. How odd. Then who lived here before?"

No answer to that. Coombe turned away, carrying the saddle into a tack room. Again Antoinette hesitated, but again she followed him.

"Coombe," she spoke in an airy, unconcerned manner. "Is there a regular coach to London from any of the villages near here? Or a train station, perhaps? I forgot to ask before I arrived, and now I find I may need to return to London earlier than I expected."

He paused in his work. "I know nothing of that, miss," he muttered, or that was what she thought he said. "I've never been to London."

"Oh?" Antoinette fidgeted a moment. "Wouldn't

you like to see the Tower and Westminster Abbey?" No, a man like Coombe wouldn't be interested in architecture and history. "There are horse races in London," she went on, hoping it was true. "And horses for sale. The best horses anywhere. Big, strong, glossy . . . horses," she ended lamely.

He was fiddling with the harness. "Big and glossy, are they?" he said with something like longing in his voice. "No one here is interested in horseflesh, not proper horseflesh."

"But you are, aren't you, Coombe? You'd like your own stable and your own horses. Racing horses. Have you never thought of that?"

Of course he hadn't. A man in Coombe's position knew his place. He would never earn enough money to own anything, let alone run his own business. But Antoinette decided she must make the offer, and follow it through if he promised to help her escape.

Coombe was standing very still, staring at the saddle in his hands; he seemed to be in a dream. Quietly she took a step closer, ignoring the pungent smell of his body.

"If you take me to London, Coombe, I will help you to get your own stable and your own horses. You see, I need to get back to London urgently. Will you help me?"

He heaved a deep sigh, then spat on the straw, causing her to leap back out of the way. "I'm only the groom," he growled. "An' I have my work to do, miss."

It was a dismissal, and yet she lingered, not wanting to give up.

"Coombe . . . ?"

"I'll think on what you've said," he said, and slouched away.

Antoinette watched him go, not entirely discouraged. Coombe had shown a definite interest in what she was offering. She would speak to him again when he'd had time to mull it over, and next time he might be more willing to listen.

Gabriel waited until her steps began to fade away before he glanced up to watch her retreat and admire her figure. To prevent her from recognizing him he'd kept his face hidden and his shoulders hunched, but he needn't have worried. She didn't have a clue. He was a groom, and that was exactly what she saw when she looked at him.

Just as well.

He knew what she was up to, the manipulative little minx. She intended to turn the highwayman over to Sir James Trevalen and see him hanged. And if that didn't work, she was hoping to bribe Coombe into taking her back to London, where she could prevail upon Lord Appleby to deal with him.

Gabriel wasn't about to let that happen.

So what next?

If he was a sensible man he'd make a run for it, sail over to France, and go into hiding, forget all about saving his home and revenging himself on

Appleby. Well, he mustn't be a sensible man then, Gabriel told himself, because he wasn't going anywhere. Antoinette Dupre might well be a ruthless, greedy woman but . . . no, there was something wrong with that picture. He realized it was the way she had ridden off to see Sir James this morning, as if the devil himself were in pursuit of her. Almost as if she was afraid.

Of him and his pursuit of the letter? Or was it the way he'd made her body sing when he'd held her and touched her last night? The way she'd bolted this morning showed a fear of her own reactions rather than his.

Antoinette was running from herself.

He smiled. This was a promising start. He remembered the advice Aphrodite had given him on the night he'd fled from London. "Seduce her," she'd commanded in her soft French accent. "Make the woman yours. Make her so hungry for you that her senses overrule her mind, and soon you will discover all she knows. I promise you she will tell you willingly."

He hadn't believed her. He was beginning to now.

Gabriel was looking forward to making Antoinette Dupre hungry for him . . . as hungry as he was for her.

Chapter 9

Antoinette woke to the touch of a man's hand in a place it oughtn't to be. Her eyes sprang open in the darkness, and she stared frantically about her, seeing only shadows. Shadows that breathed. And the hand was definitely there, warm and calloused, stroking her face.

With a gasp she jumped away.

"Now, now, my little brown sparrow, not so fast."

"You!" Her heart threatened to break free of her ribs.

He chuckled breathily. "Why are you surprised? I told you I'd be back."

Antoinette tried to find her wits. He was acting as if she should be pleased to see him, as if it was perfectly all right for a stranger to turn up in her bedchamber in the middle of the night.

"Get out!" she hissed.

"I don't think I will," he murmured. His hand brushed her cheek, his fingers sliding down to brush the soft, full shape of her lips. "We have so much to discuss, you and I . . ."

She made to jump up, but he caught her, easily subduing her. When she caught her breath again he was lying very close, the heat of his body like a banked fire, his hand back over her mouth.

"I hear you went to see Sir James Trevalen today. Did you mean to give me up?" He shifted closer still, and she was aware of the masculine, spicy scent of him. "Do you really think he can catch me? I am like smoke; I will slip through his fingers and vanish."

It was useless trying to answer him with his hand over her mouth, so she didn't try, simply narrowing her eyes at him. He lifted his hand slightly, and his fingers trailed over her mouth again. He shifted his big, warm body, leaning over her, and she felt the weight of his chest upon her soft breasts.

"I wonder . . . Do you really want to see me punished? Are you such a cruel woman?"

"You deserve to be—"

But again he covered her mouth, this time with a long finger across her lips. "No, my sparrow, let me finish. I have been pondering the question, and this is what I think. You want to see me gone because you're afraid of me."

She shook her head in denial, but perhaps her eyes told a different story.

"Afraid of how I make you feel," he went on, with a smile. "How long has it been, Miss Dupre, since you've had a lusty young man in your bed? Come, be honest with me now. I know Lord Appleby is rich, but he is definitely past his prime.

How long is it since you've been thoroughly made love to?"

Antoinette tried to squeak a protest but his words reverberated in her head. *Never,* she thought. *I have never been thoroughly made love to.*

He moved closer still, and his lips trailed teasingly over her temple. That sensation she remembered from last night was back again, inside her, softening and melting. Her skin ached for his touch, and she had to force herself to lie still and not wriggle. And that was when he swooped over her and kissed her, his mouth firm and hot.

She responded with a mixture of need and curiosity. Even while she was telling herself she shouldn't, her lips were clinging to his, savoring the feel and taste of him. A moment later he surprised her again as he slid his tongue between her lips.

Unexpected as it was, the sensation didn't displease her. The opposite, in fact. The intimacy of his action thrilled her in the way he had last night, when he sucked at her breasts through the cloth of her nightgown. Antoinette heard herself whimper softly, opening her mouth wider, daringly returning the caress of his tongue with hers.

He shifted slightly, whispering in her ear. "You dislike this intensely, don't you, Miss Dupre? Do you still want me to stop?"

"Yes," she said huskily. "Yes, I do want you to stop."

But it was a lie, and as he began to kiss her again, her mouth clung even more desperately to his. In just a few short moments this man, this stranger, her enemy, had set her body on fire to such an extent that she no longer cared what he had done or who he was. All she wanted was the pleasure she knew he could give her.

The tension inside her was building, growing tighter and tighter, but, infuriatingly, the release she sought eluded her. Was she doing something wrong?

She heard him groan softly. "Antoinette," he said. "I want to kiss your breasts. I want to spread your legs and drink deep. I want to be inside you . . ."

Antoinette knew she should be shocked. She really should be very very shocked. She tried to think of all the reasons that such a thing was impossible, reminding herself of what she had to lose.

"No."

But even as the protest left her lips, she felt him move. He was lying upon her now, but not heavily, supporting his weight. Still, she could feel the contours of his body and the hard shape of that part of him that made him a man, pressing to her belly through her nightgown. When she wriggled it butted against her, and she had the bizarre urge to giggle. Then his hand slid down and covered the mound of her breast, and she gasped instead. He made a sound of approval as her nipple jutted into his palm, as if eager for his attention. He found it with his finger and thumb, rolling it, tugging on it, until Antoinette heard herself moan deep in her throat.

"Stop. I command you to stop . . ."

"Why?" he rasped. "When we're both enjoying it so much?"

It was true, she was enjoying it, but he was her enemy and she didn't trust him. He was playing games with her, and they were dangerous games.

"Lovely, lovely Antoinette," he breathed. "Command me again."

"I command you to stop."

He groaned as if her words added another dimension to his enjoyment of her. Pleasure spiraled through her, urging her onward to who-knew-what. This was unknown territory for her, and yet the thought of entering it was exciting. His hand ran down over her belly to the hem of her nightgown, and he drew it up. Antoinette felt the cool night air caressing her naked limbs. He sat back and looked at what he'd uncovered.

"What are you doing?" she said nervously. The pleasure receded, and she tried to sit up.

He grasped her ankles and pulled her down again. Antoinette began to protest, but just then his hand ran up her inner leg, diving into the curls between her thighs, and touching her in a way that made her forget all about running away.

"You're ready for me," he whispered, stroking her.

"You shouldn't be doing this," she managed in a breathy voice. "I don't know you."

"Your body knows me," he said, and his fingers worked their magic once more. "Your body wants mine. Relax, Antoinette, and allow yourself to enjoy it. Why not?"

"I haven't . . ."

"Has Lord Appleby been neglecting you? Never mind, I will make it all better . . ."

Before she could answer or even think, one of his fingers was sliding inside her moist body, and his mouth was on her breasts, sucking first one nipple and then the other.

Antoinette clasped his head and realized for the first time that he wasn't wearing his mask. His hair was springy against her fingers, and the nape of his neck strong and yet strangely vulnerable. His clothing brushed against her nakedness, and she felt the linen of his shirt and the rougher cloth of his trousers and the leather of his belt. But most of all she felt his hot mouth and his tongue, as he worked his way down over her belly, tasting her skin as if she were a rare delicacy.

Antoinette lay bathed in a warm glow of delight. She almost believed it was a dream, or perhaps she preferred to believe that because it was safer than accepting that this was real.

He had reached the apex between her thighs, and he paused. She felt herself tense, thinking he would stop now. But he didn't.

He parted her legs. In the darkness she felt his breath against her skin, cooling her, and then his open mouth closed on her and his tongue went deep.

She couldn't speak. Once more she was in new territory, and it was beyond anything she could have imagined. Her fingers clenched in the sheets, and she struggled not to scream. He began to move his mouth upon her, teasing her swollen flesh. Heat coursed through her lower belly, and she arched off the bed as the feelings inside her gathered strength. It seemed to her that there was a cacophony of sounds inside her, growing louder, drowning out the thudding of her heart, and in a moment more she would explode and scatter into bits and pieces.

He stopped.

She made a cry of distress and heard him chuckle. "Be patient," he teased.

He bent again, and his tongue was back. Antoinette realized dizzily that she wanted him, as he'd said, inside her. Filling her. Her arms around his big body, her mouth on his, their bodies moving as one to the ultimate goal.

His tongue was doing its work on her, sliding around the swollen nub, and the tension was reaching a crescendo.

And then he pulled away. Again.

Antoinette lay still, holding her breath, waiting for his next touch, for the roll of his tongue to bring her to that place she had so recently experienced and already longed for again.

It didn't come.

She sat up, her hair loose about her, staring around in the dark. She opened her mouth to call his name and remembered she didn't know what it was. Legs weak and shaky, she rose from the bed and found the tinderbox and lit a candle. The weak light wasn't much help but it did show her one thing.

She was alone.

He had gone.

The ache between her legs told her that he had left her wanting more. Of course, she thought angrily, he had done so on purpose, so that she would be longing for him to return.

And she was.

With a sigh of frustration and annoyance with him, and herself, she walked to the window. She was glad he'd gone, and yet the ache in her body mocked her, made her think of what might have been. He frightened her, put her off balance in a way she had never felt before. How did he know why she'd gone to Sir James? How did he know what she felt when he touched her? It was as if he knew her better than she knew herself.

She looked down and gave a gasp. A dark figure stood against the stars, head back, staring up at her. He lifted an arm and waved to her, and she was certain she could hear his laughter. And then he was gone, as if he had simply vanished into the night.

Leaving her more unsettled than ever.

Chapter 10

Gabriel strode away from the manor house and into the woods, a spring in his step despite the heavy ache in his groin. He was trying to reconcile the last few moments of heady pleasure with a woman he found wildly attractive with the fact that she was the mistress of Lord Rudyard Appleby, his enemy. He felt confused, as he always was when he'd spent time with her, as if the two Antoinettes didn't quite match.

Don't get drawn into her web, he warned himself. *Don't trust her.*

But that didn't mean he couldn't enjoy her.

Pleasures of the flesh didn't necessarily mean a commitment of the mind or heart. Aphrodite would tell him that, if she were here to ask. Gabriel could seduce her and enjoy her, and when he had what he wanted from her—the letter—he would return her to Appleby without a second thought.

But the words had a sort of forced bravado, and he wondered if it would be that easy to let her go.

"Master Gabriel?"

He bit back a sigh of annoyance. Mary was waiting by his door. "Why are you out so late?" he asked her sternly, as he went inside the cottage and lit the lamp.

"No reason."

There was a note in her voice he recognized. He turned toward her, and in the soft light he saw that her fair hair was down around her shoulders and her dress was low-cut, showing off the swell of her breasts. He frowned.

"You shouldn't be here," he said.

She smiled. "I want to be here," she replied softly, and swayed toward him.

And suddenly he was angry with her and himself. He didn't want her here, and he certainly didn't want to take her to his bed. His body was crying out for release, but it was Antoinette he wanted. Mary Cooper would be second best, a means to an end, and she didn't deserve that. And he certainly didn't want to go down that road—it was against all that made him a man.

"Go back to the house, Mary," he told her sharply. "I mean it."

The protest died on her lips. She made a little sound, half sob, and turned and ran outside. He heard her steps fading through the woods until there was only silence and he was alone once more.

Glumly, Gabriel sank down in his chair before the ashes of the fire. It was only then it occurred to him that he'd been in Antoinette's room, in her bed, and he hadn't thought to search for the letter.

For all he knew it had been secreted somewhere beneath her nightgown!

A wry smile twisted his lips. No, she didn't have it on her. He would have found it otherwise when he'd touched her, kissed her, licked her . . .

The memory made him shift uncomfortably.

There had been a freshness about her, an innocence he hadn't been expecting from a woman in her position. But perhaps that was part of her charm, that illusion that he and he alone could awaken her passion. It certainly worked. He knew he wouldn't be able to think about anything else until he was in her bed again.

I command you to stop.

He smiled. Next time, he promised her silently, she would command him to do something else entirely.

Antoinette lay and watched as the dawn light peeked through her curtains. She, too, was trying to come to terms with what had happened between them. Was she insane to allow such a thing? But sanity didn't appear to come into it. Rather it was as if she'd lost her wits completely once he began to touch her. Were such things always so, between men and women? That ecstatic, dizzy joy? She didn't believe it. She had seen too much unhappiness in the marriages of her acquaintances to believe joy was a lasting consequence of matrimony.

But she wasn't thinking about marriage, was

she? She was thinking about connection. Physical congress. Making love.

He made her body cry out in a way that was new and wonderful, until she longed to be a part of him.

Whoever he might be.

And what if Sir James Trevalen arrests him?

The question made her sit up. He didn't think he could be caught; he'd said so: *I'm like smoke.* But that sounded like overconfidence to Antoinette, and Sir James appeared to be a competent man.

Outside the light was growing brighter; the day was beginning.

Of course if she discovered who he was first she could warn him. Give him time to get away before she told Sir James. It seemed like a reasonable plan. All she had to do was find where he was hiding. Antoinette didn't believe for a moment she wouldn't recognize him instantly if she saw him, however he might disguise himself—there would be some indefinable something that called to her. After such intimacy as had occurred between them, she was confident it was impossible for her *not* to know him.

She would find him, warn him of Sir James, and he would leave. Then she would be safe from his attentions.

Satisfied, she lay back, closing her eyes again, only to have them instantly spring wide open. She didn't want to be safe from his attentions! She felt as if she were wandering through a marvelous emporium, full of wondrous new objects, and she'd only just begun to explore. The image was very nice, but not quite apt. Antoinette grimaced. No, she was more like a greedy child who desired to gorge on sweets, even knowing they would make her sick. The temptation was stronger than her fear of the consequences.

As sleep claimed her, she found herself drifting back in time to the Mayfair house. It was some days after the evening when Appleby destroyed her reputation, and the morning when *the letter*, which was her only hope of escape, arrived in the post from Surrey.

She'd been expecting a letter from Miss Bridewell, and every morning she'd haunted the entrance hall, intent on getting her hands on it before anyone else. This morning the postman was early and she was still descending the stairs when the footman opened the door. Breathlessly Antoinette hurried to intercept him as he made his way toward Lord Appleby's study to lay the letters on his desk. A moment later she was holding Miss Bridewell's longed-for letter in her hands.

She already knew what it would contain. Miss Bridewell had promised to contact her old acquaintance, a housekeeper who had once worked for Lord Appleby, and pass on the mysterious details that would be the means of Antoinette's escape from this intolerable and dangerous situation.

"She knows something," Miss Bridewell promised her. "As soon as I wrote to her mentioning Lord Appleby's name and his visits, she sent a note back warning me about him."

"It may be nothing, but it's as well to follow it up," Antoinette replied. "If you hear any more, then you must send me the details at Lord Appleby's house in Mayfair."

Antoinette thought no more of it. She was more interested in the excitement gripping London as visitors from all over the world arrived to attend the Great Exhibition—Britain's might on display. She soon persuaded herself that Lord Appleby was perfectly amiable and all her doubts were groundless.

But then Miss Bridewell sent a hasty scrawled note: *Have news of serious nature. I am setting off to visit the person we spoke of as she will only discuss matters with me FACE TO FACE. I will send DETAILS as SOON as I have them. PLEASE TAKE CARE.*

The wording was dramatic. Puzzled, Antoinette wondered what it meant, but there was so much more to occupy her that she told herself it was sure to be a storm in a teacup. Shortly afterward she became aware of the gossip concerning her and Lord Appleby, and had the unpleasant task of refusing his offer of marriage. A week later he staged the scene that ruined her reputation and placed her firmly in his power.

And now at last Miss Bridewell's letter was in her hands. She only hoped whatever it contained would be the key to release her from her predicament.

A step behind her warned Antoinette of someone approaching. If Lord Appleby found her and asked to see her letter she could refuse, of course, but then he would wrest it from her. Antoinette was no longer under any illusions concerning His Lordship's ruthlessness.

Hastily, hands shaking, she pushed the letter down inside her bodice, before turning to face whoever it was with an aura of determined calm.

It was Lord Appleby's secretary, a young man with a protruding Adam's apple and an ingratiating smile. "Miss Dupre," he greeted her, his gaze dropping to her bosom.

Had he seen her deposit the letter there? Or was he ogling her figure? Antoinette didn't have time to find out. A loud jangle announced a visitor at the front door, and the footman hastened to open it. They could hear him protesting, but a moment later he was stepping back, giving way before the forcefulness of an obviously unwelcome visitor.

It was a woman in a black gown, the silk rustling as she moved, her dark hair touched with gray beneath a fashionable scrap of a bonnet. The flash of jewelry at her throat and fingers was eclipsed only by the flash of her dark eyes in her beautiful and yet haggard face.

Surprised, Antoinette watched as the woman cast her black gaze around and fixed upon the secretary. He seemed to shrink, as if he wanted to disappear, but there was no chance of that now she had him pinned. She came rustling forward and planted herself directly in front of him.

"I want to see Lord Appleby." Her melodious voice was heavy with a French accent. "I want to see him now!"

Belatedly, the secretary tried to assert his authority. "Madame, I can't possibly allow—"

"I do not care what you can or can't *allow*," she cut short his attempt, one long finger darting out to poke his chest. "Find him for me."

He hesitated, but it was clear that in a confrontation with such a formidable woman he hadn't a hope of winning. With a nod of his head, he trotted off to find his master.

The woman in black tapped her shoe and said, "Psht!" She turned, and now her gaze fixed on Antoinette. For a moment she examined her intensely, until gradually a puzzled expression slipped over her face. The woman's bright eyes slid down and stopped, and now she was frowning.

Fearing the worst, Antoinette also looked down. Oh dear, the corner of Miss Bridewell's precious letter was visible above her bodice!

She clapped her hand over it, but it was already too late.

The woman gave a delighted laugh. "Ah, a note from your lover?" She drew closer, as if they were sharing a secret. "I do not blame you for finding a little diversion, my dear. Lord Appleby is so . . . so . . ." But a suitably descriptive word escaped her, and she wrinkled her nose instead, her disgust plain to see.

Antoinette didn't answer, and perhaps that was for the best, because the next moment Lord

Appleby spoke from his study doorway in a loud and irritable voice.

"I don't see anyone without an appointment!"

The woman in black turned and stalked toward him. "You will see me!" she declared. "What do you mean by stealing my daughter's inheritance, my lord? I will not have it, do you hear me? I will not have it."

In trepidation Antoinette watched them, expecting Lord Appleby to jump into the attack, for he was certainly no gentleman and would not let his visitor's sex stop him. But he didn't. To her amazement he smiled, a smile Antoinette recognized well, as if he knew something he was going to use to destroy her.

"Madame," he said, rocking back on his heels. "Well, well, what a pleasure it is to see you. How many years has it been?"

"Not nearly enough," she retorted rudely.

"I would have visited you, you know, but I have a reputation to maintain. If I set foot in your club I'd be tainted."

"Psht! Enough. Answer my question."

His gaze slid by her to where Antoinette was hovering near the stairs, her hand still pressed to her chest. "Come into my study and we will discuss this matter privately, Madame Aphrodite."

Madame Aphrodite? The name was intriguing and Antoinette would have liked to listen to more, but that would mean eavesdropping, and she did not dare. Not now she had the letter.

Up in her room Antoinette sat by the window and hurriedly scanned Miss Bridewell's words.

My housekeeper friend remembered in great detail what happened in Lord Appleby's household in 1840, ten long years ago. He paid her to hold her tongue and so she did. But I managed to persuade her by appealing to her kind heart and her sense of duty, to TELL ALL.

Miss Bridewell then proceeded to expose a bizarre and shocking truth, and gave Antoinette the exact address in London where that truth was to be found: a house in Lambeth.

You must visit this house and gather the proof. If you take the story to those in power, then Lord Appleby would be ruined.

The governess really was a marvel. There was still the problem of giving Appleby's spies the slip, but she would try as soon as possible.

Raised voices caught her attention.

Cautiously, she crept out of her room and into the gallery and peered over the polished ebony railing. Lord Appleby and Madame Aphrodite stood below her.

"Do you really imagine you will get away with this?" The fury in Madame Aphrodite's voice was audible.

Lord Appleby seemed amused by her emotion. "Why not? You know, Madame Aphrodite, you really will have to learn to get along with me. Remember, I am your partner now."

For a moment Antoinette thought the woman would strike him across the face. Her hand was raised, while her body quivered like a bow. Lord

Appleby's mouth tightened and he leaned toward her, daring her.

"Do it. But I'm warning you that if you do I'll close you down by the end of the week. You will be on the streets, where you belong."

Madame Aphrodite seemed to sag, dropping her hand, turning her face aside. Her voice trembled. "I have friends. They will speak on my behalf."

Appleby snorted. "You are a courtesan, Madame. Who do you think they will listen to? You or me?"

"Your name is spoken of in the same breath as the Crystal Palace. You are in the public eye, my lord. People recognize you in the street. But such fame is a two-edged sword. There is always gossip, always those who will seek to pull you down." Her glittering black eyes lifted to his. "It is whispered how your young mistress was in your arms, bold as brass. Soon it will be all over London." She smiled. "The royal couple do not like men of poor moral character. Do you think they have heard the whispers?"

Appleby gave a scornful laugh, as if he didn't care. "You are clutching at straws, Madame," he mocked.

"We will see!" was her parting cry.

Two days later he came back from a visit to Buckingham Palace and called Antoinette down from her room.

"You are going away for a little while," he said, when Antoinette was standing reluctantly before him, her head held high. "I have a house in Devon. As much as I dislike Madame Aphrodite, she was right. You will stay in Devon until the gossip is forgotten, and when you come back you will marry me."

"I want to go home. Why can't you send me home?"

"Because I don't want you to go home," he imitated her voice. "I want you where I can keep an eye on you and you can't get up to any mischief. Remember, I have Cecilia. If you don't marry me, I will lock you away and take Cecilia in your place. She is quite a beauty, isn't she, your little sister?"

Shock made Antoinette's throat close over. Her sister in the hands of this wicked man? She couldn't allow it to happen. Frustration surged through her. She had the letter, but she was so closely watched, she hadn't had a chance to use it. And now he was sending her away.

"You will leave within the hour."

It made her physically ill but she begged him. "Please, my lord, let me stay. I—I can't bear to be sent away."

A puzzled frown creased his brow but he wasn't swayed. "No, Antoinette, it isn't possible. I can't risk losing royal patronage, not now. All these years I have worked toward making my fortune, and now I am on the verge of major success. My name will be famous, and orders will come in from all over the world."

Did he want her to admire him? Congratulate him? Antoinette could only wonder at such single-minded selfishness.

"Now go and pack," he said briskly, rubbing his hands together. "You have fifty-five minutes."

She turned and left him, but at the door he spoke again.

"Who knows, my dear, I might come and visit you."

"And risk the royals finding out?" she retorted with distaste.

"Devon is a long way away." He smiled, his gaze examining her in a way that made her cringe inside. "Cecilia may be a beauty but you are quite fetching yourself, Antoinette. Odd, I hadn't realized it. I think we could deal quite well together."

She didn't answer. She didn't think she could. Bad enough that everyone believed her to be Lord Appleby's mistress, but to be so in fact!

Antoinette made up her mind that she would do anything in her power to prevent it from happening, even if that meant giving herself to a stranger.

Chapter 11

Mary stood still, watching as Miss Dupre made her way along the upstairs corridor. She'd been following her for more than an hour, and so far she'd been into every room in the manor house. Now, as Mary peered around the corner of the landing, she saw Miss Dupre enter the old nursery. A few more steps and she was at the door. Mary crept closer and peeked inside.

She was opening the cupboards! Going through the contents as if it was her right. Now she'd picked up a small book and was flipping through the pages. A folded piece of paper fluttered out, and she stooped to pick it up, leaning toward the light to read it.

Mary turned and hurried back down the stairs. Miss Dupre was searching for something; something to use in her plan to send Master Gabriel to jail . . . or to the gallows. Yes, that must be it! A chill ran through Mary, and she knew Master Gabriel needed to be told as soon as possible. Maybe he would make the busybody leave, and then things could be the way they were. Mary longed for a return to the past.

Before Antoinette Dupre came to Wexmoor Manor with her bossy ways and her disapproving stare, Mary had hoped Gabriel might begin to see what was right in front of him. Why didn't he realize Mary was the perfect wife? They could reside together in perfect bliss, and the fact that Mary was the daughter of a fisherman and Gabriel a baronet's son would have no bearing on matters at all.

This naïve belief had sustained her for many years, and now Miss Dupre had come along and spoiled her dreams. Just wait until Gabriel heard about her poking and prying in his house. His eyes would be opened and he'd realize that Mary, his ever loyal and loving Mary, was the only one he needed.

Mary hurried off through the woods, confident that soon everything would be just as she wished it.

Antoinette didn't really know what she was looking for. Some clue that might help her discover the identity of the highwayman or escape Wexmoor Manor, or both? It was either that or sit twiddling her thumbs, and she was never a twiddling sort of girl.

So far she'd found a great deal that made little sense. Wexmoor Manor had definitely belonged to a family previous to Lord Appleby—the Langleys. There were memories and mementos to them everywhere, from paintings and books to schoolroom desks with graffiti cut into the old wood. "Gabriel hates sums" was one that made her smile. So uncompromising. Antoinette had disliked many of her lessons but not to the point of hatred, and she would never have defaced her schoolroom desk to prove a point.

The schoolroom kept her amused for quite some time. She was still there, examining a page of ink-stained alphabet letters, imagining the child who had labored so long over the curve of an "a" and the stem of an "l," when she realized she was no longer alone.

Her body tensed with the urge to turn and look; it was almost unbearable. But some stubbornness kept her where she was, her head bent over the yellowing pages.

"Do you wish to speak to me, or are you trespassing again?" she said, pleased her voice was so calm.

He laughed softly, and the hairs on the back of her neck rose. The next moment his steps were moving toward her across the scuffed timber floor. "How did you know it was me?"

"I guessed," she lied.

He stopped close behind her, and she was aware of the scent of him, male and healthy. Still she refused to turn. Turning would give him the upper hand in the game they were playing, and Antoinette was determined not to allow him to see how much he affected her.

"What are you looking for, sparrow? Evidence to use against me?"

"I'm sure Sir James will manage that on his own. He seems to be a competent sort of gentleman."

His warm breath stirred tendrils of her hair. "Are you afraid to look at me, Antoinette?" he whispered.

"No, I'm not afraid." Antoinette had no choice but to prove it and turn. He was right behind her. The black mask was startling on first seeing it again, but his mouth was smiling and the pale blue eyes she could see beneath it were warm and wicked. His fair hair curled untidily about his brow, and his broad shoulders blocked her escape.

"Give me what I want, sparrow."

"You know I can't." The words were out before she could stop them, and instantly regretted.

"I don't see why you can't. Unless . . ." His voice changed. "Are you under some sort of duress, Antoinette? Is Appleby threatening you?"

He sounded different, concerned and possessive, as if he was a man she could trust. Her own feelings frightened her into reacting to push him away before he could worm any further under her guard.

"Of course not!"

"The letter—"

"There is no letter," she retorted stubbornly.

"Antoinette," and now he was impatient with her, and she couldn't blame him. "We both know you have the letter. Why not give it to me and put an end to this nonsense?"

Her expression hardened, her eyes narrowed.

"It may be nonsense to you, sir, but to me it is . . ." She bit her lip at the blunder, but he was already on to it like a cat on a mouse.

"You were very nearly frank then, sparrow. Don't spoil it. What does the letter mean to you? Tell me and I can help you." His voice was so low and soothing, like a calming hand upon a turbulent sea. But she couldn't trust him; she daren't. He was Appleby's man.

"You're imagining things. I do not need your help."

His mouth was still smiling, but now his face— what she could see of it—appeared harder, more intractable. "Antoinette, give me the letter."

"No."

With a sound that was a mixture of impatience and frustration, he pulled her into his arms. Before Antoinette could protest, his mouth swooped down to cover hers, and then she didn't want to. She felt the tension inside her shiver and melt; her hands reached to cling to his shoulders, and her mouth eagerly returned the caress of his lips. Already the heat inside her was rising, the ache low in her belly intensifying.

He pulled away, breathing hard, his chin pressed against the top of her head. "I warn you," he said harshly, "I am not safe."

Antoinette leaned back to look up into his eyes. They were bright and feverish. He wanted her. She was playing with fire.

A thrill shivered through her. Her heart began to beat faster. Excitement made goose bumps on her skin. Her body was readying itself for his touch, but that was too easy. Daringly, she reached up and brushed his lips with her fingertips. His face, what she could see of it, registered surprise. Antoinette gave a laugh, and then catching up her long skirts, she turned and ran.

His footsteps followed.

She rounded the desk, gasping, slipping behind a trunk and pausing to look back from in front of the dusty windowpane. He was coming after her but without hurrying, slowly and confidently, like the predator she'd likened him to the first time she saw him.

This was madness, she told herself. She wanted him to touch her and kiss her. And at the same time she was aware of what it might lead to. She didn't know what was more dangerous, his threats or his concern.

Antoinette darted around a chair and made toward the door. He almost caught her skirt, his hand just catching the cloth, and she squealed as it slipped through his fingers.

Panic spurred her on as she ran to the end of corridor and found the back stairs. Uncarpeted, the varnish worn, these stairs were for the convenience of the servants. Antoinette took them as quickly as she dared, reaching the bottom and finding herself in another narrow passage. There was a door to her left, and she opened it and entered a shadowy room with drawn drapes. Trying to quieten her breathing, she pressed herself back against the wall and waited.

Once again the questions whirled inside her head. Did she or did she not want to be caught? The truth of the matter was she didn't know. Two Antoinettes were at war within her—the old one, the sensible one, and the newly discovered reckless one. She was afraid that the reckless one was capable of anything.

Steps outside in the hallway. Antoinette held her breath. A floorboard creaked. Silence. Another step, and then another.

Waiting and listening were much worse than being pursued. She longed to pick up her skirts and run. But then he'd catch her and . . .

Suddenly the door opened and closed again, so swiftly that the brief impression of his silhouette against the light was gone before it really registered. Antoinette pressed flat to the wall, hoping the gloom would hide her well enough to escape his notice. Then again, if he moved toward the window, she'd be able to escape.

"I know you're here." His whisper made her skin prickle. "I saw your footsteps in the dust."

He knew, or did he?

"You know what I'm going to do to you when I catch you."

She did, and God help her, she knew she was looking forward to it. Antoinette hadn't felt this wildly excited since she was . . . She had never felt like this, she thought, startled.

"Are you ready for me?" he said huskily. "I'm ready for you."

Antoinette began to slide along the wall, very

slowly, very carefully, inch by inch. If she could open the door without his seeing, then she could be out of the room and running before he realized.

"I'm going to make you scream . . . with pleasure."

She took a last step and reached out her hand.

He pounced. In an instant she was spun around and pressed front first against the closed door, her breath leaving her lungs in an oomph. He was against her back, his hands pinioning her wrists at head height, his soft laughter tickling her ear.

"Antoinette, my little sparrow, I have you now."

His body was heavy, making her aware of every contour and muscle, and then his mouth trailed down the side of her neck, and she realized the true danger. He was tasting her, making her burn, and she made a sound of denial. Or encouragement. He had hold of her skirts, hauling them up with one hand, until his fingers found her stockings and then the bare flesh above.

Bliss.

He pressed hard against her, the bulky cloth of her skirts flattening between them, and she felt the hard jut of his member. "The letter?" he said breathlessly, but it was obvious he no longer cared and certainly didn't expect her to acquiesce. She shook her head and groaned again as his fingers slid between her legs and brushed her firmly through the soft cloth of her drawers.

Hot, unbridled pleasure took away her power

of thought, of flight, of anything but longing for him to continue. He kissed the back of her neck, increasing the heated tremors running through her body, and she felt him reach down to grasp her hips, bending his knees, and sliding the long, hard length of him between her thighs, settling himself against her most sensitive places.

Antoinette groaned, unable to help herself, reaching back blindly to touch him, to hold him. He wasn't inside her but he was pressing against her, creating a pressure that was driving her to distraction. She moved, too, trying to catch his rhythm, but she felt awkward. As if she was seeking to sing a song she'd never heard before and hadn't quite got the tune right.

That aching pressure was building inside her. With his fingers about her jaw, he turned her face, arching her back so that his mouth could cover hers in a slow, passionate mating of tongues and lips.

Another moment and she would be flying. She tensed, ready, as her body gathered itself for the launch . . .

And then he stepped away.

A moment of confusion, of disbelief, and then she gave a wail of disappointment. Spinning around, she tried to grasp him, pull him back to her, but he avoided her hands. His chest was rising and falling heavily, and his muscles were hard as iron. Such self-control should have won her admiration, but Antoinette wasn't in the mood to admire him. Instead she wanted to pound him with her fists; at least that would release some of her tension.

"The letter," he gritted. "Give me the letter and I'll roger you until you can't walk."

The coarseness of his words finally reached her. Antoinette dropped her hands. The ache inside her was still there but it was draining away, being replaced by cold disgust at herself and him, and hatred of Lord Appleby for placing her in this appalling situation in which she could be mistaken for a woman whose sensual greed was more important than her honor.

"Never," she hissed.

He walked by her and opened the door. The light made her blink. She couldn't see his face, only the shape of him, as he left her.

"Never is a long time, sparrow," his voice drifted back.

She stood there in the silence after he'd gone. Anger ravaged her, making her hate herself and him, but gradually her emotions began to cool. Her mind took over.

Why was she allowing him to treat her like this? He was teasing her, manipulating her, using her. It was time she turned the tables on him and began to do the same to him. He'd shown himself to be vulnerable to her charms, hadn't he? Antoinette might be an innocent but she was no fool. She knew he wanted her. Why not use his desire against him just as he was using hers?

But the question was: *How?*

Frustrated at her own lack of sexual knowledge, she almost gave up the plan—and then she remembered something. When she was in the library looking for a hiding place for her letter, she'd noticed some books in the corner of a high shelf. They were the sort of books gentlemen collected—her gentle Uncle Jerome had several and called them "art," but since they had titles like *The Journey into Desire* and *Ladies of the Rod*, Antoinette had her doubts on that score. Now such tomes might actually come in useful if they gave her hints on how to play the highwayman at his own game.

In a purely educational manner, of course.

Antoinette smiled to herself as she left the room and sauntered down the hallway. Just wait until next time. She'd show him what it was to suffer the effects of unsated passion!

Gabriel didn't know how he managed to hold back. He hadn't planned to, he'd wanted her so much, but at the last moment his pride had stepped in.

Of course now he was in agony. Again! Was it possible to die from unsatisfied lust? And the unfairest cut of all was that Antoinette had wanted him just as much as he wanted her.

He pushed open the side door and strode out into the cool air, breathing deeply, trying to still the trembling in his limbs and the heavy ache in his groin. There was the letter, he reminded himself. The letter was why he was here, not to slake his lust on Appleby's mistress.

Jealousy burned inside, and he clenched his fists. He wanted her, he accepted that, but what worried him more was that he didn't want Appleby to have her. He wanted her all to himself, just him and no one else.

Gabriel knew he was in trouble.

Chapter 12

The books were where she remembered, just out of reach on a higher shelf, but with the titles plainly visible. Antoinette peered upward through her spectacles. *Erotic Poses and Positions*, she read. *Nights in the Sultan's Harem*. She dragged the stepladder into position and climbed up to remove the books and carried them to the table.

They were dusty, and after she mopped at them with her handkerchief, she opened the first one. The illustration that confronted her made her blink. Several times.

A naked young woman with her back to a half-open door, glancing around over her shoulder with a wicked little smile at the man who was standing in the shadows watching her.

Antoinette cleared her throat nervously, and glanced over her own shoulder. She'd locked the library door, but she still felt as if someone would burst in upon her and demand to know what she was doing with obscene material.

"I'm teaching myself the arts of seduction," she

said aloud. Feeling better, she turned over the page and took in the next image.

A woman reclined on a chaise longue, her long, dark hair spread across her breasts, her head arched back, and a look of dreamy pleasure on her face as a man leaned over her, his fingers between her thighs.

"Oh my . . ." Antoinette closed her eyes and swallowed. She turned over the page. The same woman was seated on the chaise longue while the man stood before her, his manhood jutting toward her open lips. She looked at it as if—Antoinette peered more closely—she was going to suck on it like a giant lollipop. An irresistible giggle broke from her.

Quickly she turned the page.

The pictures were amazingly educational. Who would have thought some of those feats were even possible? And when she imagined doing them to the highwayman, she found herself growing warm. Her breasts began to tingle, and she pressed her hands to them, closing her eyes and remembering their encounter in the darkened room.

Looking at pictures was all very well, but Antoinette preferred the real man to pretend images. Remembering the taste and scent and texture of him made the flesh between her legs begin to ache. Antoinette told herself she had more study to do, and opened the second book.

Lots of women in scanty harem trousers and tiny blouses, cavorting with leering men similarly dressed and with amazingly large . . . swords.

Hurriedly she closed the book, and then sneezed when dust rose up in a cloud into her face.

Antoinette was certain she now knew enough to put her plan into action, but whether she would be brave enough to actually do it when the time came . . .

That was another matter.

Wexmoor Manor was sleeping. Gabriel climbed the stairs, avoiding the creaking board on the landing from long practice, and moved silently along the short passage to Antoinette's room. For two days he'd waited, allowing himself to cool down. Or so he thought. In truth, as soon as he stepped into the manor, that ache of desire began its familiar throbbing and his hopeful body began to ready itself for release.

He'd been strong, but he didn't know if he could be strong much longer. She had the letter and they both knew it, but how could he persuade her to part with it? This way wasn't working, not unless he wanted to be driven mad with unfulfilled lust. Perhaps he should have gone with violence after all, he thought, and shook his head with a wry smile, knowing he could never hurt her.

He was still smiling as he quietly unlatched her door and swung it inward.

She was asleep, breathing softly, the night breeze stirring the curtains that were drawn back from her open window. Sally Wonicot had told him about the window and Antoinette's refusal to close it. He smiled. She was an unusual woman, his sparrow, and not one to do as others did just because that had always been the way of things. She made her own decisions and lived her own life, and he found he liked that about her.

He was beginning to feel as if he understood her, and he was aware that bullying her into handing over the letter would only make her more stubborn and determined not to give it to him. She was a strong woman who thought for herself, and he admired her for it. Antoinette Dupre was an honorable enemy.

Gabriel strode softly over the old Turkish rug toward her bed and stood staring down at her. She didn't move, her hand flung out on the pillow, her hair in a single braid across her shoulder, her lashes like dark crescents on her alabaster skin.

She looked so innocent and yet so desirable, both at the same time. It made no sense, but that was what he felt. Before he could stop himself, or even try, he stooped over her and kissed her soft mouth. Savoring her taste, taking his time, enjoying the exquisite sensations she created within him. Because in a moment he knew she would wake up and demand he leave, and then . . . then the whole push and pull between them would begin again, with both of them determined to be the victor.

She was stirring. He kissed her again, drawing her gently into his embrace, and with a sigh she lifted her arms and draped them about his neck. He felt her lips smile, saw the flicker of her lashes as her eyes opened and she gazed into his.

"You," she murmured sleepily.

"Yes."

"I thought I was dreaming."

Her voice was soft, sweet, and for some reason the sound of it brought a new ache to his chest. Not lust this time but something else, something he didn't have the time or the courage to explore too closely. Besides, her lips were brushing his, her fingers twining in his hair, and he let her have her way.

Gabriel was completely unprepared for what happened next. He felt her give his chest a sudden shove, and then he was falling off the bed and landing hard on the Turkish rug. Surprise slowed his reaction, and before he could get to his feet she was on top of him, landing hard, and driving the breath from his body. For a moment she lay sprawled over him, her nightgown rucked up over her legs, and her soft breasts in his face. He was enjoying the sensation so much he forgot to struggle. He even reached for her, intending to carry on.

But Antoinette had other ideas.

She sat up, straddling his waist, her palms pressed to his chest for balance, her single braid swinging down to tickle his chin.

"Now it's my turn, highwayman," she said in a triumphant voice. "You've had your way for too long. Lie still and do not struggle, or I warn you, it will be the worse for you."

She sounded so dramatic he began to laugh, he couldn't help it, and he couldn't stop. She laid her hand across his mouth to silence him, and her face swooped down to within an inch of his, her dark eyes round and bright and full of anticipation.

"Lie still," she ordered. "And do not fight me. I *will* have my way."

Gabriel blinked. It was the first inkling he had of what she intended to do to him, and he wondered if he should be afraid of her. But he didn't feel afraid. Instead excitement tingled down his spine, and his body, already eager, leaped once more to attention.

Antoinette took his silence for acquiescence. She removed her hand from his mouth and began to undo the fastenings on his shirt, before tugging the garment over his head. His bare torso seemed to fascinate her. She brushed her fingers lightly over his chest, tracing the curve and dip of bone and muscle, before she bent her head and began to blaze a new trail with her lips and tongue.

He tried to clasp her to him but she pulled away, firmly removing his arms and laying them down at his sides, and shaking her head.

"No. I told you. I will have my way."

The order was not so difficult to obey. Gabriel grinned and shrugged and lay back, closing his eyes, and after a moment he felt her fingers trailing over his skin once more, down over his ribs to his stomach, and then lower to the fastenings of his trousers. Despite himself he shifted uncomfortably, his member so engorged it was a wonder it didn't shred the cloth in its eagerness to escape.

"Ah, my highwayman," she mocked, "can it be you wish for my touch? Here?" Her hand glided over the bulge in his trousers. She drew back with a gasp, pretending to be shocked. "Oh my, how big you are. All the better to . . ." She didn't finish the sentence, smiling instead.

"Antoinette," he groaned, his body on fire. She was torturing him, and by the expression on her face she was enjoying it.

"What? Don't you like what I'm doing?" she said, widening her eyes in pretended surprise. "Should I stop?"

"You know I don't mean that," he growled.

"Then hush and let me get on with it."

And she was touching him again, slowly tracing the shape of him, leaning over him as if she was making a study, her lips parted, her braid dangling against the naked skin of his stomach and tickling him.

He bore her torture as best he could, but when she circled her hand about his length and gently squeezed, it was too much. Gabriel cried out, arching up from the floor. "Put me out of my misery, Antoinette, I'm begging you."

Startled, she turned from her inspection and looked into his face. There was something so dreamy about her expression, and her lips were reddened and parted. He wanted to drag her down and kiss her senseless. But then her face hardened and her eyes narrowed and she laughed. "So the boot is on the other foot now, isn't it?"

"Hardly the same . . ." he protested breathlessly.

She smiled and began to undo the buttons. "Oh yes, it is the same. Do you want me to stop and walk away, just as you do?"

"You know I don't," he groaned.

Her smile broadened as she opened another button and then she hesitated, almost as if she was afraid or she hadn't seen a naked man before. Which, Gabriel told himself, was plainly ridiculous. Or was there something here he was missing? The next moment her hand slipped inside his trousers and closed over his bare flesh, and he was no longer capable of thought at all.

Antoinette was proud of her boldness. The books she'd read had shown her things, explained things, but she was still an innocent playing at being a demimondaine. And it was so different from what she'd expected. The pictures were flat and cold, but this was close and intimate. He was warm and alive and so . . . well, beautiful. Who would have thought a man could be beautiful? But his body was young and strong and healthy, and he seemed like a creature from a fairy tale rather than simply a man.

The fact that he wanted her as much as she wanted him was far more exciting than she could have imagined. The more she touched and caressed him, the hotter grew her own desire. The thought of making love with him, their bodies entangled, giving and taking pleasure . . . She'd seen in those books how it could be between a woman and a man, and far from being shocked and disgusted, as no doubt a proper and genteel young lady should have been, she was intrigued and eager to take part.

Her hands began to tremble and her breath to quicken. She was on a knife edge, and at any moment she would lose her balance and her control over this dangerous situation.

"Tell me quickly," she said desperately.

"Tell you what?" he croaked, gasping, his chest gleaming with sweat.

"Who you are, why you want the letter, where you will take it?" she answered him with sharp impatience.

He opened his mouth and she leaned forward, waiting breathlessly. And waited. He closed it again. He shook his head, his jaw clenched, his eyes squeezed tight shut.

Torture. Agony. And yet with the promise of such pleasure as he had never had before. Gabriel waited for her to do her worst . . . or her best.

With a deep sigh, Antoinette laid her cheek upon his stomach, and he felt her breath on his member, cooling his heated and sensitive skin. He groaned softly, wondering if he could get any harder, and knew it was unlikely.

All he needed to do to put a stop to this was tell her what she wanted to know.

But if he gave her the information she wanted, he'd never get the letter, he thought bleakly. She'd pass the information on to Appleby, and next thing he'd be arrested and charged, or forced to leave the country, and his hope of recovering Wexmoor Manor would be gone.

Gabriel swallowed hard. She was touching him with her tongue, delicate little licks, like a cat. He rolled his head to the side. Watching her made it worse. Her mouth closed over the tip, enveloping him, and Gabriel knew he couldn't hold out any longer.

Tell her, tell her, tell her . . . His feverish brain was on fire.

But instead of telling her, he reached out and caught hold her. He swung her around, lifting her easily, and planted her directly on top of his aching body, just where he needed her most. She gasped, reaching out to steady herself, her hands slipping on his damp chest, her knees striking the carpet on either side of his hips. He looked up into her face and saw her eyes widen at the sensation of him against her aching body, slick flesh against slick flesh, naked skin against naked skin.

Ecstasy.

Involuntarily, Gabriel thrust upward against her, and felt a good half inch of his member nudge inside her. Oh yes, this was what he wanted. No more games, no more winners and losers. Just pleasure, pure and simple.

Antoinette knew she should fight and run. This wasn't what she'd meant to happen. He was supposed to suffer as she'd suffered. The trouble was she was suffering, too. Now she understood. This was how he'd felt as he gave her pleasure, wanting her while denying himself. Her new knowledge didn't help her feel any better.

The muscles in her thighs trembled as she held herself up off him while his hands on her hips urged her down. He nudged her again with his sleek strength, and entered her a little bit more. Antoinette felt a moment of resistance, as if he'd come up against a barrier, but whatever it was, was breached quickly and painlessly, and he slid in deeper still.

"Let me make love to you," he begged hoarsely. "I can give you more pleasure than Appleby's capable of, I promise you."

It felt so good, him inside her, his hands on her skin, and she didn't want to stop. *Why should you?* The Antoinette inherited from her wicked ancestress was in her head, reckless, eager. *You take after me; you know you do.* And then he reached up and cupped her breasts, and she was lost.

The stumbling footsteps outside the door were shockingly loud. The pair of them froze, staring toward the sound, as Wonicot went by, breaking into a few lines of song as he passed. He was drunk. "Sally," he called. "I'm home, Sally . . ."

Antoinette put her hand over her mouth and held in her laughter, but when her eyes met those of the highwayman, she could see he shared her feelings. He grinned.

And that was when Antoinette came to her senses.

Pushing away from him, she got to her feet. She expected him to protest and struggle, to try and coerce her, but he didn't. Perhaps he sensed the danger, too, and didn't want to betray his master by making love with his mistress. A moment later he sat up and pulled his clothes together. Sprawled on the rug, he ran his hands through his hair and briefly dropped his face into them.

"This was a mistake," she said, to herself as well as him. "I thought I could make you feel what I felt. I didn't know that I would feel such a strong desire for you. Every time we are together it grows stronger. More difficult to resist."

He met her eyes as he pushed himself to his feet, but he didn't come any closer. Obviously he was just as aware as she of the dangers of their getting too near. "This wasn't a mistake," he said. "*Stopping* was the mistake."

"Lord Appleby—"

"—isn't here."

She tried to read his eyes but it was impossible. "I need to return to London. Will you help me?"

He smiled and shook his head. "No, little sparrow. You are here and here you will stay. Once I have the letter in my own hands you can go wherever you like and I'll gladly take you there. I promise."

"You promise!" she spat. "I don't believe your promises."

He laughed, not at all insulted. "Wise sparrow."

Enough, thought Antoinette. They were going around in circles.

"I'm tired," she said. "You should go back to . . . wherever you sleep." Curiously she added, "Where *do* you live? It can't be far."

"Do you plan to visit me? I warn you, Antoinette, if you do there will be no stopping. Next time I will have you."

He sounded as if he was making a vow, and she wrapped her arms about herself and shivered. But she set aside thoughts of kissing and touching and his body sliding into hers, and thought instead of driving him away. She didn't trust him, but she knew he didn't trust her, and that was what she'd use.

"If you tell me where you live," she said sweetly, "I might well visit you."

"Oh?"

"So suspicious? Do tell; I won't repeat it to anyone else."

He reacted as she'd expected. "So you can hand me over to the magistrate and see me hanged? No, thank you."

Instinctively Antoinette shook her head. "I don't want to see you hanged," she said earnestly.

He observed her with a faint smile. "Now if I was an easily led fool I'd believe you, but I'm not. Of course you want me hanged. Once I'm out of your way you can return to Appleby and reap the benefits."

His words were puzzling, but she shook her head, more intent on convincing him she wasn't the bloodthirsty creature he imagined her. "Well, perhaps I do want you out of the way, but I don't want you hanged."

He moved closer, tipping up her chin with a fingertip and searching her face in the moonlight. "I almost believe you. You are a most unusual woman, Antoinette Dupre."

"These are most unusual circumstances," she murmured, meeting his pale eyes and refusing to look away from his searching gaze.

He leaned over her, until his mouth was only a breath away from claiming hers. "I want you and you want me," he said. "You know it's only a matter of time before we are lovers."

"But not tonight. Wonicot has seen to that."

He let her go. "I don't care about your past," he said quietly.

Again she tried to understand what he was really saying, but she was tired and fraught, and she just wanted him to leave her alone. She turned to stare out of the window, and a moment later her door closed and she heard his steps retreating.

This time when he appeared outside in the courtyard, he didn't turn and wave at her. He walked away, into the woods, and Antoinette knew that the light she had seen that first night was his. He was living out there, somewhere.

If she could find his home she might well discover his identity, and then she could force him into forgetting the letter and leaving her alone. He would have to leave if he didn't want to be arrested, and she would be safe.

Suddenly "safe" didn't have the same comforting feel. In fact, Antoinette was beginning to wonder if being safe was really something to be desired. And whether she was the sort of person who preferred to be very unsafe indeed.

Chapter 13

"**G**abriel."

Sir James Trevalen's smile was a shade anxious as he greeted his visitor. Perhaps, thought Gabriel, he was expecting some ravaged, desperate creature, unshaven and shabbily dressed, more used to hiding out in the woods than to polite company. If he was, then he was mistaken. Gabriel was shaven and clean and far from desperate.

"Sir James, I had your note. You wanted to see me?"

"Yes, Gabriel, I did." He sat down, gesturing for Gabriel to return to his own seat by the fire. The day had turned chilly, and outside the wind tossed treetops and bowed the taller perennials in the garden border. "I thought I owed it to your father to speak with you and to see how you are managing in the current difficult circumstances."

"I am managing," Gabriel replied levelly.

"You know all your friends are doing what they can for you. There has been a gross miscarriage of justice, and we will not rest until it has been righted. Unfortunately, because your father signed over Wexmoor Manor to Appleby, supposedly willingly, there's not much we *can* do. By the way, I have tried to discover from your father the truth of the matter, but he will not speak to me."

Gabriel gave a harsh laugh. "I'm not surprised, Sir James! It is a matter of a lady's honor, you see."

"Ah."

Gabriel preferred not to air the possibility of Appleby being his father, not even to an old family friend, and both men fell silent. After a moment Sir James rallied, changing the subject slightly.

"I had a visit from a Miss Dupre."

"Miss Dupre, dear me, don't believe everything that little bird says. She is Appleby's mistress, sent down here so that his reputation with the royals won't suffer. As soon as the Great Exhibition is over, you can be sure Miss Dupre will be heading back to London and her cozy life."

Sir James studied Gabriel's face. "You sound bitter. Do you dislike her so much? Or is it the man who keeps her you dislike?"

"Both," he said uncompromisingly.

"I have to say she didn't seem the type to put herself in Appleby's power. In fact, if I had met her anywhere else, and known nothing of her life, I would have said she was a well-brought-up young lady. A little intense, perhaps, and too frank to be popular at afternoon tea parties, but a lady nonetheless."

"Don't be deceived. Miss Dupre is a clever minx who can make you believe whatever she wants."

Sir James tilted back his head and folded his hands across his lean paunch. "You obviously don't admire her then?"

"No! Yes . . . I don't know." Gabriel stood up and peered from the window as if the weather might help him make up his mind. "I find her interesting, that's all. My life at the moment is difficult . . . uncertain. I find studying Miss Dupre takes my thoughts off my own misery."

An image of her perched above him, her body clasping his, eyes wide with surprise and wonder, shot into his brain. He pushed it out again before it had the inevitable effect on his physiology.

"Your family has a weakness for fallen women. Or so your grandfather used to say," he teased.

"You mean the story about the king's mistress? Yes, my grandfather believed if it wasn't for our ancestor's weakness we'd be titled now. Dukes or some such." Gabriel raised an eyebrow. "Are you worried I might form an attachment for Miss Dupre? You needn't be."

"You haven't asked me why she came to see me, Gabriel. Perhaps you already know. The lady wished to report an outrage perpetrated on her during her journey to Wexmoor Manor. It seems that she had already told the Wonicots but they weren't taking her seriously—a prank, they called it. She wanted me to discover the identity of the man who committed the outrage and arrest him. She seemed quite keen that I do so."

Gabriel continued to stare out over the garden. "And what did you say?"

"I agreed, of course."

"What do you want from me? A confession?"

Sir James made an impatient sound. "Gabriel, I know the man was you; what I don't know is why you would do such a thing. Miss Dupre may be Appleby's mistress but she doesn't deserve to be molested—"

"She wasn't molested!" he said, turning back to the room. "She had something hidden upon her person that I wanted. I asked her for it, politely, but she refused to hand it over. I offered her threats, although I had no intention of carrying them out, and she still refused. I was playing a part, remember. I suppose I wanted to frighten her into complying. I touched her and . . . once I began I . . . I couldn't seem to stop."

"Good God, man!"

Gabriel gave him a sickly smile. "Yes, a worrying development. But don't fret, I didn't hurt her, even though a woman who shares a bed with Appleby must be used to far worse than I dealt her. Anyway, we have made up now. I assure you, she is perfectly satisfied with the situation."

"I did wonder . . ." Sir James cleared his throat. "I wondered whether she was less keen to have you arrested than she appeared. It was almost as if she saw incarceration as a way of removing a threat to her peace of mind. Are you disturbing the lady's peace of mind, Gabriel?"

He laughed. "I hope so."

Sir James shook his head and reached to pour them both a brandy. "I will make inquiries. That should satisfy her. And I'll pay her a visit and see for myself that she is 'perfectly satisfied,' as you so intriguingly put it."

Gabriel took the glass.

"I don't suppose you are going to tell me what she was hiding on her person that you wanted so badly?" he went on. "Something to do with Appleby, I presume? And your father . . . ?"

"I was given information that Miss Dupre was keeping something safe for Lord Appleby, and I've searched everywhere else. It seemed a reasonable bet that the evidence I was seeking—a letter—was with Appleby's mistress. It would be just like him to use her like that, no matter what danger he put her in the way of."

"Are you sure it isn't a trap to catch you, Gabriel?" Sir James said mildly.

Antoinette as the bait in a trap? An interesting thought, but it didn't make him want her any less. "If it is a trap, then I will take the risk."

"I wouldn't have thought Wexmoor Manor was Appleby's type of place," Sir James went on thoughtfully. "Not flash enough."

"My father also owns a half share in Aphrodite's Club in London. Appleby has appropriated that, too."

"Aphrodite's Club?" Sir James's puzzlement cleared. "Yes, I see that would appeal to him."

"As a business investment, do you mean? I don't think that's the full reason. From what Aphrodite says he's a vengeful man. Years ago she slighted him in favor of my father, and he's remembered it all this time. Now he finally has his chance of revenge."

"Yes, I see. Take care, Gabriel," Sir James said, leaning forward intently. "Appleby is not a man to take lightly. He is ambitious and ruthless, and he seems to feel a deep dislike for your family."

"Could that be because I caressed his nose with my fist?" Gabriel spoke dryly.

"You joke about it," Sir James warned, "but it is not a game. Appleby doesn't play games, Gabriel. Be very careful."

Gabriel smiled. "I intend to be."

"With Miss Dupre, too. Intriguing as she is, I don't think I would trust her entirely. There's a great deal more to her than she's letting us see."

"I know. That's part of her charm."

Far away in London, Lord Appleby was strolling through Hyde Park and feeling well pleased with himself. He had just come from a meeting with Prince Albert. This time the prince consort made no mention of any scandal, although he must have heard the gossip, but it seemed that Antoinette's speedy departure for the country had done the trick.

His factories were currently turning out cast-iron tubing as fast as they could, and still could not keep up with the orders. His name coupled with the Crystal Palace had done the trick. He knew he'd taken a terrible risk, borrowing so heavily and going deeply into debt so that he could tender for the contract of supplying the Great Exhibition with the cast iron needed in its construction. If he hadn't won the contract . . . He shuddered to think of the consequences. He would have been abandoned like a sinking ship, until eventually his creditors tore him apart in the rush to get what was owed them.

But the gamble *had* worked. Oh yes, he still owed money, more than he could believe possible, but his creditors were showing signs of being willing to wait a little longer. At least until he married Antoinette Dupre and used the Dupre fortune to pay them off—and he'd certainly been dropping plenty of hints to that effect.

All was well with Appleby's world. The prince had even complimented him at the opening of the Great Exhibition, in front of all his peers and so-called betters, and Antoinette herself.

"I like this very much," he'd declared, gazing about him as they strolled through the vast interior of the Crystal Palace. "It is a miracle of glass and cast iron and steel. So beautiful and yet so strong. I am impressed, my lord. You must be very proud of your part in it."

"Thank you, Your Majesty."

The prince's gaze sharpened. "You are a self-made man, I hear. Pulled yourself up from nothing. Men like you are the backbone of England. You own and run the factories and the mills, you are never too fine to get your hands dirty. I like that, Appleby, indeed I do. There are far too many gentlemen about with lots to say and little to show for it."

"I consider myself very lucky to have been given this opportunity to serve my country, and you, sir."

Perhaps he'd gone a bit too far there, because Prince Albert gave him a long, steady look, as if he was trying to see into Appleby's mind. There had been that little upset when rumors about Antoinette and him got about, but now she was gone they had settled down nicely. When the wedding was announced, no one would be surprised, and even if she did protest, no one would listen.

A woman who was foolish enough to lose her reputation should know what was required of her. Marriage, and as soon as possible!

The way Appleby saw it, this was his way out of trouble. His continued success and solvency were more important than Antoinette and her sister. Antoinette must be made to see that her only option was obeying him.

And if she didn't?

Appleby paused to tip his hat to a passing acquaintance.

If she didn't, then it would be so much the worse for her. This wasn't the first time he'd come close to financial ruin and escaped by the skin of his teeth.

And his superior intelligence.

The memory made him uncomfortable, and he pushed it aside. There was no time for sentimentality in business; he'd learned that from a young age. When he was a child he'd gone hungry and suffered the back of his father's hand whenever he complained. He'd promised himself then that he'd escape from the cruel world he'd been born into, and so he had.

There was no possibility he would ever go back there, to the dirt and the filth and the unbearable misery. The London blue bloods might laugh at him and his pretensions and his love of fine things, but they didn't understand what it was like to go without. In his heart Appleby knew that he would fight to the death before he went under.

In such circumstances everyone and everything was expendable.

Chapter 14

Someone was following her. The familiar feeling had been building ever since she left the house and entered the woods. She found herself glancing over her shoulder, carefully observing her dark and creepy surroundings, even pausing to listen intently for footsteps. Despite her precautions she'd seen nothing to suggest she was under surveillance, although that didn't stop her from experiencing an increasing anxiety.

Of course it was possible that the Wonicots were spying on her again. They were Lord Appleby's creatures, after all, and they'd shown her from the beginning what they thought of her. Coombe might not be quite as bad—she still had hopes of bringing him over to her side—but neither did she trust him. Not yet.

As she wandered deeper into the thick woods, Antoinette came to the conclusion that if the Wonicots were watching her they were cleverer than she'd thought. She had not spotted them once. And she could not really see Mrs. Wonicot darting behind tree trunks, or Wonicot shuffling through the undergrowth with a spyglass.

No, whoever it was, was far cleverer than the Wonicots. For a moment she considered turning back, but she needed to do something.

Once again she paused, glancing about her, listening to the wind, the rattle and clack of the branches, the rustle of leaves, the sway of the tree-tops. Eerie. The woods were much thicker and far darker than she'd expected, full of shadows and noises that preyed upon her imagination.

After last night Antoinette had determined to find the source of the light she'd seen, and which she suspected belonged to the highwayman, and despite the blustery, unwelcoming day and her growing unease, she meant to complete the task she'd set herself. It made sense that the highway-man was in hiding. The attitude of the servants had hinted at a man who kept to the shadows, whom they were protecting.

She'd been thinking he was Appleby's man, bought body and soul, and sent to retrieve the letter. Perhaps he really was an outlaw, but she no longer believed he was Appleby's creature. This man had a mind and heart of his own, and that was what made him so dangerous to her. If she found his dwelling in the woods, it might give her a clue to his identity.

Something with his name on it, perhaps.

Something she could show to Sir James Trev-alen, or use to threaten the highwayman with disclosure. He'd have to leave then, and she would be safe from his kisses and caresses, and her increasing attraction to him and the delights to be found in his arms. Safe, before she lost her wits completely and failed herself and Cecilia.

Antoinette liked to think she was stronger minded than to fall for his charms, but the truth was she was in serious trouble. And the only way to get out of it was to run away—she was working on that—or to get the source of her trouble removed.

The path she was following through the woods was barely discernible, and now and again she would stop to make certain she hadn't strayed from it. As she walked her long skirts trailed through the leaves and debris littering the ground, and try as she might to hold them up, there was always something attaching itself to the hem that she then had to shake free. The latest fashion in skirts was for length—they were meant to trail. Irritably Antoinette wondered, as she pulled her skirts free yet again, whether those who set the fashion for what women should wear had ever tried traipsing through a dense wood.

She looked up at the sky, or what she could see of it through the crisscrossing leaves and branches, and decided it was growing gloomier by the minute. There was a feeling of dampness, too, as if a great deal of rain was coming, and wryly she wondered how she'd cope with her long, trailing skirts if they were soaking wet.

A moment later, to her surprise, she stepped

out of the woods and into a clearing, and there before her stood a cottage.

It looked like something from a fairy tale, the sort of fairy tale where the wicked witch was lurking in her cottage and waiting to trap unwary children. Old and dilapidated, the two-story building had an unhealthy slant to its slate roof, while overgrown shrubs formed a hedge about the perimeter. Blank black windows stared out at her from the ground story, while those at the top were either broken or boarded up. No smoke drifted from the chimney. The overall effect was one of desolation.

Perhaps she had the wrong house? Perhaps there was another one about somewhere, because she certainly had not imagined the light glowing in the middle of the woods.

Antoinette hesitated, not anxious to go any nearer, but she supposed that now she was here, she should take a closer look. She was not normally a coward, but something about the silent and gloomy sky, the woods, and the house in the clearing, made her edgy.

Suspicious, alert for danger, she made her way across the clearing. The cottage wasn't as decrepit as it first appeared. Someone had cleared away the weeds from in front of the doorway, leaving just enough of the tangled mess to disguise the fact, and those panes of glass that hadn't been broken were sparkling clean. The cottage might appear deserted but it was just a disguise.

A disguise such as the clever highwayman might devise.

Antoinette pushed at the solid old door and found it unlatched. It swung open without a creak, and she stepped inside the mysterious cottage, blinking against the gloom, her shoes barely audible on the stone floor. Dust motes danced in the wedge of light from the doorway, and she could see a table and a couple of chairs and a dresser filled with old crockery. The scent of herbs filled the air, old but still powerful, as if whoever once lived here had surrounded himself with aromatic plants.

Fascinated, forgetting caution, Antoinette took another step inside.

There was a noise behind her from the doorway—a footstep—and then a strong pair of arms came about her, pulling her back against a broad chest, and a familiar voice whispered in her ear.

"Little sparrow . . ."

Gabriel felt her jump, her body tensing. She tried to break free and run but he held her fast against him, enjoying the sensation of soft, warm, female flesh. Lucky, he thought, he had caught sight of her through the trees as he was heading home. He had his mask with him, and the visit to Sir James had ensured he was not wearing his Coombe clothes, so there was nothing to connect him to the smelly groom.

But as much as he was enjoying holding her, the fact that she was here, poking about where she had no right to be, irritated him. He hadn't known she was aware of the cottage in the woods, and he was certain no one had mentioned it to her. Now that she had discovered his hideaway she would broadcast it far and wide, demanding he be arrested, putting Sir James Trevalen into a difficult position. He'd have to leave and find somewhere else, and he didn't want to. Between Antoinette and Appleby, he was being driven from his rightful home.

"Do you know what happens to curious little sparrows?" he said in a low, menacing voice.

"No, what happens to curious little sparrows?" she said in a voice that strove to be calm, but he could hear the tremor in it.

"They are locked up in cages." He lifted her feet off the floor and swung her around once, hearing her gasp of surprise. Her fingers clung to his arms where they were folded about her waist, her nails digging into the sleeves of his jacket.

"Let me go," she said.

"This time it's you who are trespassing," he mocked, and spun her around again, her skirts belling out around them.

She gave a squeal, kicking her feet, and clinging harder.

Gabriel sighed and set her feet back down on the floor, but he didn't release her. He didn't want her fear. He wasn't the sort of man who found pleasure in making others afraid of him. Instead he rested his chin lightly on top of her crown, once more enjoying her scent and the feel of her soft body nestled against him. Desire shot through him and as if it had a life of its own, his cock twitched and hardened. Frustratingly, he was back to feeling just as desperate as he had last time they were together.

"Antoinette . . ." Gabriel groaned softly.

She tried to turn her head to see him, and when he wouldn't let her she grew impatient. "Are you injured?" she demanded. "Has someone shot you while you were robbing his coach? I should say it serves you right but . . ."

"But?" he repeated huskily, more interested in her curves and the way in which they seemed to fit to his harder, tougher body so perfectly.

"But I don't enjoy bloodshed, even when the blood is yours."

Gabriel opened his mouth to tell her that she needn't worry, he was perfectly well, and then he changed his mind. There was concern in her voice, a sharp note of worry that hadn't been there before. If he was as lacking in conscience as she thought, then he'd use this chance to punish her for finding his hiding place.

Only he couldn't do that . . . could he . . . ?

Gabriel staggered slightly, leaning his weight heavily on her. She gasped, turning in his arms and trying to support him. Her face was turned up to his, and he could see the darkening of her eyes as she searched for signs of an injury.

"Sit down," she urged. "I can't hold you; you're too big."

Gabriel was wearing his mask and there was

nothing about him to hint at his true identity, even if she did know who Gabriel Langley was. With a wince for good effect he let her help him to the wooden chair by the table and sank gratefully into it.

"Thank you," he gasped. "I wouldn't blame you if you walked out and left me."

"I won't do that."

Through the slits in his mask he watched her, her expression a mixture of worry and doubt. She was wearing her spectacles—who would have thought those little round pieces of glass could make him feel so hot?—and wild tendrils of her hair framed her face. The bottom half of her long skirt was filthy, and there was a tear where the cloth had caught on something sharp.

Gabriel didn't know why he thought her perfect when she was obviously far from it. But he did.

"I've behaved very badly toward you," he said, with a shudder.

"Yes, you have."

She was leaning over him now, and he tried to ignore the lush curve of her breasts, so close that if he leaned forward an inch he could rest his face against them and breathe in her sweet scent.

"Will you forgive me?" he whispered, gazing into her eyes.

They were beautiful eyes. Her spectacles had slipped down her nose, and he could see the warm brown color of her irises. A smile creased the corners, but a moment later was gone.

"Where are you hurt?" she said, a note of impatience in her voice. As if she wanted him to stop this nonsense so that she could do something practical to help him.

He shook his head and turned his face away. "Leave me here," he said with a heroic grimace. "I deserve to die like a dog."

She touched his shoulder, her fingers gentle. "No one deserves that."

"You don't know half of what I've done, Antoinette. I wouldn't soil your ears with the details. A man like me was born to be hanged."

"Even so . . ." She was watching him uncertainly, as well she might. His acting was appallingly bad but she believed him to be a highwayman, willing to go to any lengths to achieve his goal. She didn't know he was Gabriel Langley, son of a baronet . . .

Or maybe he wasn't the son of a baronet at all. He was a man without a name, without the home he loved, and this woman was the mistress of his arch enemy. He closed his eyes and began to writhe in his chair as if he were in his death throes.

"Please . . ." Her hand tightened on his shoulder, and then she touched his hair, stroking the untidy curls. When he opened his eyes and looked up at her, she was gazing down at him, and, just for a moment, he thought she looked like an angel. An angel wearing spectacles. And then desire took over again and she was all woman, *the* woman for him.

"Tell me where it hurts?" she said, enunciating

the words clearly and slowly, so that even a man in his perilous state could understand.

He made a vague gesture downward.

Antoinette frowned as she tried to see where the wound was. She pressed her hands carefully to his chest, then his stomach, glancing up at him for guidance. He shook his head. Her hand rested lightly on his knee as she knelt before him on the floor.

"Tell me," she begged. "I cannot help you if you will not tell me."

"Up," he groaned, with another spasm.

Her hands crept up over his thighs, her worried gaze searching his limbs for wounds or signs of trauma. He thought he might die. He remembered her mouth on him, and his discomfort doubled. Gabriel was no longer pretending to be in pain.

"There," he gasped, pointing.

She actually reached out and laid her palm over him—who would have thought her such an innocent!—before realizing she'd been made a fool of. The next moment she leaped to her feet, eyes flashing, fists clenched, the image of womanly fury.

"You beast!"

Gabriel shook with laughter. Behind the mask his eyes were streaming.

"I cannot believe I was concerned for such a . . . a . . ." she stammered, so angry she couldn't go on.

"Such a beast," he offered, and took a shaky breath. "I didn't know you cared, Antoinette."

"I don't!" she half screamed.

Laughter left him, and abruptly he stood up. She eyed him uneasily, backing away. "You're lying," he said coolly.

"No."

Were those tears in her eyes? Impossible! And yet he felt his heart soften at the thought that they might be.

"Last night . . ." he began.

She turned her back on him. "I don't want to discuss last night."

"You enjoyed it. You can't hide that from me."

"I shouldn't have—"

"Because of Appleby?" he scoffed. "Why are you so loyal to such a man?"

She glanced at him over her shoulder. "You sound as if you hate him."

She sounded surprised, and he in turn was surprised that she wouldn't expect him to hate such a man. Of course he hated Appleby! Hadn't His Lordship told her his plans? But perhaps he hadn't. And Antoinette didn't know she was speaking to Gabriel Langley, the victim of Appleby's vengeful plot. In her eyes he was nothing but a thief.

Perhaps it was time he explained.

"The letter—" Gabriel began.

"I'm tired of the letter!" she burst out. "I'm tired of you, and I'm tired of Lord Appleby. You're both as bad as each other."

Gabriel's heart went cold. *I'm not like him. He's not my father.*

"It's because of the money," she added quietly, her mouth drooping.

Was that her excuse for siding with Appleby? Money? He understood she had to live, but surely there were other ways?

"You're right, I do hate him," Gabriel said harshly. "But it's not because of the money. I hate him because he has you."

She looked as surprised as he felt. The words had burst out of him, and now it was too late to take them back. He wanted her. Gabriel told himself that an experienced woman like her probably already knew that, and she would use it against him.

He didn't care.

He could still feel the brush of her fingers against his flesh through his trousers, tantalizingly close but not close enough. The time for game playing was over.

"Come here Antoinette," he said, and knew his decision was in his eyes for her to see.

She turned and fled.

Gabriel went after her.

Chapter 15

As Antoinette reached the edge of the clearing, she gave one desperate glance back. It was enough. He was gaining on her. She plunged into the gloomy woods. Her long skirts snagged on twigs and low bushes, and violently she wrenched them free. Behind her she heard him curse as he stumbled, crashing through the undergrowth. Another quick glance behind her showed him several yards away.

Her heart was thudding, a curious mixture of excitement and fear pumping through her veins. She knew she should be terrified of this man and what might happen if he caught her— she'd read the hot desire in his eyes. But she wasn't. She'd run because she was just as afraid of herself as of him. When he looked at her, the melting sensation inside her body had been warning enough to send her fleeing.

It was either that or fling herself into his arms.

Besides, she was angry with him for making her think he was wounded, and just as angry with herself for letting him see how much it mattered to her.

A tree loomed up in front of her, and at the last moment she darted around it, pushing against the trunk as she passed. She didn't need to glance behind her this time to know he was closing in.

She'd lost the path through the woods. Now the trees were closer together, and the undergrowth was thicker, catching at her clothing, blocking her way so that she had no choice but to force herself through, or pause long enough to find an alternate route. Far above, through the swaying branches, the sky was darkening. At any second Antoinette expected the storm to break.

On she ran, blindly, praying she was heading for the manor, and that in another moment she'd burst from the woods and find sanctuary.

Or would she? He'd follow her inside. He'd chase her upstairs and force open her door. He'd kiss her mouth and touch her skin and . . . and the truth was . . . she wanted him to.

Something gripped the back of her skirt and brought her up short. She swung around, fighting, trying to free herself, and promptly slipped over, landing on her back in a soft pile of leaf mulch. The smell of earth and vegetation rose around her, and with it an herbal scent similar to the one she'd detected in the highwayman's cottage.

Dazed, she looked at her hand, and saw that when she fell she'd grabbed at a nearby plant. The sweet aroma was coming from that.

"Can we stop now?" he pleaded.

She looked up. He was on the ground, too, crawling toward her, the black mask hidden in the shadows. He shrugged off his jacket and threw it to one side, his chest rising and falling from the chase. The damp air was causing his fair hair to curl wildly around his head—an angel's halo.

Only he was no angel.

As if in agreement there was a deep rumble of thunder, and then the heavens opened. Rain came down, heavy and soaking, dripping through the trees and falling on her face as she lay gazing upward.

Breathlessly she began to laugh.

He grinned down at her, water dripping from his hair and trickling down the mask. His shirt clung to his broad shoulders in wet patches, and he pulled it over his head and flung it aside with the jacket. His skin glowed palely, muscles rippling as he knelt at her side.

She desired this man as she had never thought to desire any man, and as she looked at him her mind became crystal-clear. Lord Appleby planned to marry her, and he'd already ruined her reputation. Even if she finally escaped his clutches, it was doubtful a respectable gentleman would ever propose to her now—she was not naïve enough to believe all could be mended. But she could still win. By giving herself to the highwayman, at least she would deny Appleby the pleasure of taking her maidenhead. And at least she would have made her own choice as to who would be her first lover.

"Kiss me," she whispered.

"Sparrow," he groaned, and, bending his head, obeyed.

The combination of storm and man was exciting, as if she were caught up in something stark and primeval, where civilized behavior had no place. At this moment anything was possible. The past and the future ceased to exist, and there was only here and now.

His kisses made her ache, and she helped him unbutton her bodice, as eager as he to have his mouth and hands upon her. At the first touch she knew this time it wasn't going to be enough. He was right; they must consummate this passion between them. And if there was a cost, then she would worry about it later.

He gathered her breasts into his hands, and they felt heavy and swollen, so sensitive when he brushed her nipples, and then bent to suckle upon them, that she made little sounds of want. Such pleasure. Antoinette sighed, fingers tangling in his hair, and he lifted his head and smiled into her eyes. Their mouths fused, tongues mating, and he rested his weight lightly upon her.

She felt his hand tugging up her skirts and petticoats, and she wound her legs around his as best she could, but it wasn't nearly enough.

Not for him, either.

He moved away and sat staring down at her, enjoying the sight of her dishabille and her mouth swollen from his kisses. Then, with a wicked smile, he began to work on her fastenings once more. The bodice was soon removed; the long, tight sleeves came free with a sharp tug or two. Her skirts and petticoats were more difficult, but he freed her, and then slid her stockings down over her legs slowly and with minute attention, before untying the waist of her drawers and slipping them off.

She was naked.

As Antoinette lay before him, letting him look at what no other man had looked upon before, she wondered at herself. She'd always expected to feel embarrassed at such a moment, self-conscious in regard to her shortcomings, but she wasn't. Instead the expression on his face made her very aware of her sensual beauty. She felt confident and feminine, and in control of her own destiny.

He brushed the curls between her thighs with his fingertips and smiled when she gasped softly. He began to unbutton his trousers, his smile broadening at her rapt attention. His cock sprang free, rising up eagerly. She reached out toward him, but he caught her fingers in his and instead raised them to his lips.

"You're too clever with these little hands. I'll lose control," he said. "I don't want to make love to you like a lusty youth with no finesse, Antoinette. I want to pleasure you as you've never been pleasured before."

He began to kiss her again, and she lost herself in his slow, deep caresses. Soon he lay down on top of her, and his body molded itself to hers, his skin hot and hard where hers was soft. His thighs opened hers, and she felt his member press against her core. Antoinette went still, quivering.

"I can feel you," he murmured, bending to nip at her lips. "So warm and wet and ready. Are you ready, Antoinette?"

"Yes." She had never been so ready for anything in her life.

He pushed inside some more, then withdrew, slowly, the stem of his manhood teasing her aching bud. That familiar tension was building inside her, clenching in her lower belly and making her thighs tremble. She arched up against him, knowing she needed more from him, but he held her hips steady, refusing to allow it. His member slid inside her again, and he groaned into her mouth.

"You're mine, all mine . . ."

"Yes, yes, all yours."

She felt as if she had a fever, trembling and aching and delirious. If he didn't bring her to the peak she so desired this time, she'd scream, she told herself. He slid deeper, filling her, and her body was able to accommodate him perfectly. She didn't want him to withdraw, tightening about him to hold him inside.

Beneath her fingers she could feel the warm, damp skin of his back, and she reveled in the touch and smell of him. Everything combined to increase her desire. The way the tips of her breasts brushed against the hair on his chest, the movement of his muscular thighs within hers, the weight of his body, which could have been frightening and claustrophobic and dangerous, and yet now felt almost protective.

With a deep breath he withdrew again, every muscle rigid with the need to control his own pleasure. "Oh," she wailed, "don't stop."

"I want to make you feel better than you've ever felt before," he said, his jaw tense. "I want it to be like the first time."

She managed a laugh. "I promise you it will be."

He thrust into her again, deeper this time, and a hot, aching pleasure rose up inside her like a tide. He reached down, his fingers finding her swollen bud, and suddenly the tide surged up over her and she cried out in ecstasy. Her body spasmed, squeezing him like a fist as she climaxed.

Somewhere beyond the languid sense of pleasure she knew he was still driving deep inside her, and then he gave a shout as he, too, found his peak. For a moment his weight was heavy on her, his mouth against her neck, his breath hard and hot, and then he eased himself from her and, turning her on her side, wrapped his arm over her and lay pressed against her back. She felt his face nuzzling her hair, and his hand reached up and cupped her breast.

He hadn't noticed she was a virgin.

Not that Antoinette wanted him to, but she'd heard enough whispered conversations and half-caught confidences between married friends and servants that it could be painful, that first time. Thinking about it, she wondered now whether he had breached her maidenhead when she was seated upon him, and that was why she'd felt no discomfort.

His fingers rolled her nipple, tugging at it, and his open mouth moved over her cheek. She turned her head, and he kissed her. After a moment she was aware of his body shifting, his member rising hard against the globes of her bottom. To her surprise she felt her own flesh begin to tingle and ache, and the place between her legs, although a little sore, melted once more.

She should tell him no. She should get up and dress and leave before things could get any more complicated. But he was already turning her over, slipping his body over hers and into hers, and Antoinette welcomed him with an eagerness she couldn't disguise.

Her enemy, the highwayman, the man sent by Appleby to take away her one chance of freedom, was now her lover. And if that was an odd and dangerous twist, then it didn't feel like it. As he drove deep inside her, Antoinette knew it felt absolutely perfect.

Chapter 16

"Miss!"

Antoinette had crept upstairs to her bedchamber, thinking to take solitary sanctuary there, but as she closed the door, her relief was short-lived. Mary's shocked cry made her jump. She turned with an involuntary shiver, goose bumps rising on her wet skin, her dark hair a wild, bedraggled mess.

Mary's dark eyes were enormous. "You're completely drenched, miss! Whatever happened to you?"

Fortunately, Antoinette had prepared her story on the way home. "I was out walking when the storm came. I tried to shelter but . . . well, you can see. I waited for ages for it to stop, but when it didn't I ran for it."

She tried a self-deprecating laugh but broke off in the middle to give another shiver. Mary began to work on buttons and hooks and eyes, muttering about unnamed others who'd caught chills in weather such as this and their ensuing long, slow, and painful deaths. "That's what Mrs. Wonicot says at any rate," she ended, as if that was the final word on the matter.

"I have always been blessed with good health," Antoinette assured her, and sneezed.

Mary stripped her of her dress. "I wouldn't be surprised if this was ruined," she said reprovingly. "Just like the other one."

"Like the other one?"

"The other dress that was ruined, miss. Torn in the . . . the accident in the coach on your way here. Two dresses ruined seems very careless."

"Careless" was not the word for it, but Antoinette couldn't be bothered arguing.

Mary began work on petticoats and other undergarments, soon stripping Antoinette to her frozen white skin. Gratefully, Antoinette accepted the quilt Mary drew from the bed, wrapping it around herself and perching on a chair in front of the fire.

"I suppose His Lordship buys you lots of pretty things, miss."

Antoinette opened her mouth and closed it again.

"A ruined dress would mean nothing to you."

She ignored Mary's envy, holding out her hands to the flames, but she felt stiff and awkward, as if the truth was written in big black letters across her white face.

"Where were you walking?" Mary was sorting the clothing into sodden piles, oddly intent.

"In the woods. I stepped off the path. The trees were so thick, so close, I was lost. It took me a while to find my way back."

"You shouldn't have gone into the woods." Mary spoke sharply, but when Antoinette looked around at her in surprise, she forced a smile, softening her tone. "They do say as the ghost of Miss Priscilla Langley roams those woods. She was something of a witch, even though she was the only daughter of Sir John Langley."

Mrs. Wonicot's Sir John.

"Who were the Langleys? Did they live here for a long time?"

"They were the lords of Wexmoor Manor for hundreds and hundreds of years."

"Did Sir John own Wexmoor Manor before Lord Appleby took over?"

"No, that was Sir Adam. Sir Adam Langley was . . . is Sir John's son, and it was him that owned the manor before Lord Appleby took it over. His son, Master Gabriel, was meant to inherit, but . . ."

Her voice trailed off, and instead she began busying herself again with Antoinette's clothing.

Antoinette's shivers were fading as the warmth of the fire seeped into her cold flesh. She was even becoming drowsy. She'd closed her eyes and was close to drifting off when Mary spoke again.

"I wouldn't go into those woods again if I was you, miss. You might fall and hurt yourself, and no one would find you. Except the ghost of the witch, of course."

"I don't believe in witches," Antoinette said sleepily. "Besides, Priscilla was probably an herbalist." That would explain the lingering scent of herbs in the cottage.

Mary ignored her. "If you fell down and hurt yourself, Lord Appleby might think you'd run off, miss," she said, with an odd little laugh. "I reckon he'd sack the lot of us, and then we'd all be looking for new jobs. So you see, miss, we can't let you wander around alone in the woods."

The girl was giving her a warning. Antoinette drew her quilt closer about her, as if for protection. "You don't need to say anything to anyone about what happened, Mary. I feel foolish enough as it is. Let's just forget it, shall we?"

Mary hesitated. "I'd like to say yes, miss, but surely it's my duty to tell His Lordship if I think you're putting yourself in danger?"

"Mary, I wasn't in danger."

"But, miss, it isn't just ghosts to be found in those woods. What if some man was roaming about and he saw a pretty lady like you? I wouldn't like to think about what might happen to you. What he might do to you. And how would I tell His Lordship that?"

She knew. Antoinette gripped the quilt tightly, her knuckles white. She didn't understand how, but Mary *knew.*

It was no use confronting her, or confessing. The girl might feel compelled to act. But there was another way. "If . . . if you like you can have another of my dresses. Not the ruined one, but perhaps the royal blue? I believe it would suit your coloring very well, Mary."

Mary had bent over to gather the wet clothing into her arms, hiding her face. "If you say so, miss," she said tonelessly. "I never refuse a gift, and as you've so kindly offered . . ." She paused. "Maybe I'll have the green instead. I've always fancied myself in green."

"Very well, Mary. I'm sure the green will look just as good on you. And . . . thank you for your circumspection."

But Mary didn't answer, and the door closed behind her.

Alone, Antoinette sat and stared into the flames. Mary had guessed, but once she'd got what she wanted she seemed to lose interest. Antoinette hoped she wouldn't say anything to the Wonicots, and more importantly she didn't want Lord Appleby to know. If he decided to take her back to his house in Mayfair and force her into marrying him, she would be lost.

One dress seemed a small price to pay.

Antoinette snuggled into her quilt and sighed. Outside the rain was still falling, but softly now, gently running down the windowpanes. The sound was soothing, lulling her into forgetting her troubles, and remembering instead the pleasure of being in *his* arms. Her body ached in strange places, and she smiled. She'd told herself she was giving herself to the highwayman to take the initiative from Appleby, but that was far too simplistic. As was "giving." They had given and taken from each other.

Did all women feel thus? She couldn't believe it. There were too many unhappy wives in the world for that. If, she thought smugly, they all had a man like the highwayman waiting in the shadows, they wouldn't have to be unhappy.

She stretched. Would he come to her again? Remembering the burning kiss he'd given her as he left her at the edge of the woods, she thought that he probably would. And anticipation made her smile.

Mary had to stop when she reached the landing, the wet clothing clutched tightly in her arms. She was shaking and the skin across her forehead felt tight, and there was a burning sensation behind her eyes as she held back tears. But they weren't tears of sorrow.

Mary was angry.

Miss Antoinette Dupre hadn't been lost in the woods. She'd gone there on purpose. She and Master Gabriel had lain down together in the leaves and joined their bodies. Mary had known as soon as she saw the higgledy-piggledy way Miss Dupre's clothes were fastened, and the stains. She'd seen what men and women did when she was at home, in her village, spying on the beach when the young people went courting. Mary had always imagined herself and Master Gabriel, together, when she remembered those images.

Now Antoinette Dupre had stolen him from her.

She didn't blame Gabriel for what had happened. Men were easily swayed by a clever woman's tricks; she accepted that. It was the woman who was at fault, and this woman was another man's mistress. She had everything. She had no right to set her sights on Mary's Gabriel.

The tears overflowed and spilled down her cheeks. She bent her head, wiping them away on the wet clothes, furious with the world and everyone in it. What did she care for dresses, whether they were blue or green? Her dreams for a rosy future were ruined. In tatters. Like her heart.

No! I won't let her have him!

She thudded down the stairs, heading toward the laundry. Master Gabriel was hers and always had been, and she wasn't about to give him up. She had never doubted that one day Gabriel would marry her, and they would spend the rest of their lives together, here at Wexmoor Manor. It was meant to be, and nothing was going to interfere in their predestined future.

Mary thought again about how she'd tricked Miss Dupre into more or less admitting that something had happened in the woods. She'd been so quick to agree to give Mary the dress, to stop her telling. And that was because she was afraid of what would happen to her if Lord Appleby heard about her tryst with Master Gabriel.

And what *would* happen? Mary decided he'd have to come and take her away, or at least take her somewhere else, well away from Master Gabriel. *Take her away* . . .

Suddenly Mary smiled. Her future wasn't ruined, after all. In fact her future was safe in her hands. If Lord Appleby was to take Miss Dupre away, then Gabriel would be hers again. So Lord

Appleby must be told, and she would be the one to tell him.

Mary knew Lord Appleby lived in London—as did anyone important—but she didn't know his exact address. She could question the Wonicots, but she didn't want to stir their curiosity, and she didn't want them to stop her. Perhaps she didn't need an address? Lord Appleby must be a well-known figure in the capital, and therefore a letter would surely reach him? Just as a letter to Sir James Trevalen addressed Devon would surely find its way to his home. It made sense to her, and she decided it was worth the risk.

Yes, she would write to Lord Appleby and tell him what his mistress was up to. She'd not only be keeping her dreams intact, but she'd be saving Master Gabriel from the clutches of a woman who wasn't nearly good enough for him.

Because Mary Cooper was quite certain that the only woman good enough for Gabriel was Mary Cooper.

Chapter 17

Gabriel propped his bare feet up in front of the fire and raised his glass of Lord Appleby's expensive brandy. "To Antoinette," he said, and smiled. What a woman! He'd never met anyone like her. One moment she was the sensual mistress, and the next a wide-eyed innocent. Just when he thought he had worked her out, she'd surprise him again. He felt permanently off kilter. And permanently aroused.

Here he was ready for her again, despite being barely able to stagger home after their encounter in the rain. If she was standing before him now, he'd pull her onto his lap and spread her legs and love her as he wanted to. His pocket Venus; he found her perfect in every way.

Except that she was Lord Appleby's mistress.

With a frown, Gabriel took another sip of his brandy and brooded. There was also the problem of the letter that she possessed and he wanted. If he didn't get it, then he would lose Wexmoor Manor, and Aphrodite would lose Aphrodite's Club; Appleby would make certain of that. Ga-

briel had made a promise to her the night he went
to see her in London, after he punched Appleby
and then ran from his Mayfair house in the rain.
He had to have the letter, and if he couldn't persuade Antoinette to give it to him out of the goodness of her heart, or the power of her passion, then
he would have to take it by force.

And Gabriel knew that Antoinette would hate
him if he did that. He would lose her forever—
always assuming he had a chance of possessing her
for more than a brief while. He needed Aphrodite
to advise him, he told himself with a wry smile. She
was good at giving advice on matters of the heart.

He imagined the infamous courtesan sitting
before him.

"Consider, Gabriel. This woman is Appleby's
mistress. She thinks with her head, not her heart,
but she is still a woman. What if you woo her,
seduce her, show her what she is missing? You are
a man who can persuade women to do anything,
Gabriel. She will melt like butter in your hands,
and then you can persuade her that it is in her best
interests to give up her secret to you."

"Madame . . ."

"You don't believe me? This woman may be
Appleby's mistress, but you are young and handsome, everything he is not. Of course she will be
attracted to you. And then, if you accustom her to
being made love to by a lusty younger man, she
will very soon do whatever you want her to."

Aphrodite had said much the same at their last
meeting, but even then Gabriel had thought it an

unlikely scenario. As it turned out he was right; Antoinette was not a woman easily persuaded.

He could spend a lifetime with her and never grow bored.

After he'd fled from the terrible confrontation with Lord Appleby, Gabriel had gone straight to Aphrodite's Club and taken shelter there to lick his wounds. Aphrodite, Sir Adam's former lover and mother to Gabriel's half sister, Marietta, was someone he'd always known and liked. His was a strangely tangled family, but having grown up with it, Gabriel didn't give it much thought. Although Aphrodite now had her own life, happy with her true love, Jemmy Dobson, he'd known she would welcome him.

And so she did.

"I have many friends, Gabriel, and they are happy to help me out when I need it. One of those friends has a son who just happens to be Lord Appleby's secretary."

"That's very useful, Madame."

"Extremely. I asked Jemmy to call upon him last night, to explain matters to him so he understood he would be doing me a tremendous favor. He was eager to help—I do not think he is very happy in His Lordship's employ. So this morning he bribed one of the servants to let me into Lord Appleby's house—with a little acting, of course."

"Of course. Why?"

"I wanted to see for myself. I can tell you that Appleby hates me. He is revenging himself for past slights, real and imagined, and he will not stop. We are in a great deal of trouble, *mon ami*."

She then told him that the secretary had told her that Lord Appleby did indeed have the letter written by Gabriel's mother, and that he was very secretive about it. The letter had been on his desk the day before, and by evening it was gone.

"Gone where?"

"There is a woman living in Lord Appleby's house in Mayfair. Rumor has it she is his mistress. Very shocking, *oui*?"

"But . . . I saw her!"

"So did I. And it so happens she had a letter hidden down the front of her bosom." She placed a hand lightly against her own chest and smiled. "Appleby is clever; he will know we are seeking the letter and will do anything to get it back. What better place to hide a secret than upon your mistress's body?"

Gabriel had laughed, he remembered, not realizing then what was to come. "What do you intend to do, Madame?"

And she'd told him. Once Appleby's misbehavior reached royal ears, he would need to send his mistress away for a time. Aphrodite would see to it that his secretary whispered the name Wexmoor Manor in his ear. "Isolated and safe from the prying eyes of his enemies," she mocked. "It will seem to him the perfect solution, and a little amusing joke, too, to be using your home, Gabriel."

Gabriel sipped his brandy and stared into the fire. His wet clothing had begun to steam nicely, and he felt warm and sleepy on the outside, but inside the familiar brooding anger was bubbling away.

Appleby hated him. He had no doubt about that. His mother believed it was because he'd wanted his son with him, and if he couldn't have that, then he'd hate him instead and punish them both. Aphrodite, on the other hand, believed Appleby knew Gabriel wasn't his son after all, and that was why he hated him.

"You are a Langley through and through," she declared. "Do not doubt it."

He felt like a Langley. He desperately wanted to believe it. Whenever he began to doubt he felt his heart turn to lead. His grandfather John had believed he was a Langley and raised him to inherit Wexmoor Manor and love it as his own.

If he ever escaped the mess he was in, he'd do just that. Wexmoor would become his home, and he'd repair the crumbling stones and bring the rooms back to life. The garden would bloom again, and the old maze would be tamed. He'd live here content, happy, and never give Antoinette Dupre another thought.

But he knew in his heart he was lying.

He was a Langley, and the Langleys were notoriously attracted to dangerous women. His ancestor had fallen in love with the king's mistress and married her, although it nearly ruined him, and now Gabriel was heading down a similar path.

And there was an inevitability about it, a sense of fate. As if he'd set his course on having Antoinette and nothing could now alter it.

Chapter 18

Two nights later Antoinette heard the soft click of the door in the darkness behind her, and smiled. She was standing by the window looking out at the clear night. The moon hung, half full, over the woods. She hadn't been able to sleep. There were too many things to think about, too many doubts and questions, and a strange tingling happiness that had been with her ever since she found the cottage in the woods. And now here he was.

Her secret lover.

He slipped his arms about her waist and nuzzled her hair, as if enjoying her scent. She leaned back against him and wondered how it could be that she felt so comfortable in his arms. So safe. When had she forgotten that this man was her enemy?

"Antoinette," he murmured, kissing the curve of her neck.

She felt the hard texture of his mask. "Can't you take that off?" she whispered. "Does it matter if I see your face?"

He hesitated, and then she felt him shake his head. "Better not," he said.

"I don't understand."

"I think you understand more than you're willing to admit."

Well, what did that mean? Antoinette turned to ask, but he bent and kissed her instead, and the heat of his mouth and his body made her dizzy with her newly discovered need of him. Who would have thought she could so quickly become such a sensual woman? Or had this side of her nature always been there, waiting, hoping to be allowed out?

Perhaps the man kissing her was more important to her metamorphosis from staid miss to woman of the world than someone of her independent character wanted to believe. Her flesh tingled and her blood burned when she was in his arms. She melted and ached, but only he could soothe her heated body. And as for the soaring pleasure . . . it was beyond words.

Would she feel this way with someone else?

At the last moment her mind skittered away from the question. This was not an affair of the heart, she told herself. There was no question that she felt anything more than desire. And just as well, because this was Appleby's man and she could not trust him. Not for one single moment.

He bent her over his arm, arching her neck and back, and rained kisses on her throat and bosom.

Antoinette had the curious sensation that this had happened before, but the memory eluded her, until he said:

"The first time I ever saw you, you were being held like this."

She pulled away from him. In the moonlight his face was still and his expression unreadable behind the mask. "You were there that night in Mayfair?" she whispered. "You were there!"

His smile had no humor in it. "Yes."

She tried to force herself to think, to remember the faces of all the guests, but there were so many of them, and later events had driven most of her recollection of the evening from her mind. He could have been one of the gentleman in evening wear—he spoke like one—or was he one of the tribe of faceless servants that Appleby employed to run his house?

Something else occurred to Antoinette. After she'd rushed upstairs to rage and weep over Appleby's perfidy and the destruction of her reputation, there had been an incident downstairs. Something had happened to Appleby, because the next morning his nose was reddened and bruised and his eyes bloodshot.

Someone had struck him.

"A private disagreement," he'd said shortly, when he saw her staring, and she didn't dare ask more.

They'd had little to say to each other that morning anyway, but Antoinette remembered wishing that whoever had hit him, had hit him harder. And more than once. If she'd taken boxing lessons she might have done it herself.

But Lord Appleby's nose couldn't have had anything to do with the highwayman, who was his man, after all.

No, the highwayman was probably one of the servants. She could imagine him watching her all along, his eyes secretly lusting after the proper lady he'd thought her—or the improper lady, seeing he appeared to believe she truly was Appleby's mistress. Then when His Lordship gave him this task, to fetch the letter from her, it would have been the perfect opportunity to taste the forbidden fruit.

But it still didn't seem to fit. The highwayman didn't have the air of a servant; he was an independent man, a man more used to giving orders than taking them, and with a gentleman's manner.

"Who are you?" she said. "What are you?"

He was watching her, reading the expressions flitting over her face, but he didn't answer.

"Why are you living in the witch's cottage in the woods? Are you hiding from someone?"

"Witch's cottage," he said with a laugh. "Who told you that?"

"Mary."

"Priscilla was a wise woman, perhaps a white witch, but she only ever helped the people who came to her."

"You sound as if you knew her?" Antoinette said.

"Curious little sparrow," he mocked. "Careful what you ask; you may not like the answer."

There was a mystery here, and she longed to have it resolved.

But before she could ask any more questions, he reached out and ran his finger across the swell of her breasts beneath her nightgown, and then all sensible thought left her as physical sensation took over. He hooked his finger over the neckline of her gown and drew her toward him, slowly, inexorably.

"That night when I saw you in his arms," he murmured, "I knew then I had to have you."

"I don't understand . . ."

"You don't have to understand. Just feel . . ."

He cupped her breasts, pushing them up, and bent to plant openmouthed kisses on them through the cloth. She trembled as he unfastened the nightgown and slipped it from her shoulders, exposing her upper body to the cool night air drifting in the window. Her nipples peaked and hardened, and he bent and took one of them in his mouth. She caught her breath, stroking his hair with her fingers, drawing him closer.

He finished what he was doing, leaving her in a state of aching need, and demanded in a low voice, "Does Appleby do this to you? Does he make you feel like this?"

Confused, she didn't know whether to answer him or not. Should she tell him the truth, that he was her first-ever lover, and Appleby had touched her only once? Or should she prevaricate and allow him to believe the worst, as he already did? Confiding in him suddenly seemed far too dangerous—she felt as if it might open a door she did not want to go through. No, it was better to say nothing.

His fingers were sliding up her thigh almost roughly, and then he cupped his hand between her legs, stroking her slickness, brushing back and forth against her swollen bud while she clung to his shoulders, trembling and trying not to scream.

"Does he?" he growled. "Answer me."

She shook her head feverishly. "No. No, he doesn't . . ."

That seemed to please him because he gentled his touch, fingers moving up inside her now, filling her. She wrapped her arms about his neck and clung as her knees buckled, shamelessly opening her legs to the delights he offered. Behind his mask his eyes glittered.

"Tell me you want me." It was an order.

"I want you," she mewed, her mouth seeking his.

He broke the kiss with a triumphant laugh and picked her up in his arms, carrying her to the bed. The mattress dipped beneath them. He knelt above her and stripped off his shirt, and then began to unbutton his trousers, but Antoinette sat up and brushed his fingers aside.

"Let me help," she murmured, with a smile upward. Her smile broadened when he immediately acquiesced. The buttons came free one by one, and she slipped her hand inside, feeling the velvet steel of his body. She made a sound in her throat, a purr of anticipation, and his warm flesh quivered in her hand.

She bent close, breathing in his musky scent, and licked the tip like a cat lapping cream. She licked again, and made a murmur of pleasure. He cupped her head in his hands, and she opened her mouth and took him inside. He jerked and groaned, as if she'd hurt him, but when she made as if to stop, he said, "Please, Antoinette . . ." in such a husky, pleasure-filled voice, she ached with desire.

Was this what a real mistress would do? Imagining Lord Appleby in the place of this man made her go cold. But then a real mistress would have to be a good actress because she'd be playing a part and concealing her true feelings. Antoinette knew, as she caressed and sucked at him, that she couldn't do that.

Gently he lifted her head and kissed her deeply. He lowered her backward onto the bed, his body following hers down, and entered her with a single deep thrust. Her body spasmed, clenching around him, and he stilled, letting her settle, before he moved again. He was drawing out the pleasure, building the sensations, making her wait.

She could feel his naked body sliding against hers, hard where she was soft, rough where she was smooth. Her breasts ached, her nipples incredibly sensitive, and when he clasped the globes of her bottom and tilted her slightly, so that he could go deeper still inside her, she knew she would never feel this for another man.

Highwayman, stranger, servant, gentleman . . . it didn't matter what he was. Something old and primeval inside her recognized him and claimed him as her own.

"Tell me," he whispered in her ear.

Was he able to read her mind now? Antoinette gasped, fingers clenching on his back, not caring if her nails cut his skin.

"Tell me," he insisted, and thrust harder, deeper, pushing her toward a place she had never been before.

"There's never been anyone like you."

The clenching spasms took her then, the pleasure so great she lost awareness of everything but her own body and his. She felt him thrust once, twice, and then arch above her, his head thrown back, his mouth open as he cried out.

After a moment he rolled over on his side and took her with him, still inside her, his arms holding her close, his lips soft against her hair. Limp, replete, Antoinette closed her eyes and went to sleep.

Gabriel listened to the sound of her breathing. Something had happened between them, but he didn't want to think about it. The truth was he knew he'd never felt like this before. He'd forced Antoinette to say something of the sort, although she probably would have said anything to get him to give her release, but it was Gabriel who was changed.

And now he was trapped and it was his own fault.

There had been women before, plenty of them. He was a healthy young man, and women enjoyed his company, and certain types of women were willing to share his bed, some for payment but others simply for the pleasure it gave them. He'd never fallen in love with any of them, not even a little bit. Physical pleasure was one thing, emotional attachment another, and the two sides of the coin were just that—separate. Until now.

Antoinette Dupre was different. He found her attractive, surprisingly so. Not because she wasn't a lovely woman but because she was different. True, she was a pocket Venus, but her hair was glossy brown rather than the fair he favored, and her eyes were brown not blue, and she wore spectacles and gazed at him in a steady, fearless manner rather than simpering and flirting. And yet he found everything about her made him want her more.

He was like a climber in the Swiss Alps, standing beneath an avalanche and watching it rumbling toward him and yet unable to run. In a moment he'd been overtaken, overcome, swallowed up. And he couldn't wait.

Gabriel groaned softly and stared up at the canopy of the bed above him. King Charles's bed had a lot to answer for. He remembered his grandfather telling him that it was here he'd begun his married life with Gabriel's grandmother, and afterward he never looked at another woman. Perhaps he should blame the furniture for his predicament?

No, there was no one to blame but himself. He'd set out to seduce Antoinette to recover his mother's letter, and now he was the one seduced.

Antoinette woke sometime later, replete, and found him still naked beside her, deeply asleep, lying on his back with his masked face turned to hers and his arm outflung.

Antoinette half sat up, watching him, and enjoying being able to do so without his being aware of it. He was well made, and she didn't think it was her lack of experience that made her think so. Even when he was clothed, he put her other male acquaintances in the shade. Although, to be fair, she hadn't seen his face properly, not without the black mask. For all she knew he might be hideously scarred . . .

The urge came to her. She hesitated, excited and yet oddly reluctant. What if he *was* hideously scarred? What if he awoke and caught her?

Just then he let out a little snore, and she made up her mind. Antoinette leaned over him and felt at the back of the mask. There were fastenings, thin leather ties, that were used to secure it around his head. With great care she began to undo them, expecting him any moment to wake and demand to know what she was doing.

But he didn't.

Suddenly the mask loosened, and carefully, holding her breath, she eased it from his face and laid it on the pillow.

The bedchamber was too dark. She slipped from the bed and went to the window, drawing the curtains apart. The moonlight was still bright, and when she turned back to the bed, her heart thudding, she could see him almost as well as in daylight.

Young, of course. No scars, no villainous sneer. His face was handsome, a straight nose with thin nostrils, high cheekbones, dark eyebrows in contrast to his fair hair, and his lashes were also dark. His chin was stronger without the mask, a stubborn chin, giving his handsome face character and strength, while his lips were sensual.

Despite his obvious masculinity, he looked vulnerable in his sleep. Antoinette lifted her hand, her fingers hovering, but she did not touch him. She did not dare. But she could see on his cheek the beginnings of a beard. She wanted to kiss him, to take him in her arms and ask him what was happening to them.

Swiftly, lightly, she pressed her lips to his brow.

He moved, his eyelids flickering, and murmured, "Marietta . . . ?"

The name startled her and she drew back. *Marietta?* Another woman? Well, of course he would have a woman somewhere, a man like this. Did she really think she was the only one? She was being very naïve. She was a distraction; he thought her Appleby's mistress and perhaps there was a frisson of excitement in being with her, especially if he envied his employer, but any deeper emotion was out of the question.

The idea depressed her, but she forced herself to be practical and shrug it off.

No, she must not begin to think of love. They were using each other. Soon enough she would find a way to escape, and then she would never see him again.

But all the same, the woman's name—Marietta—lodged in her chest like a stone. Uncomfortable, immovable, and unbearable.

Chapter 19

Gabriel woke suddenly in the growing dawn. The air was cool against his bare skin, and he shivered and turned his head, wincing as the ties on his mask tightened on a caught strand of his hair. Antoinette lay curled up beside him, her hand under her cheek, her loose hair across her face. He reached out and gently smoothed it back. She looked young and innocent, not at all the kept woman who slept with men like Appleby for the comfort and wealth they provided her.

Sir James had said something of the sort, he remembered. And his reply? He'd warned Sir James that she could play any part necessary to get what she wanted and could not be trusted. Gabriel knew he should take heed of his own advice, but things had come too far.

He climbed out of the bed and stretched, yawning. His body was relaxed and replete, but in contrast his feelings were raw. Confused. And he didn't want to delve into them too deeply. He'd been dreaming about Aphrodite's Club and his half sister, Marietta. In his dream she'd been crying, begging him to save her inheritance, and he'd promised he would.

"All you care about is that woman," she retorted.

"I'm seducing her to gain control over her," he explained. It was half true, but Marietta didn't understand.

Ironically, Antoinette would probably understand his motives only too well. For all her eagerness, he guessed she had her own secrets where he was concerned, keeping him too occupied to care about the letter being a big one of them. Well, he was in her bedchamber now; why didn't he make a search? Prove to himself he hadn't forgotten his real purpose in being here.

Prowling about the room, he could see no obvious papers lying about. He began to peer inside furniture, rifling through neatly folded clothing. There were some truly breathtaking undergarments, constructed of the finest silk, in a mouthwatering array of colors. But no letter. He could also swear the letter wasn't concealed on her person—he'd caressed every part of her. His conclusion was she'd hidden it somewhere in the manor, and the only way to get her to give up her secret was to persuade her to hand it over to him.

Next time . . .

Gabriel pulled on his clothing, leaving his shirt unfastened and his feet bare, and carefully opened the door. When he found himself pausing to glance back for one last look, he knew, with self-disgust, that he really was in trouble.

* * *

Mary saw him leave the house, stopping to pull on his boots before striding away into the woods. His head was bent, his face pensive, and he didn't even notice her standing outside the stillroom.

Her own face felt stiff and taut, and a headache was still throbbing behind her reddened eyes. She knew where he'd been; with *her*. The knowledge of their affair was like a torment that never left her. At night she tossed and turned, tears on her cheeks, and during the day she could barely function. Her hatred and anger were eating her up, and she knew there was only one thing she could do to stop it.

Rid them of Antoinette Dupre.

It was clear to her—or as clear as possible in her sleepless, frenzied state—that once Antoinette Dupre was gone, then Master Gabriel would return to her. He would be able to see again, and the first thing he would see was Mary. She had been his love once, and she would be again.

She'd even visualized the scene.

He would gasp and smile and call her name, and she would turn expectantly, and then she would be in his arms, held so tightly she could barely breathe. "Mary, Mary," he would cry, "how could I have been so blind? Will you forgive me and forever be my wife?" And of course she would forgive him and they would walk about the garden hand in hand, making plans for their future here at the manor. Then, in time, there would be children and gray hairs and . . .

But it was usually around this point that Mary foundered. She sometimes wondered, too, what they would talk about in the evenings. Gabriel was an educated gentleman who knew the world, and she was a fishing village girl with little education and little experience. Would he smile and look at her as if she was funny and quaint? Or would he grow impatient with her, and stop talking?

Mary didn't want that, but somewhere deep in her heart she already knew her hopes weren't practical. Lord Appleby owned Wexmoor Manor now, and Gabriel was a fugitive. Besides, educated gentlemen didn't marry lowly serving girls—they might do other things to them but they didn't marry them. But she refused to accept her dreams were just that, dreams. "We'll jump that hurdle when we come to it," she told herself firmly. "Gabriel will know what to do." She believed in him; she must trust him. Yes, once Antoinette Dupre was gone everything would fall into place.

She'd sent the letter.

Mary remembered the long hours she'd spent over the wording, before copying them out on a sheet of Lord Appleby's writing paper in her best handwriting. Still she wasn't completely satisfied. Her attendance at the village school had been brief and she knew such things didn't come easily to her, but she did her best. As soon as Lord Appleby understood the urgency of the situation here at Wexmoor Manor, he'd leave London and travel full tilt to Devon, she had no doubt about it. And then . . .

She smiled as much as her aching head would allow.

. . . Then Gabriel would be hers again.

By the time Antoinette woke the morning was well advanced. She didn't usually sleep late—she was an early riser—but after last night she could understand why she was so tired. Sexual connection, it seemed, was better than hot milk and honey when it came to guaranteeing a good night's rest.

The sky was clear and bright, and she decided it was the perfect day to go horse riding. Quickly she rose and washed and dressed, hurrying downstairs and startling Mrs. Wonicot, who was just on her way up.

"Miss Dupre?" she said. "I was coming to wake you. Miss Dupre!" her voice grew more strident as Antoinette strode by, heading for the door. "Don't you want your breakfast?"

"Later." Antoinette waved her hand airily and kept going, smiling at the thought of Mrs. Wonicot's furious expression.

At first glance the stable building appeared to be empty. She made her way toward the stall where the mare she rode last time was watching her over the door, and then she heard a sound. There was Coombe in one of the far stalls with a pitchfork, cleaning out the mucky straw and replacing it with clean.

"I'm going riding, Coombe," she called.

He barely glanced up at her. "No, you're not, miss. I have my instructions."

He was wearing a grubby jacket with that cap pulled down low over his face, his coarse black hair sticking out in all directions. Did he never brush it? Antoinette knew she should cultivate Coombe if she wanted him to help her escape, but it was difficult to get enthusiastic. She could smell the earthy, horsy smell of him from several feet away.

She took a shallow breath as she stepped closer. "Then come with me. I'd like an—an escort," she declared brightly. "I don't feel safe since the highwayman held up my coach. Coombe, do please ride with me?"

He stopped pitching the soiled hay into a wooden barrow, resting on the fork and staring at his boots. "Ride with you?" he repeated in his almost incomprehensible accent, as if the concept was as foreign to him as bathing.

Antoinette laughed at the note in his voice. "Good heavens, Coombe, don't tell me you *can't* ride? I certainly won't believe you. Especially when I know you're such a racing enthusiast."

He gave a snort and finally looked at her.

Just for a moment, a heartbeat, she thought she knew him. But the impression was gone an instant later. This was Coombe, she reminded herself. His face was sweaty and streaked with dirt, and some of his black hair had fallen into his eyes. His kerchief was tied around his mouth and chin;

she supposed to save him the dust, or the smell, of his task. Although if the truth be told, if anything smelled it was Coombe. He needed a good long scrub. Her tongue itched to tell him so but she couldn't afford to upset him. He was her one hope.

"Well then . . . ?" she said impatiently, tapping her foot. "Will you come with me? Or do I have to take Wonicot, and watch him fall off his mount after ten paces?"

Coombe's hunched shoulders shook as if he might be laughing but he made no sound. With elaborate care he rested his pitchfork against the wall and slouched past her to saddle her mare. Antoinette gulped in fresh air as soon as he'd moved on.

"I'll come with you, miss," he growled. "If that's what you want."

Antoinette beamed a smile. "Oh, I do, Coombe, I really do."

Gabriel was glad he'd made such an effort with his disguise this morning. In hindsight, something had told him she might be seeking out Coombe when she woke. He remembered that whenever she was with the highwayman her next move seemed to be a desperate need to escape. So he'd donned Coombe's filthy jacket and he'd rubbed mud onto his face, just enough to disguise his appearance, and pulled on the hideous concoction of cap and horse hair. The final touch was the red kerchief.

His own mother wouldn't know him. Better yet, she wouldn't want to get within a mile of him, and from the expression on Antoinette's face, she felt the same.

It was amusing, watching her trying to ingratiate herself with him while at the same time holding her breath. He knew very well she was only wheedling him into going with her because she wanted something. Well, he was happy to while away the hours playing the country dolt. It would give him the chance to learn what she was up to.

She was a good rider, he admitted critically, as he followed her from the stable yard and out onto the road. Her back was straight, her hands up, and she moved well. Wherever she came from, she'd learned to ride like a lady.

Gabriel was well aware that the courtesan Madame Aphrodite was from poor and difficult circumstances and had transformed herself into a lady, learning to talk and walk and pass as a gentlewoman. He didn't think it was the same for Antoinette Dupre. Her behavior was so instinctive, and she had a touch of arrogance—as if she was used to being treated with deference. In his opinion she was born a lady, however low she might have fallen.

Gabriel was well aware that some women were forced into selling their bodies by poverty and family circumstances, gentlewomen as well as those from less privileged backgrounds. A friend of his family had run off with a suitor after her parents refused them permission to marry. Unfortunately the parents were right, because the girl was abandoned by the scoundrel, and without the protective shelter of a wedding ring, she was considered ruined. Subsequently her family refused to take her back, and she found herself with no option but to seek work. But her education and upbringing hadn't trained her for anything apart from being a gentleman's wife. For a time she was employed as a governess, underpaid and badly treated, but eventually the position wore her down and she left. After that she slipped out of the circle of his friends and acquaintances, and into the murky world of the demimondaine. She became the mistress of the owner of several drapery stores, a man whose wealth had lifted him higher than the class to which he'd been born, and who felt her ladylike ways contributed to his social status.

Had something similar happened to Antoinette?

Had she, abandoned and alone, had no option but to seek her livelihood by using her wits and her body? Or was he making excuses for her, trying to turn her into a fallen angel, someone who had gone to Appleby without a choice, someone he could save. Gabriel admitted it was quite possible she'd leaped into her profession with both feet, perfectly happy to trade her favors for cold hard cash and a comfortable lifestyle.

He didn't blame her, nor did he despise her. Since his own life had become precarious, he'd grown to understand so much better a longing for all the comforts he'd once taken for granted. And he was by no means destitute or abandoned. How much worse must it be for someone who was? How much greater the temptation?

"Hurry up, Coombe!"

She sounded impatient. She'd been riding ahead of him, but now he saw that while he'd been woolgathering she'd stopped and turned to see why he was dawdling. Quickly Gabriel assumed Coombe's blank expression and kicked his mount into a gallop, coming level with her and then passing right by. Her surprised gasp made him want to laugh out loud, but a moment later he heard the pounding of the mare's hooves as she made up ground on him.

"I didn't think you had it in you, Coombe," she called breathlessly, as she came level with him again.

He grunted, holding on to his cap with one hand, so it didn't fly off.

"You're wasted here at Wexmoor Manor. You should be in a stable with horses that win races."

Ah, back to her agenda, he thought, hiding a smile. Did she really see Coombe running a racing stable? Gabriel tried to picture the groom in a well-cut jacket and breeches, with shiny riding boots and a cigar clenched between his teeth as he shouted out orders. No, he couldn't see it, no matter how hard he tried. Antoinette's imagination must be far more vivid than his.

"I happen to know someone who owns such a stable," she said airily. They'd slowed their horses now and were ambling along under the leafy boughs of the trees that lined the lane.

"They wouldn't take me on, miss."

It took a moment for her to interpret what he'd said, but she managed, more or less. "Of course they would, Coombe. I'd put in a good word for you, you can be sure of that."

But I'd have to help you run off to London first, wouldn't I, my pretty lady?

"I'm not asking you to do anything you don't want to do," she went on, oblivious to his mocking thoughts.

He slowed to let her go ahead, the lane narrowing into a path leading to the top of a rounded hill. The magnificent view opened up before them. It was one of Gabriel's favorites, but Antoinette was too wrapped up in her scheming to notice.

"Coombe . . ." She turned to him, a frown wrinkling her smooth brow. "Do you think you'd like a life like that? Of course, it would mean leaving Wexmoor Manor, but there's so much more out there in the world. I'm quite certain you wouldn't miss it."

He hunched down over his horse's neck, twisting the reins between his gloved fingers, making himself look miserable. "This is me home, miss. I was born here. My—me ma died when I was a little 'un and Sir John took me in. I've never known any home but here at the manor."

Her expression softened. He'd touched her heart, it seemed, or else she was a very good actress. "I know this is your home," she said gently, "but sometimes it's necessary to leave the past behind, if you want to better yourself."

"Is that what you did, miss? When you went to be Lord Appleby's bedmate?"

Her eyes flashed but she tamped her anger down. "In a way, I—I suppose . . . But we're not talking about me, are we, Coombe? We're discussing you. Don't you want to better yourself?"

"Better meself? I have a warm stable to sleep in and Mrs. Wonicot's cooking. How can I do better'n that?"

Her impatient sigh was clearly audible. "I meant to make a better life for yourself. Sleep in a proper bed, for instance, and eat in a dining room instead of in a corner of the kitchen. Wear fine clothes, live in a fine house with—with servants."

"Is that why you sleep in His Lordship's bed, miss? To make a 'better life' for yourself?"

No, she definitely didn't like to be reminded of that. He saw the color stain her cheeks as she struggled not to give him a sharp set-down. But he'd spoken with such guileless innocence she could hardly reprimand him for insolence, even if she didn't have the added agenda of keeping him sweet.

"I . . . Well, not quite," she managed at last through tight lips. "You shouldn't listen to gossip, Coombe."

He decided to push her a bit further. "Oh aye? Mrs. Wonicot says you're bad, miss. She says a woman like you might make me do things . . . things I oughtn't."

Antoinette's eyes narrowed. "Indeed."

"But I don't think you're bad," he added hastily. "You've always been kind to me. Once Mrs. Wonicot gets an idea in her head, then there's no stopping her. Me and Mary have a laugh about it sometimes. Mary's very pretty, don't you think, miss?"

Her face brightened as she saw a chance to bring the conversation back to her favorite subject. "Do you have a girl, Coombe?"

A girl? Hmm, there was a question.

"I like girls, miss, but they don't like me."

He waited. He could imagine what she was thinking but she could hardly be honest, not if she wanted his help.

"Perhaps you haven't yet met the girl who will accept you for what you are, Coombe." She spoke carefully but with a kindness that he found touching.

"How will I know when I meet her, miss?"

"I don't have a great deal of experience in such matters, but I think you'll know because you'll want to please her, Coombe. Chores that seem tedious and boring will fly by because you'll be seeing her. And when you look into her eyes and touch her hand, when you kiss her, you'll feel as if you are sharing something very special."

They were silent, both looking out over the breathtaking view of green fields and woods and distant blue hills.

"This is beautiful," Antoinette said, as if only just noticing what was before her.

"Yes, miss. Barnstaple is over that way, we go
there sometimes to market, and once some visitors came to the train station and we had to col-
lect them in the cart. St. Nells is over there, on the
coast. It's not so far. And London is beyond Barnstaple, that way, but you can't see the smoke and
soot of the chimneys from here, so Mrs. Wonicot
says."

He was attributing a lot to Sally Wonicot, but he
didn't think she'd mind.

"London." Antoinette sighed.

"Aye. Is there a special reason you want to go
there, miss?"

She turned to him, and the expression in her
eyes was one he'd seen before, on the day he'd
opened the door of her coach and confronted her.
She looked as if she was trapped and desperate
but refusing to give in, with a courage he found
admirable. Something in his chest clenched so
hard it hurt, and he wondered if it could possibly
be his heart.

"I am asking you, no, *begging you*, to help me to
get to London, Coombe."

"I told you, miss, I've never been further than
Barnstaple," he muttered, uncomfortable.

"But you just said that the road to London runs
through Barnstaple. Or else I can catch the train.
Yes, the train would be best. I know it's a great
deal to ask, but if you help me, then I promise to
help you."

If he was really a man like Coombe, what
would he think of that? Gabriel shot her a quick

glance from under the peak of his cap. Behind her spectacles her eyes were bright with worry, and she was chewing her full bottom lip. Coombe, he decided, would probably fly to the moon for her, if she asked him to.

"Why do you want to go to London, miss?" he said, needing to know.

"I have something very important I must do there." Her expression was no longer open, and she turned away to gaze again at the view.

"But you could ask His Lordship to fetch you home, couldn't you? It would be safer that way, and he'd pay your fare."

"I—I suppose I could, but I'd rather not. It is a private matter, and I don't want His Lordship to know I am traveling to London."

Puzzled, he watched her profile. What was she up to? If she was telling the truth, then there was more to her situation than he'd thought. Could she and Appleby have had a falling out? Perhaps she resented being hidden away down here to save his reputation? And if she and Appleby were estranged, then why wouldn't she hand over the letter to Gabriel? Surely if that was the case there would be no reason for her to hold on to it, and it would give her a chance to pay him back.

In Gabriel's experience, women were very good at revenging themselves on the men who upset them, using anything from tears to screaming obscenities. He shuddered, remembering one such incident, when he refused to give a pretty dancer the necklace she demanded.

Suddenly Antoinette turned, catching him staring, and he hastily cleared his throat and spat, to distract her. It worked; she looked away.

"Will you give me an answer, Coombe?" she said quietly. "I need to know soon."

"I'll think on it," he muttered uneasily. " 'Tis a big step, miss."

Again he sensed her frustration, but she held it in check. "I will need my answer, Coombe. I can't wait forever."

"Aye, miss."

She could do nothing but nod her understanding, but he could see it wasn't the ending she wanted. Together they rode back in silence. He thought she looked sad and pensive, and she spoke only a brief good-bye before leaving him to unsaddle the horses.

As Gabriel worked he thought about what she'd said and what he should do. If he agreed to her request, then he might be able to slip beneath her guard and discover what she was up to. And then again, if he helped her run away, she would have to take the letter with her, and he could persuade her to hand it over to him, or take it by force. Of course that would mean revealing himself to her as Gabriel, not Coombe, and she'd be justifiably angry.

And if he refused to help her? She'd lose her faith in Coombe and stop talking to him, but she would have to stay here at Wexmoor Manor, and he'd have to make sure that the watch on her was intensified. The letter would remain here in the manor, hidden, and he'd continue with his efforts to persuade her to give it up. Their pleasurable trysts would go on.

As far as Gabriel could see, whatever decision he made meant he would win. Now he'd just have to decide what he wanted more—Antoinette or the letter.

Chapter 20

The garden at Wexmoor Manor was a wild affair. It must once have been trained into neat borders and beds, but now it more or less did as it pleased. Shrubs were overgrown and perennials reached to the sky, while roses bloomed in mad profusion, climbing over and through other plants.

To her surprise, Antoinette found its chaos charming. Her own garden in Surrey was perfectly behaved—if a blade of grass grew too tall, someone would clip it off. But here at Wexmoor Manor the garden was king.

She pottered about, perfectly happy, admiring flowers and wondering what some of the more unfamiliar herbs might be. Were these planted by Priscilla Langley, the witch of the woods? Did she wander in this same garden, feeling the sun warm on her head, enjoying the scents and the sounds of the birds?

Gradually, though, she began to feel a tingling at the back of her neck. A sense that she was not alone. She caught a glimpse of the highwayman slipping behind a grove of apple trees, and smiled. Lately she was always being watched by one of Appleby's cronies, but that flush under her skin only occurred when *he* was watching her.

She turned toward the maze—too overgrown now to attempt to find one's way in, much less out—and told herself to ignore him. He would have to show himself, eventually.

Sure enough, as she was bending to inspect another of the herbs, a voice spoke so close behind her it made her jump. "Sparrow, you have petals in your hair."

Antoinette turned so quickly she nearly fell over, and he had to catch hold of her arm. "I wonder there are only petals," she said, breathless. "This is a wilderness, not a garden. Does no one prune or check anything here?"

"We believe in nature taking its course."

Antoinette broke his hold, moving away, but he came after her. He was out of place here, in his dark clothing and his mask, like a ghost in the daylight.

"Have you robbed any coaches today?" she said, a sting in her voice. She was still smarting over Marietta.

"Several, thank you, darling."

"There must be a great many wealthy gentlemen here in Devon."

"And beautiful wealthy ladies. I prefer to rob them."

How did he know just what to say? It wasn't that she was jealous, she told herself, goodness me no! She felt sorry for the ladies, if the truth be told, to be tricked by a smooth-tongued rogue like him.

"If I were you I would find one you like and persuade her to marry you," she said. "An heiress in the hand is worth two in the bush, so they say."

He looked puzzled, his head cocked to one side, and then he smiled. "Are you making a jest, Antoinette? Or are you a little jealous? Don't you like the thought of me spreading my favors far and wide? Believe me, of all the women in Devon, you are my favorite."

Foolish, the way her heart jumped about. She turned away, wanting only to escape him before he saw just how much he affected her.

But he was too quick for her.

He caught her hand in his. As she tried to pull free he was running with her toward the overgrown maze, tugging her off balance so it was all she could do to stay on her feet. A moment later they were inside the living walls, greenery towering over them.

"Let me go!" she cried, trying to free herself.

He ignored her, circling around and around, zigzagging through narrow pathways where the sides of hedge almost joined together. "This maze was built for a famous lady, a king's mistress," he said.

"Built for her?" Antoinette gasped.

"For love of her." They turned another corner and then he stopped. "Here we are," he said with an air of reverence. "In the very heart of the maze."

Antoinette was panting, trying to catch her breath. The light in here had a green tint, almost as if they were under water. "Well, now you can turn around and take me out again," she said furiously.

"The idea is to find your own way out."

There was a glint in his pale eyes she knew all too well. He was planning something she wasn't going to like—or perhaps she would like it a little too much. She began to shake her head. "No—"

"You haven't heard my proposition yet," he pointed out.

"Then tell me. But the answer will still be no."

"I will require one piece of clothing for each time I show you which way to go to get out. If you're lucky and don't go the wrong way too often, you may still have your stockings by the time you reach it."

Antoinette could hardly believe what she was hearing. Shocking! How could he make such a suggestion? But deep inside her, where the other Antoinette slept, excitement was stirring. Of course she couldn't let him see that, and there was no way she could agree to such a proposal.

She pursed her lips. "Most definitely not. Show me the way out immediately."

He shook his head and began slowly backing away from her, one foot after the other. Her heart began to thump at the prospect of being left here, alone, at the heart of this wilderness.

"Good-bye, Sparrow," he said, his mouth turning down in pretended regret, and then he turned and was gone.

"Don't leave me . . ." But it was a whisper, not loud enough for him to hear. Antoinette sighed. She supposed he thought she would scream and weep and agree to anything if he'd save her. But Antoinette was used to taking control in such situations—she had been her own mistress for a great many years now. This was not the time to become hysterical. Slowly, cautiously, she began to retrace her steps.

It can't be all that difficult.

But it was. Every path appeared the same, and she'd not taken note of the direction as the highwayman led her in. She'd been more interested in preserving her dignity. But she persevered, following her instincts. Just when she was sure she was on the right path, she came to a dead end, and had to retrace her steps. But for every wrong turn she became more and more confused. To make it worse, some of the hedge had grown so tall it made an arch and blocked out the sky, so she was walking through green shadows.

It felt like another world. A world of elves and creatures of nature, waiting to pounce. Antoinette, who was too levelheaded to be frightened by fairy stories, began glancing over her shoulder at every step and starting at every sound. A couple of times she thought she heard laughter, a woman's laughter, and a man's soft chuckle. As if she were sharing the maze with ghosts of the past.

"Hello?" she tried calling out, softly at first and then increasingly louder.

No one answered.

"Help!" she bellowed, but still there was no reply. She even called for Coombe, but the groom must have been busy elsewhere today. The one time she wanted to be followed, there was no one following her.

I'm lost, she thought despairingly, as she turned another corner.

The highwayman was seated on an old wooden bench, smiling at her, his pale eyes gleaming wickedly through the slits of his black mask. But she'd seen his face now, and her secret gave her a small surge of power in what seemed a hopeless situation.

"Do you need help, Antoinette?" he asked sweetly.

"You know I do," she said crossly.

"Are you willing to accept my proposal? Every time I point you in the right direction you will pay a forfeit of a piece of your clothing. Agreed?"

Her eyes narrowed. He was altogether too pleased with himself and she would have liked to refuse, but the maze was beginning to frighten her badly. Besides, what he was suggesting was exciting and dangerous, and it was quite possible she might best him. Once she reached familiar ground she could find her way on her own and walk out without losing very much at all, and then it would be he who looked foolish.

"I agree."

He stayed where he was, but his gaze slid slowly over her body, assessing her items of clothing. "We'll start with your dress, I think."

Antoinette hesitated. She was wearing petticoats and chemise, as well as numerous other undergarments. If he imagined she would be overcome by the removal of her dress, then he was wrong. Swiftly she began to unbutton her bodice.

He paid her flattering attention.

She tugged her sleeves over her hands and eased the dress down over her hips and stepped out of it, leaving it where it fell. And then she stood before him with her back straight and chin up, and waited.

He grinned and stood up, holding out his hand. Slowly she placed her fingers in his and was drawn toward him. "This way," he said, and led her down a pathway that looked exactly the same as all the others.

What followed was a battle of wits and wills. By the time they reached an area she thought she recognized, she had removed all her petticoats and her chemise, as well as her shoes. Now, in only her drawers and stays and stockings, she was finally sure of her direction. Antoinette halted, and when he turned to see what was the matter, she gave him a broad smile.

"Thank you, sir, but I believe I know the way from here."

A quizzical look, and he shrugged and folded his arms. "Go ahead, darling. Surprise me."

Antoinette took her time, peering one way and

then the other. She remembered this junction, and if she wasn't mistaken—and she was confident she wasn't—*this* was the way out. With a final triumphant glance over her shoulder, she made her choice.

She was wrong, but she didn't know it.

Gabriel watched as her confidence began to melt away, drop by drop, and her steps faltered. Did she know how gorgeous she looked? The stays were tight, pushing up her breasts until they threatened to overflow, and her drawers hugged her waist and flared out over her hips and bottom. Her stockings were fine silk, and the curve of pale thigh between their tops and the drawers made his mouth water.

When she finally stopped and turned, admitting her mistake, he was right behind her. "Oh!" Her eyes widened, her lips parted. It was too tempting for him. He drew her into his arms and began to kiss her.

She didn't struggle. She stood up on her tiptoes and clung to his neck, and her mouth opened eagerly under his. He cupped her bottom, lifting her higher, settling the hard length of his cock against the warm niche of her thighs.

She made a soft sound of need, and he knew if he didn't get inside her he was going to burst.

"I was so sure," she gasped. "How did you know I was wrong?"

"I've walked this maze since I was a child."

"But . . ."

"Hush," he said arrogantly. "It is time to pay your forfeit in full, Antoinette."

He kissed her again, fingers in her hair, drinking from her lips, but this time she wouldn't let him work his magic. She twisted away and ran back the way they'd come, turning in the direction she'd spurned before. He followed, at first walking, certain she'd stop, and then running to keep up when she didn't.

As he expected, eventually she took another wrong turning and arrived at a dead end. And that was when Gabriel pounced.

He came up behind her and slid an arm about her waist, pulling her delicious curves in against him and pinning her there. She doubled over, slapping at his arm with her hands, kicking her legs. Every movement she made intensified the pressure in his groin, until he thought he'd burst, and with a groan he let her go. She stumbled, fell, landing on her hands and knees, and suddenly it was perfect.

He dropped to his knees behind her, covering her back with his chest, his thighs fitted to hers, her soft bottom cushioning his cock. She turned her head, mouth open in protest, and he leaned down and kissed her.

"Let me," he murmured, kissing her again, nuzzling at her nape, her hair, pushing his hips hard against her so that she could feel him.

"Oh," she whispered, understanding.

It made him smile, as he loosened the back of her stays and slid his hands beneath her and cupped her breasts. Her nipples were hard with excitement, and when he gently tugged them, she arched her back in pleasure.

"This wasn't . . . part of the . . . forfeit," she managed.

"Wasn't it? You knew it was, darling."

He slipped down her drawers, hands cupping the globes of her bottom, parting her thighs. His fingers slid between them, finding the slick core of her, feeling her tremble.

She clenched her muscles about him, moving to gain the most pleasure, and he knew he couldn't wait. Hastily he freed himself and thrust deep inside her, all the way, and groaned aloud with the exquisite pleasure of it. She pushed back against him, gasping. And in the green, secret shadows of the old maze, with one arm about her waist, the other cupping her breast, he took them both to sensual heaven.

"Miss Dupre!" Sir James Trevalen rose from a chair in the parlor, smiling in greeting.

It was morning of the following day, and when Mary had come upstairs to inform her that Sir James was there to see her, she'd immediately imagined the worst.

"Sir James." Her eyes were round behind her glasses. "Have you come to tell me you've arrested the man who—"

"No, I'm sorry, I haven't been able to discover the wretch."

She was so relieved, she only just remembered

not to let him see her emotion. "But . . . you are still looking?"

"Of course. It is my job as magistrate to see that justice is done."

At that moment Mrs. Wonicot brought in a tray with tea and cakes, and was duly complimented by Sir James. He seemed to be on good terms with her, and although unsurprised, Antoinette was certain it was not because he was friends with Lord Appleby. The two men were worlds apart.

"You knew Sir John Langley?" she ventured, when the housekeeper had gone.

"Yes." He looked surprised. "A grand old gentleman."

"He seems to have been well regarded. Did he have any family?"

Sir James hesitated, but when he spoke his voice was even and without subterfuge. "There was the daughter, Priscilla. She never married and went a little odd. She used to concoct all sorts of herbal remedies for the villagers. Then there was a son, Adam. I haven't seen him for a very long time."

"How old would Adam be now?" she inquired.

"Oh, fifty years and more, I should say. Why do you ask?"

"I don't know. Curiosity, I suppose. So there were no other children here? No other family members who made this their home?"

Sir James tapped his cheek. "Children? I suppose some of the servants had children, and the tenants." He gave her an innocent look.

Antoinette gave up. If the highwayman was telling the truth, and had walked the maze as a child, then she wouldn't discover his identity from Sir James. She hadn't seen her lover since he tricked her into the maze and pleasured her so thoroughly, but she intended to question him the next time.

"And now Lord Appleby is the owner of Wexmoor Manor," Antoinette said quietly, watching Sir James's face.

His smile didn't shift. "He is. Quite a prize, having such an important and wealthy man moving down here. We're hoping he will interest himself in local affairs."

Antoinette smiled back, but she didn't believe him. He was lying. Everyone at Wexmoor Manor was lying, and they couldn't all be in league with Lord Appleby.

When the tea was poured and cake offered, Sir James leaned forward and said, "You seem more content than you did when you last visited me. I hope you are recovered from your, eh, shock. It would be a shame if it spoiled your stay here."

"A great shame." Antoinette sipped her tea.

"Have you been inside the maze yet?"

Her cup and saucer rattled. Did he know? But how could he? She and her lover had been alone, lost in ecstasy, or so she'd thought. In truth she'd been so caught up in the moment, the Coldstream Guards could have marched through the maze and she wouldn't have noticed.

"I—I believe it is difficult to find your way out again." She tried to brazen it out.

"Well, yes, so it is. You need a guide, Miss Dupre."

"Can you recommend someone?" she asked sweetly.

He opened his mouth, then closed it again. The name in his mouth was the one she wanted to hear, and she knew it as positively as she knew her own name.

The identity of the highwayman.

Chapter 21

Gingerly, Lord Appleby took hold of the single sheet of paper by one corner. The writing was blotted and smudged and so poor as to be barely legible, but it was surprising how many of his customers had poor literacy skills. Some of the wealthiest men in the land could barely pen two sentences.

He began to read.

At first he couldn't accept what he was seeing, so he read it again, slowly and carefully. The letter was from a servant at Wexmoor Manor, and she declined to give her name. She was a woman wronged, according to her own description. Her lover had fallen in love with Antoinette Dupre. She begged His Lordship to remove his mistress and to punish her for her immoral behavior. Wasn't she supposed to be true to only him?

The question was rhetorical, it seemed, because when he turned the page over, to see if he could find an answer, he couldn't.

His face darkened and the paper crackled as he tightened his fist. He sat staring at nothing, reliving the moment when Antoinette refused his offer. She'd been polite about it, trying to disguise her shock and disgust, but he'd seen how she really felt. He knew it was that insult as much as her fortune that was now driving him into an enforced marriage. How dare she act as if she was better than he!

She'd taken a lover.

It made his blood boil.

She'd refused him, and now she'd given herself to a nobody. Hardly the actions of a lady, and yet that was what he'd believed her to be. His visits to her home in Surrey, the way she conducted herself there, her affection for her sister . . . Appleby had been impressed and hopeful that a happy marriage with such a woman might be possible.

Her uncle had certainly thought her a remarkable specimen of womanhood. Appleby remembered Jerome raving on endlessly one afternoon at their club in London. It was Jerome's description of the Dupre fortune that first caught his attention and caused him to begin circling the two sisters. At that time he had other possibilities in mind, but his need for money was becoming critical, and the other heiresses he'd chosen were either surrounded by too many watchful relatives, or were too well known. Orphaned and living quietly, the Dupre girls seemed perfect for his purposes.

He couldn't change his mind now; it was too late. Appleby knew he had no option but to go ahead with his plan. But could he still marry Antoinette if she had taken a lover? Could he stomach soiled goods?

He looked down at the letter, crumpled in his fist, and began to straighten out the thick paper. He worked methodically, patiently, as he did everything, and as he worked he knew he could still wed Antoinette. In fact her bad behavior made it seem as if he was doing her a good turn by marrying her and scotching any scandal. And if she didn't like it, if she kicked up a fuss, people would think her ungrateful. Of course if she had developed a taste for low-class men . . . no, he couldn't tolerate that. He'd wait until he had her fortune in his grasp, and then he'd deal with her.

It wasn't as if he hadn't dealt with an inconvenient wife before.

His mind made up, Lord Appleby rang for his secretary. He'd leave tonight to go and fetch Antoinette back to London and he would do it personally. If he took the train and then hired a coach, he could be at Wexmoor Manor by morning. It was time they were married. When Appleby had broached the subject today with the prince consort, he had more or less given his approval. If it seemed overhasty, then people would believe Appleby had fallen in love—autumn and spring; it was not unknown. They might laugh behind his back and call him an old fool for hitching himself to Antoinette, but they wouldn't dare do so to his face. And it would amuse him to know the truth, that in reality he was far from foolish.

And if she refused . . . ?

But no, her wish to save her sister from a similar fate would ensure her cooperation, no matter how unwillingly. She would marry him and probably think to pay him back by making his life a misery. Appleby smiled grimly. Well, let her. She'd only have herself to blame in the end.

He let himself imagine the moment when Antoinette realized how clever he was. Would she fall to her knees, begging for a second chance? He hoped so, he really did. Revenge could be very sweet.

But in the meantime, he believed he'd done his best to prepare for all eventualities. He slid the wrinkled letter into a drawer and rose to his feet, as his secretary knocked and entered the room. Out in the hall, a very pretty young woman with fair curls and sparkling blue eyes was removing her gloves while servants carried in her luggage.

"Cecilia, my dear!" he declared with real pleasure.

Cecilia Dupre, beautiful and innocent and far easier to deal with than her sister. He'd invited her to London as soon as Antoinette left for Devon, and he was very much looking forward to getting to know her better.

Lord Appleby rubbed his hands together. Oh yes, he was prepared for all eventualities.

"Sally, you are the best cook in the country," Wonicot said with a sigh, patting his belly as he settled back in his chair.

But Sally wasn't of a mind to be complimented. She'd been moody all day. Wonicot had a feeling it was all to do with Master Gabriel and Miss Dupre being together. It was none of his business; that was the line he preferred to take. Sally thought differently, and after she'd insisted that Wonicot interrupt them by playing at being in drink, she'd hoped the trysts might stop.

They hadn't.

"Lord Appleby didn't think I was a good cook," she said now. "He hardly touched a thing when he was here."

"Does his opinion count for more than mine?" Wonicot tried to turn it into a joke.

"It'll be His Lordship who decides whether we stay on."

Mary, half listening to their chatter, looked up in surprise from her sewing by the fire. "But he won't send us away! Why would he? We've been here forever. It's more *our* home than *his*."

"But if he sells Wexmoor Manor, Mary," Wonicot explained gently, "then there'll be no need for us. New owners tend to want their own servants around them. We were lucky that His Lordship kept us on for so long, but it can never be like it was when Sir John owned the manor. Those days are gone."

"But I thought—" She bit her lip, looking positively stricken.

The two Wonicots exchanged a puzzled glance. "What *did* you think?" Wonicot asked.

"I thought that Master Gabriel would get

the manor back and then we could all go on as before."

"Well . . . we hoped for that, too, but Lord Appleby is a very wealthy man with powerful friends. As far as I'm concerned Master Gabriel can stay here and I'll do my best to hide him, but if His Lordship sells the manor, it will be hard to keep his being here a secret. If Lord Appleby finds out he's here he'll have him arrested and sent to jail, and nothing Sir James Trevalen says or does will make any difference."

It was a big speech for Wonicot and was followed by a respectful silence.

"But Lord Appleby can't sell!" Mary cried, crumpling the sewing in her hands.

"Mary, we can't tell His Lordship what to do," Sally chided, irritation wrinkling her brow, "and if we did he wouldn't take any notice of us."

"Perhaps he won't sell, not for a while," Wonicot soothed. "We don't know what his plans are, do we? Let's just hope that nothing upsets him," he couldn't help but add, with a grimace. "He seems like a vengeful type of gentleman to me."

"What could upset him?" Sally mocked. "We have Master Gabriel hiding here and he's been spending all his time cavorting with His Lordship's mistress. Upset him! Of course he'd be upset . . . if he knew!"

Wonicot gritted his teeth as pots and pans were clashed violently on the stove. His wife was worried; it was understandable. Mary shot him a sympathetic look and stood up, quietly leaving the room. She looked wan, he thought, but soon forgot it in the need to soothe Sally.

Gabriel woke with a start. Someone was in the house with him. He could hear steps on the old stairs, creeping closer. He barely had time to jump out of bed and find his weapon—a hefty slab of wood—when his bedroom door cracked open.

Candlelight spilled in, and he saw who it was. Relief made him sag, and then a new sort of tension tightened his muscles. He set the wood down and, bare-chested, went to meet her.

"Mary? What on earth are you doing here?"

She'd been weeping. With her reddened eyes and the stains on her cheeks, she was like a child. Instinctively he drew her into his arms to comfort her. Gabriel also felt a pang of guilt. The girl had been acting peculiarly of late and he'd found himself avoiding her, not wanting to have to hurt her with another rejection, or to explain himself where Antoinette was concerned. But now she was in obvious distress, and all he could remember was that they had once been friends.

"Mary," he said again, gently, "what is the matter?"

"I've done something very bad, Master Gabriel," she whispered into his shoulder, and he felt her mouth tremble. "I—I was angry and jealous and I . . ." She took a shaky breath. "Don't hate me, please don't hate me!"

His heart sank, but at her final words he rallied. "As if I could, Mary. You know I would never hate you. But you need to tell me what you've done. Come on, trust me. Perhaps it isn't as bad as you think."

"It is," she wailed, and clung closer, her body trembling.

Gabriel sighed, waiting, holding her until she calmed. Slowly the trembling stopped, and the tears, and she lifted her woebegone face to his.

"That's better," he said brightly, forcing a smile.

"No, it's not," she retorted, her face wrinkling up, but somehow she held back the tears long enough to tell him, in a small staccato voice, what she'd done. "I sent a letter to Lord Appleby. About Miss Dupre. That she has a . . . a lover."

He went still, staring down at her. "Mary, what do you mean, 'that she has a lover'?"

Silently Mary begged him for forgiveness. "I meant *you*."

His eyebrows rose high. "But . . . how did you know?"

She gave something between a laugh and a sob. "I know everything about you, master. I was jealous and I thought if I told His Lordship he'd take her away and then we could . . . could . . ."

He'd stopped listening. "So Appleby knows?"

"Aye."

Gabriel dropped his arms, his mind racing. He knew Appleby too well to expect His Lordship to ignore such news. Antoinette's behavior would lodge in his black heart like a thorn, and from that moment on he'd be planning his revenge.

Mary was babbling, and some of what she was saying caught his attention, enough for him to understand that quite a lot of her tears were self-pitying, for her own situation. Instead of being angry, Gabriel felt relieved to know she wasn't truly in love with him after all.

"What will happen to me?" the girl cried. "I didn't think of anything but him coming and taking her away, and that we would be back to the way we used to be. But now I know I was wrong. Nothing can be like it was, can it? And if His Lordship finds out the lover I was talking about is *you*! Oh, Master Gabriel, I'm that sorry . . ."

Gabriel cut her short. "He won't find out from me. Don't worry, Mary, you've done the right thing by telling me. Now, I'll have to go away for a time, and I'll have to take Miss Dupre with me. But I promise you that one day I'll return and all will be well. Do you believe me?"

Mary nodded miserably but he could see she didn't.

"Go back to bed. If Lord Appleby turns up and starts asking questions, then just say you have no idea who the lover is. No, wait . . ." He grinned. "Tell him it was Coombe."

She gave a tentative smile back. "Yes, Master Gabriel."

"And that you think Coombe will take Miss Dupre to Truro in Cornwall because Coombe has relatives living there. Be sure the Wonicots know what to say, too."

"Where will you really be going, Master Gabriel?"

He touched her cheek. "I can't tell you, Mary. If you don't know, then it can't slip out. I don't want to put you in danger."

"I'll miss you," she said woefully.

"No, you won't." He laughed and spun her around. "A lovely girl like you, Mary, must have dozens of suitors. You've been so busy wasting your time with me, you haven't noticed them. Just wait and see if I'm right."

Dazed, she let him accompany her to the door, and with another reminder to be careful, Gabriel sent her off into the night. He felt energized. Alive. At last something was happening. He hadn't realized until this moment just how much he'd begun to sink into a mire of his own making. A stodgy soup of subterfuge.

Gabriel grinned as he hurried upstairs to get dressed and pack some of his belongings. Appleby was on his way, probably getting closer by the moment, and he needed to get Antoinette away.

He paused. How was he going to do that? She'd argue, and at the very least demand an explanation before she set foot outside the front door. Now wasn't the time to go into detail; all that must wait until they were somewhere safe and secure.

Gabriel knew there was only one way to make her trust him enough to leave with him.

He'd have to be Coombe.

Chapter 22

Antoinette had been tossing and turning, dreaming but unable to drag herself fully awake. There were wolves chasing her through the dark woods but their faces weren't animal faces, they were the faces of the people currently in her life—Lord Appleby and the highwayman, Mary and the Wonicots, Cecilia and her late uncle. She ran but the wolves were too fast and too strong, and finally they cornered her. But just as she was about to be torn asunder, Coombe's hand reached down to her from above and she was drawn up into the trees. "You'll be safe now," he said, and she looked up into his grubby face and wondered if it was true. Because there was something about him, something so familiar . . .

The knocking on her door broke into the dream. Startled, she called out, "Who is it?"

"Mrs. Wonicot, Miss Dupre. Please let me in."

Antoinette sat up, her hair in her eyes. "Come in," she said.

The door rattled and then the knocking began again, louder and more urgent.

What was wrong with the woman? Antoinette struggled out of the tangled bedclothes and padded across the floor on bare feet. That was when she saw the dresser blocking the doorway, and remembered how she'd dragged it there last night, thinking to spare herself the complication of another of the highwayman's visits. Besides, that name still rankled: *Marietta*.

Now she heaved the dresser back out of the way and opened the door. Mrs. Wonicot stood outside holding a lamp, a paisley shawl draped over her voluminous white nightgown. Her plump face appeared to have grown new lines since Antoinette last saw her, and her eyes were ringed with tiredness.

"Coombe wants to see you, Miss Dupre." She was breathless from the stairs and all the knocking. "He's downstairs in the kitchen. I told him such a request in the middle of the night is very irregular but he says you'll agree to speak to him."

"Coombe?" Antoinette tried to gather her wits.

"Do you want to see him?"

"I . . . yes. I do. I'll be down directly."

Coombe was wanting to see her? He must have made up his mind about her request for help to return to London. Why else would he be here? And yet why respond so dramatically? He'd had plenty of time to ponder the matter. Surely his decision could have waited until the morning?

Something must be very wrong.

With a sense of urgency Antoinette pulled on a dress and swung her scarlet shawl around her shoulders. She twisted her hair into a knot and stuck in some pins to hold it. Her gaze slid involuntarily to the window and the dark woods beyond. No light tonight. But of course it was late, and even the highwayman needed his sleep.

Had he tried to visit her and found his way barred? Probably not. She'd likely dragged that heavy dresser about for nothing, and when he heard what she'd done he'd be laughing. "There's always the window," he'd say. His voice in her head was so exact that it gave her a start and she glanced behind her, wondering if he was right there in the room with her. Of course he wasn't. The room was empty; she was alone.

Coombe was hunched before the kitchen fire, attired in his familiar smelly jacket and muddy boots. When he saw her he stood up. Antoinette was surprised Mrs. Wonicot allowed all that dirt in her kitchen, but the formidable cook seemed to have a surprisingly soft spot for the groom. Cautiously she sat down a short distance from him and waved her hand for him to resume his chair.

"What is it, Coombe? What do you want to see me about?"

He was watching her, the firelight shining in his eyes in the shadow of his cap and that atrocious hair. "We need to go tonight, miss," he said. "His Lordship's on his way. You said you wanted help to get away, remember? Well, we need to do it now."

"Now . . .?" The full meaning of his words struck her like a dash of cold water. "Lord Appleby is coming here!" she cried, jumping to her feet, ready to run.

"Calm yourself, miss," he said sharply, in a very un-Coombe-like voice. "We'll manage it, don't you fret."

"How will we manage it? He will find us and—" She stopped herself, not wanting to tell Coombe what Appleby had in mind for her. The less he knew, the better for them both.

"I know this countryside," Coombe said with smug self-confidence. "Lord Appleby'll never find us. Now, you go and pack. Not much, mind. Just the one bag."

She nodded a little wildly. "Yes. Yes, of course. One bag."

"That's it, miss."

Antoinette hesitated. The highwayman didn't know she was leaving, and she realized she couldn't tell him. Being Appleby's man, he'd be obliged to stop her and tell his master, and she couldn't allow that. It was more than likely she would never see him again.

"What is it, miss?" Coombe was looking at her strangely, as if he read her mind. "Is there someone . . . something you've forgotten?"

Antoinette shook her head with finality. "No, no one and nothing."

"Well, don't fret," he repeated as she bolted out of the room.

Something about his tone struck her as so familiar, like the dream she'd had earlier, but Antoinette didn't have time to consider why that was. There was just too much else to think about. Once in her room she turned into a whirlwind, throwing her belongings about, cramming a few bits and pieces into her carpetbag, hardly aware of what she was doing.

Until she remembered her most important possession of all.

The letter.

She swung her cloak around her shoulders and fastened it at her throat—the attached hood would help to disguise her. A last glance about at the chaos of her room, and she was snatching up her carpetbag and hurrying for the stairs.

The Wonicots were huddled together in the entrance hall but they stopped speaking as soon as they saw her. What were they planning to do? Tell Lord Appleby where she was going? Well, she could hardly stop them. Right now it was everyone for him- or herself.

Antoinette rushed past them and into the library. The letter was where she'd left it, and with an exclamation of relief she tucked it down inside her bodice.

She was ready.

Back outside in the hall the Wonicots were still standing together, rumpled from sleep, but now Coombe had joined them. He didn't look any different, and, obviously, washing before he set out on their journey wasn't one of his priorities. But Antoinette said nothing. He was helping her to return to London with her precious proof of Appleby's evil intent, and in the circumstances she wouldn't have cared if he had two heads.

There was a sound. Startled, Antoinette turned and noticed Mary for the first time. The girl was sitting in a chair against the wall, smothering a yawn with the back of her hand, her fair hair spilling out from beneath her crooked mobcap.

She jumped up and dropped a little curtsy. "I wanted to wish you good luck, miss," she said, with a flicker of a glance at Coombe.

"Why, thank you, Mary." Antoinette smiled, touched by the girl's kindness. Ever the organized chatelaine, she had set aside some coins for the moment of her leaving, and somehow she'd remembered to bring them with her. Now she handed them out among the grateful Mary and the unwilling Wonicots.

"Thank you, I'm sure, miss," Sally Wonicot sniffed, while he husband gave a quick nod of his head.

"I'm sorry my stay here wasn't under happier circumstances," Antoinette said, and then she turned and walked to the door to wait for Coombe. There were murmurs from the group behind her and a muffled sob from Mary. This seemed surprising—the girl had never shown any partiality for the groom—but again Antoinette didn't have time to think too hard about it. A moment later Coombe was by her side, throwing open the door, and she was setting off for the stable, with him slouching along beside her in the darkness.

"Is Lord Appleby really on his way?" Antoinette turned to ask him. "How do you know?"

"I do know, miss. Trust me, we've no time to waste."

"No, of course we don't," she murmured, and tried to shake off her doubts. Suddenly she smiled. "I was dreaming about you tonight, Coombe."

He seemed startled. "About *me*, miss?"

"Yes." She heard herself give a very uncharacteristic nervous giggle. "In the dream you saved my life. Perhaps it was an omen. What do you think?"

He was as silent as he was probably wishing she was.

"Anyway," she went on, unable to stop herself— his lack of conversation seemed to cause her to want to talk twice as much, "I think it bodes well for our journey. I was running through the woods and . . ." Suddenly a thought occurred to her and she frowned. "Do you know about the witch who once lived in these woods, Coombe? Her name was Priscilla Langley. Did she have a son?"

"I don't know nothing about no witch, miss," he muttered in a tone that suggested she was losing her mind.

Perhaps he was right, but what if the highwayman was Priscilla's boy? Something about the way he behaved, apart from his verbal hints, the familiarity he displayed with the manor and the cottage and the woods that surrounded them. As if he belonged here. If he was Priscilla's son, then he would be a bastard with no real claim to the Wexmoor estate, but Appleby might use his hopes to force him to obey his orders. *Get me the letter and I will give you Wexmoor.* That sort of thing.

It was a stretch of the imagination, Antoinette thought, as she blew warm air into her gloved hands, and watched Coombe saddle the horses. She was trying to turn the highwayman into an angel, a good man who'd been forced to act out of character under difficult circumstances. Antoinette knew she'd feel far less guilty about their encounters if he was such a man.

But did it really matter what motivated him? She was never going to see him again. And just as well! He'd end up hurting her, abandoning her, and leaving her heartbroken. Then he'd go off to this Marietta woman, and Antoinette would be left at the altar with Lord Appleby.

"Let me help you, miss." Coombe reached for her arm. "Miss?"

She was still lost in her thoughts, but at his touch she found enough strength to give a brusque nod. Once she was in the saddle, she settled herself, waiting for him to finish attaching her carpetbag. As they rode from the yard, Antoinette glanced over her shoulder and saw a flickering light in one of the manor windows. A moment later it was extinguished, and the old house lay in complete darkness.

Antoinette turned her face resolutely forward, telling herself that whatever had happened to her here was finished, and now she must learn to forget.

* * *

Gabriel rode as fast as he dared. Fortunately Antoinette was a good horsewoman and could keep up, although she looked tired and pale, with lines of strain about her eyes and mouth. He had a sudden urge to take her in his arms and promise her he wouldn't let anything bad happen to her, and whatever she was frightened of, she could tell him and trust him.

Of course he didn't.

She'd probably scream and scratch his eyes out, or freeze him with one of her looks. He'd have to be very careful not to slip out of his Coombe character so she didn't suspect anything until they reached their destination. When she was nice and safe with no chance of escaping, he'd reveal himself.

He was looking forward to it.

They had been riding for almost an hour, the dawn light beginning to envelop them with birdsong as the new day appeared, when ahead of them the growing rattle and trot of a horse-drawn vehicle announced someone approaching them at speed.

Before Antoinette could say a word, Coombe grabbed hold of her reins and dragged her off the road and into a field. There was a high stone wall, and they slipped off their mounts and crouched down behind it. Coombe seemed to expect her to protest, but she didn't. They were barely in position when the vehicle came around the corner and rushed toward them. Four horses and a coach with lanterns still lit on either side; someone was in a hurry to reach his destination. And the only destination she knew of in that direction was Wexmoor Manor.

"Lord Appleby," Antoinette whispered.

"Aye. He's in a right hurry."

"We only just left in time." Her relief was obvious.

Coombe gave her a sharp sideways glance. "I thought you was His Lordship's lady. Why don't you want to meet up with him?"

Antoinette watched as the coach raced into the distance. "There are some things I'd rather he didn't know," she said. "If I come face-to-face with him, then I'd have to tell him."

It sounded like nonsense, and he wasn't being put off that easily. Damn it, he wanted to *know*. "What things?"

She turned to look at him. He could see her making up her mind whether to tell him the truth or to lie, but when she finally spoke, he still wasn't sure which option she'd chosen. "He—he is a very jealous man. I—I have someone else in London, another gentleman. That is who I am going to, you see. Lord Appleby will be very angry with me. He probably already knows about this other man, and that is why he has come to Devon. Now do you understand why I can't see him, Coombe?"

"Another man, miss?" Gabriel didn't believe her; he didn't want to.

"Yes."

"And is this one a lord?"

"No, he's a duke," she retorted. "I am making my way up through the peerage."

He stared at her a moment more, then turned away, and Antoinette noticed a hint of disgust in the set of his shoulders. Was Coombe sitting in moral judgment upon her? She told herself it didn't matter what a groom thought of her. As long as he did as she asked and helped her to escape, he could despise her all he wished. When the time came he'd have his reward, she'd make certain of that, and they'd go their separate ways with relief.

When the noise of the coach had faded completely, they remounted, and Coombe led her back onto the road. She noticed after that, he dropped the courtesy "miss." She didn't care; this was hardly the time for social niceties.

"We need to hurry," Coombe said, kicking his horse into an urgent gallop. "Once His Lordship reaches the manor and finds us gone he'll come after us. If you really don't want him to catch you . . . ?"

"I *really* don't."

They set off, Coombe in front and Antoinette following, trying her best not to think about Lord Appleby in hot pursuit. With luck they would reach Barnstaple and be long gone before Appleby discovered in which direction they'd traveled.

She pressed her hand to the letter inside her bodice and felt reassured. She was on her way to London, to save herself and Cecilia. All other considerations, even men who wore masks and made her body sing like an angel, must be forgotten.

Forever.

Chapter 23

Antoinette remembered little during the ride that followed, just the ever-present fear they would be caught. Now and again Coombe would glance behind him to make sure she was keeping pace but she always was. Soon they left the main road, following a maze of smaller lanes and paths until she was completely turned around. Sometimes it seemed to her that they were heading west rather than east. Once she questioned Coombe about that, and their present whereabouts, but he just shrugged and said that as far as he knew they were going in the right direction.

"Don't you trust me?" he said.

Do I have a choice? Antoinette thought her dream, as far as he was concerned, hadn't been as clear-cut as she'd pretended this morning. But there was no point in antagonizing her only friend by suggesting he was taking her in the wrong direction.

"Yes, of course I trust you, Coombe," she said, forcing a smile. "I wouldn't be here if I didn't."

After a while she realized that the smell of salt on the wind had grown very strong. They must be closer to the coast than she'd thought. She drew in a deep breath, weary and yet determined not to ask Coombe to stop for her.

It was only when they came to a village that it occurred to her they'd been avoiding towns and villages up until this point. As they rode slowly down a steep cobbled street past cottages huddled on the hillside, Antoinette looked up and saw the sea. The screech of gulls filled her head and she blinked, taking in the harbor with its curved protective wall around the flotilla of moored boats, and beyond the green water, stretching as far as she could see.

"Coombe," she said cautiously, shading her eyes against the glare. "This can't be Barnstaple."

"No, 'tis St. Nells," he replied calmly, as if it was perfectly fine to have changed his plans without telling her. "I didn't expect Lord Appleby to get here so fast. He'll be after us now, and he'll catch us on land. We're going by water. Water's the only way."

What he said made sense so she smothered her doubts. "Do you know someone with a boat?" she asked anxiously, knowing even as she spoke that he wouldn't be so foolish as to come all this way to the coast if he didn't have a means of sailing away.

"Aye." There was a note of amusement in his deep growl, and his mouth curled in the shadows of his upended jacket collar.

Again that sense of recognition came over her, stronger than ever, and with it a confusion of other emotions. But once again there was no time for it to make sense. Down at the harbor, boats, large and small, bobbed within the safety of the stone wall, and Coombe dismounted and helped Antoinette down. Her legs gave way as they touched the ground and she stumbled, clinging to him. He was big and strong, his hands firm about her waist, his shoulders broad beneath her grasping fingers.

As her nose pressed into the vee of his shirt it occurred to her that he didn't smell so bad after all. It was the jacket that smelled, not the body beneath it. But a moment later he was grasping her hand and tugging her along behind him, toward a small tavern facing the sea.

He turned to her. "Wait here." He spoke as if it was an order and he was used to giving them.

Surprised, confused, she nodded without answering. He disappeared inside. Antoinette stood, aware of the smells of hot food and ale, mingling with those of the harbor. She was weary and she would have loved something to refresh her, not to mention a hot bath, but she didn't want to risk lingering if it meant Appleby might catch them. For all she knew he could be on the outskirts of the village right at this very moment.

A short, bowlegged man appeared from the low doorway with Coombe following. Coombe handed him the horses' reins, and a murmured conversation took place. At one point the man shook his head and laughed. Finally, with a glance at Antoinette, the stranger led the horses around the back of the tavern and Coombe rejoined her, carrying her carpetbag in one hand and his saddlebags in the other.

"The boat is ready," he said. "She's tied up at the jetty, so we won't have to row out to the mooring."

Antoinette tried to read his face but he kept it lowered, his coarse hair flopping over his forehead and into his eyes. She needed to ask questions, but even as she opened her mouth he was turning and moving away, calling over his shoulder that the boat was in that direction.

Coombe walked swiftly. She panted along behind him, holding up her skirts with one hand to prevent herself from tripping over them, and holding her bodice with the other, as if afraid the letter might fly out and sail away over the sea. By the time she reached him he'd jumped down onto the deck of a boat tied up to the narrow wooden jetty that ran along the harbor front.

Except the boat wasn't just a boat. It was a yacht, built on sleek lines, the timbers glossy from the care lavished upon them, ropes carefully coiled and sails lashed to the masts. As her gaze took everything in, Antoinette's mouth fell open in astonishment.

Coombe had already jumped down and was standing on the deck, his feet apart as the vessel rocked, like an old sea dog. He reached up his hand. Instinct caused her to give him hers, and the next instant she felt his strong grip. Almost at the same time she experienced a sense of danger so intense that she tried to pull away. But it was too late. He gave a hard tug on her hand, and with a shriek she fell forward. He caught her, hands gripping her waist, and swung her down onto the deck beside him.

She tried to catch her breath, stumbling as the yacht rocked with their movement. "There's plenty of room below," Coombe said, proceeding to a hatchway and sliding it open. "Go down and settle yourself while I get her under way."

Antoinette stared at him. With every passing second he seemed to be expanding beyond the Coombe she thought she knew. His shoulders were no longer hunched and he was moving confidently about the yacht, unfurling ropes, checking equipment. He wasn't the same man, and yet how was that possible?

She looked beyond him, to the jetty and the tavern, but she could hardly climb back up there now. She was stuck on the boat with Coombe, and she no longer trusted him.

Reluctantly Antoinette went below. In one room—cabin, she supposed it was called—there was a bed built into the wall, with cupboards above and a lantern swinging from the low ceiling. When she peered into the other cabin she found a table with bench seats, more cupboards, and the means to cook and prepare food.

This wasn't just any boat and it certainly wasn't a fishing vessel or a coastal trader. It was clear this was a yacht belonging to a man of means. Hardly a description of Coombe.

Something was very, very wrong.

Coombe was a groom, a man of few words and fewer wits. Remembering how he had busied himself on deck, his confidence and sense of purpose, she felt a terrible dread squeeze her chest.

Slowly she climbed back up the companionway, and popped her head through the open hatch.

He'd cast off and set one of the sails and was now busy hauling on the ropes as the yacht turned and began to move slowly out through the narrow harbor entrance. He had his back turned to her and he'd stripped off his jacket and rolled up his shirtsleeves, the muscles of his arms rippling with his efforts. There was a pistol tucked into his belt at the small of his back. He'd taken off his cap, too, and his hair wasn't coarse and dark after all, but curly and fair. In fact—her eyes widened—his cap lay discarded on the deck and there were tufts of coarse dark hair attached to the sides.

As he turned his head to check they weren't too close to the wall, Antoinette took a hard look at the man's profile, and she could no longer doubt who he was. The highwayman, and her lover. A sick sensation twisted in her stomach as she understood the extent of his betrayal.

"You!" Her voice shook with emotion.

He finished negotiating the boat past the wall before he turned to face her, one hand on the tiller. His expression was watchful, as if he wasn't quite sure how she was going to react.

"Sparrow, don't be angry. If you'd known the truth you would never have come with me . . ."

"You tricked me!" she cried. "How could you do this to me? Why did you bring me here?"

"Because you asked me to help you get away," he said evenly.

"You're taking me to Lord Appleby, aren't you?" Her hands were clenched into fists.

The yacht rolled as it hit the swell beyond the safety of the harbor and a burst of spray peppered the deck. "No, I'm taking you away from him. I promised I would. You said you trusted me."

"I don't understand. You're Lord Appleby's man. Why would you—"

"I've changed my allegiance," he said.

She didn't believe him. "Let me off."

"Too late, Miss Dupre," he said, and there was that smile she knew so well. "I hope you don't get seasick. It looks like we're in for some rough weather."

As if to illustrate his warning, another burst of spray came up over the side of the yacht and washed across the deck, all the way to the hatch. It soaked Antoinette's hair, trickled down her face, and the salt water splashed her spectacles.

She spluttered and choked, and he laughed at her.

"Let me off!" she shrieked, just as the boat rolled again. Her feet slipped on the companionway and she fell, landing on her bottom on the steps, and bumping the remainder of the way down.

As Antoinette sat, dazed and wet, a shadow fell over her. She looked up, and he was peering down at her. "Are you all right, darling?"

She pushed herself to her feet, clinging to the safety railing on the wall, her hair sopping and sticky. "I think so."

"Good." His eyes narrowed and grew almost cruel. "I wouldn't want to deliver damaged goods to your duke, now would I?"

And then he was gone and there was only a square of sky above her.

Tears stung her eyes. Coombe or the highwayman or whoever he was had planned this all along. He'd tricked her. The rest of them must have known, too; she saw it all now. The Wonicots and Mary, sniggering away at her expense, while she attempted to bribe Coombe into helping her escape. How they must have laughed!

Remembering some of the things she'd said, Antoinette felt outraged and humiliated by the trick that had been played on her. Oh, he'd been clever, keeping her at a distance, changing his mannerisms and his way of moving, as well as his voice, so that although she might occasionally feel he was familiar, she never actually connected the two men.

She was trapped. Here she was, on board a yacht, with nowhere to go but into the sea. Even if she could swim, Antoinette doubted she would be brave enough to leap into those cold, deep waters. And she still didn't know what this man planned to do with her, despite what he said about changing allegiance. It was quite likely that once he had the letter from her he would throw her into the sea himself.

The tears began to drip faster down her cheeks, and she let them come. There was no one to see her. She was frightened and alone, and her lover had lied to her and betrayed her. She didn't know what to do or whom to believe, and now the rolling of this dreadful boat was making her feel sick.

Eventually she began, shakily, to make her way toward the cabin with the bed in it. The boat was rolling even worse now and the movement threw her about. She clung to anything that was fastened down and finally reached the bed. As she lay down she told herself she would rest but she wouldn't sleep. No matter how weary and miserable she was, she mustn't sleep. She needed to keep alert and watchful, then if he was going to hand her over to Lord Appleby, she'd be ready.

Except if he'd been going to do that, then why did he leave Wexmoor Manor? Antoinette hadn't known Appleby was on his way until he told her. If he was Appleby's man, then he didn't need to tell her and he didn't need to help her run away. So he wasn't going to give her up. That part of his story must be true at least. He'd spoken of the duke, but that was just something she'd made up for Coombe's benefit, although now it might be useful to her. She might be able to bribe him by promising him recompense from the "duke."

But that still didn't tell her what he wanted from her.

She supposed it was possible he'd heard she was wealthy and wanted her money, or perhaps he really did want to own a racing stable and expected her to find him one. It was all too much to take in, and as hard as she tried to keep her eyes open, they began to drift shut. Despite the rolling of the boat and the wash of the waves, Antoinette sank into oblivion.

Chapter 24

Gabriel sat back in the cockpit with one hand on the tiller, steering his yacht and breathing deeply of the salty air. The weather was blustery and perfect for sailing, he couldn't have asked for better, and they were making good progress down the coast. He was enjoying himself and he felt free again, knowing he was beholden to no man out here. It was the first time he'd felt this free since he learned the news from his father and had gone storming to Appleby's house in Mayfair.

Where he'd first seen *her*. Antoinette.

She'd stayed below since she'd had that soaking as they left the harbor, and the only time he'd ventured down to check on her, he'd found her fast asleep in his bed. She looked so sweet, so peaceful and innocent, he was almost ashamed at the hot imaginings that sprang into his head. And then he remembered the duke and he felt like wringing her neck.

He shifted the tiller slightly to port, and the flapping sail filled again as they heeled over, the wind buffeting them along at a cracking pace.

Of course she'd been very angry when she finally realized who he was. And he'd expected anger, yes; he'd even been looking forward to meeting it head-on. But that shattered expression . . . he'd wanted to wrap his arms around her and hold her and tell her over and over how sorry he was.

Except he hadn't done anything wrong. In fact he'd done exactly as she asked him: helped her run away from Appleby. After she'd recovered from her shock he was expecting some gratitude, some sweet, passionate kisses.

Until she'd mentioned the other man.

At that moment something inside him had begun to burn, a slow, intense heat that threatened to consume him. Antoinette had lain with him, sighing and moaning, clasping him in her arms, and all the time she wasn't thinking of Gabriel, and she wasn't thinking of Appleby. She was thinking of the duke.

No doubt he was everything Gabriel was not, could give her her heart's desire and more.

His hand clenched on the tiller, and it was only as the boat began to shift off course that he realized what he was doing and straightened her up. What was the point in speculating? He'd get the truth out of her. There was plenty of time. Gabriel meant to drop anchor at dusk and spend the night in one of his favorite sheltered coves. They'd be far from Appleby's reach, just Gabriel and Antoinette . . . and the letter.

He knew she'd never have left it behind. It was

here, somewhere, and he was going to get it from her. After all, what possible use could she have for it now? And once he'd regained Wexmoor Manor and persuaded Appleby not to pursue any charges against him, he'd be able to live the life of a wealthy landed gentleman.

Would a man like that appeal to Antoinette?

Gabriel despised himself for thinking it, but he couldn't help it. He wanted her, and he'd use all the weapons in his possession to win her.

Antoinette sat on the edge of the bed, trying to decide what to do. Her stomach lurched. She'd awoken confused and disoriented, wondering where she was. The next moment she made a dash for a bowl she'd noticed earlier. It was probably used for washing water, and fit securely into the top of a wooden chest, but Antoinette found another use for it. The retching made her feel a little better, but as soon as she straightened up, nausea returned.

Seasickness. Antoinette moaned and closed her eyes. She needed fresh air, and to get that she'd have to go up on deck where *he* was. No matter what he said to the contrary, she didn't trust him. Another roll of the boat and her stomach lurched again. With a whimper she headed toward the companionway.

Gabriel raised his eyebrows in surprise as her face appeared through the hatchway. It was an interesting shade of green. She swallowed, a hand covering her mouth. She wasn't wearing her spectacles and her eyes were enormous.

"I wondered if you might have something to help my stomach," she said in a stiff little voice, as if she was afraid of opening her mouth too far.

Gabriel felt like laughing but he bit his lip—he didn't think she'd appreciate his humor just now. Getting to his feet, he crossed the deck and reached out for her hands. Reluctantly she gave them to him, and he helped her up through the hatchway and, with an arm about her waist, led her back to the cockpit. The sunken space had a built-in seat made comfortable with cushions, and he settled her there before correcting their course again.

From the corner of his eye he could see her trying to breathe, her eyes closed as she lifted her face to the brisk wind. The air was cold and she shivered, wrapping her arms about herself.

"Poor sparrow," he murmured.

She shot him a suspicious look, as if she mistrusted his sympathy.

"Do you think you can steer us while I go below and find you a blanket or two? You'll soon get frozen up here."

"Steer the boat?" she croaked.

"Don't worry, you won't capsize us. At least I don't think so. Here, hold the tiller right here. Remember, you have to push it in the opposite direction to the one you want to go. But you shouldn't need to do that; just hold it steady."

Tentatively she placed her hand on the wooden

tiller and he covered it with his, feeling her cold skin and the tremble in her arm. Sweet, bossy Antoinette Dupre was in a bad way.

"That's it, keep her steady," he said gently.

"Like this, do you mean?" She sat up straighter, concentrating. Above them the sails flapped as the wind gusted and the boat cut through the green water, flying along. It was invigorating, and, studying her face, Gabriel thought she was actually beginning to enjoy herself.

"Just hold it there. I'll be back in a moment."

She looked a bit panicky and her fingers tightened as he removed his. He felt her tension as he left the cockpit and made his way to the hatchway and slipped below.

He stripped some blankets from the bed, and while he was there also grabbed a flask of liquor and a tin of biscuits, perfect food for the seasick. Carrying his bounty, he returned to the deck. Her nervous gaze was fixed on the hatchway, waiting for him, and when he appeared she couldn't disguise her relief.

"All right?" He sat down beside her and began to wrap the blankets around her, tucking them in carefully about her feet.

"Yes. Thank you." She sounded stiff and formal, avoiding his eyes.

"Have a sip of this." Gabriel unscrewed the flask and handed it to her. She sniffed it suspiciously. "Brandy," he said. "It'll help settle your stomach."

She looked as if she might refuse, but changed

her mind and took a sip anyway. After a moment she took another. He handed her a biscuit.

"Nibble on this. Nothing worse than an empty stomach when you're seasick."

This time she didn't argue. "Do you ever get seasick?" she said, after a long pause.

"Only if it's very rough."

"I thought you said this was rough?"

"There's some rough weather coming but not today. This is just brisk, Antoinette."

She mulled over his information. "Is this your boat?" she said, watching as he adjusted the tiller.

"Yes. She's called *Sea Witch*."

"Oh."

He could see the question on her lips and decided to put her out of her misery. "And no, I'm not Priscilla Langley's son, legitimate or otherwise. And yes, the boat is named after her."

"Was she really a witch?" she asked dreamily, snuggling down into the blankets and the cushions, closing her eyes.

"I wonder that myself. She was an herbalist, and people came to her for help; even the local doctor deferred to her on some matters. She had a way of getting to the heart of a problem that was uncanny, and sometimes she seemed to know what was going to happen before it did." He smiled, remembering her prediction that a brown bird would be his downfall. He wished now she'd offered him some more advice on how to keep that little bird by his side forever.

Gabriel glanced at Antoinette and found she'd

fallen asleep. Careful not to wake her, he slid his arm about her and drew her closer, so that her head was resting on his shoulder and her body was snuggled into his. She was soft and warm, and a strand of her hair blew across his face, bringing with it her sweet scent.

He wanted to protect her and look after her. The feeling was new to him, but it felt good, it felt right. The pity was she belonged to someone else. Or claimed she did, he thought, holding her closer. She made a murmur and wriggled against him, a smile on her lips. Gabriel decided he'd have to persuade her differently. Her body already knew she was his; all he had to do was convince her heart and mind.

With one arm wrapped about her and the tiller in the other, he steered his boat, and for the first time in a long time he felt completely happy and content with his world.

Antoinette vaguely remembered being carried below deck and tucked back into the bed. At least the boat seemed to have stopped its dreadful rolling, and her stomach was calmer. The brandy had helped, making her sleepy, and she sighed as Gabriel began to unbutton her clothing. If he expected to find the letter, then he was going to be disappointed—she'd hidden it as soon as she came down there.

He slipped off her dress and loosened her petticoats and stays, leaving them on her. The bedclothes were warm and comfortable as he pulled them over her, and she could smell the sea on them and him. Then his lips brushed her cheek and he was gone.

A long time afterward she heard the rattle of a chain and knew he must have dropped anchor, and then his footsteps moving about on the deck and the sounds of equipment being tidied up and stowed away. Eventually he came back down to the cabin and slid into the bed beside her, reaching out to draw her against him.

Antoinette had planned to reject him, accuse him of all manner of crimes, but her limbs felt so heavy and her eyelids refused to open more than a fraction. So she nuzzled against his naked shoulder and smelled his warm, spicy scent. Her tongue flicked against him and she tasted salt.

At her touch he slipped a finger under her chin and tilted her face up and kissed her.

She didn't mean to return his caress, but before she knew it they were locked in a hot and hungry kiss. He removed her remaining garments, kissing and caressing each new inch he exposed, until she was twisting and gasping and begging him to make love to her. His muscular thigh slid between hers, and she felt the familiar stirrings inside her. It was so easy to lose herself in her growing passion, far easier than trying to think and reason and decide what to do. His lips on her breasts, his fingers finding her most sensitive spots, his body moving inside hers, taking them both to that place where there was nothing but ecstasy.

But as always she had to come back to earth, eventually, and this time the bump of her landing was harder than usual.

"Where are we?" she demanded.

"Safe." He sounded sleepy now.

"How do you know?"

He moved to touch her face but she pulled away, putting distance between them, glaring at him. She felt an unstoppable need to push and prod at him, forcing him to give her answers. Somewhere deep inside her, Antoinette longed for him to admit he'd abducted her because he couldn't live without her. Even though she knew it was foolish and ridiculous and impossible, still she longed to hear him say it.

"What do you want from me?" she went on, moving to sit up, pulling the covers awkwardly over her naked breasts. "Why am I here?"

"Antoinette, please, not now . . . Sleep. We can discuss this in the morning."

"I want to discuss it now. I need to know what you're planning to do with me. I-I'm expected in London."

His voice, so warm a moment ago, was suddenly cold. "You mean your duke is expecting you?"

Marietta? Who is Marietta? The question was on the tip of her tongue but she couldn't force it past her lips.

"I want the letter," he said, when she didn't answer, the familiar refrain. "That's why you're here. Did you think there was another reason?"

"The letter. Yes, of course." She'd forgotten the

letter. How could she forget it when it meant so much to her? But she had.

He climbed out of bed and stood naked in the pale light from the lantern that swung gently from its hook in the ceiling. His eyes were pale blue, his face as handsome as she remembered, but he was a stranger. Not the highwayman and not Coombe, but someone else, someone she didn't know at all.

"Why won't you give it to me?" he said in that same harsh voice. "You can't need it now. Do something unselfish, Antoinette, and give me the letter."

"No! I need it. Without it I'll never get away from Lord Appleby."

There, she'd told the truth. She watched him, wondering what he would make of it and what questions he would have to ask. But to her dismay his expression grew even colder and harder than before, and any hope she had of winning him to her side vanished.

"So you intend to blackmail him with the letter, is that it?"

Did she? "Blackmail" was a horrible word but Lord Appleby was a horrible man.

"Where is it?" He turned and looked about him. Seeing her clothing spread about the cabin, he bent and picked up each garment, piece by piece, shaking them and searching them, even rending the padding in her petticoats to see whether the letter was hidden inside. Antoinette watched him, silent, holding her protests inside. When he finished with her clothes he grabbed her carpetbag and tipped it upside down on the bed, spilling out the contents.

Seeing her personal belongings rolling about was too much. "Stop it," she said angrily, reaching out to stop him. But he wouldn't be stopped. Everything must be searched and examined and then tossed aside, right down to the last hairpin and stocking.

"This is what I should have done in the very beginning," he said in that hard, angry voice she didn't recognize. "I would have saved myself a lot of wasted time and trouble."

So that's how he thought of her? A waste of time. No doubt he considered the times they'd made love a waste of time, too. Antoinette forced her own anger to fire up again, to disguise her misery.

"I wish you'd said so before, I wouldn't have bothered pretending you were the world's greatest lover. Frankly, you could do with some lessons."

"Antoinette," he said through gritted teeth.

She folded her arms over her breasts and glared back at him. "I think it's about time you told me the truth. What has Lord Appleby got that you want?"

He took a shaky breath, calming himself. "I want the letter, and in return he will give me Wexmoor Manor."

There was a knife in her heart, or so it seemed. He mustn't see it or know how she felt; she wouldn't give him the victory. "Well, that is unfortunate. For you," she managed in a light, chilly voice.

Gabriel wanted to shake her. Or kiss her. Her insults stung but he didn't accept them. He might not be the world's greatest lover, but she couldn't fake what she'd felt when they made love. It had been special, and if she wanted to deny it now, then she had other reasons. Perhaps she needed to pretend it meant nothing so that she could go to her duke and play her part. In a way he could understand her need to do that even if he couldn't accept it. But the letter was a different matter. She was going to take it to her new protector and use it as a bargaining tool, to keep Appleby from making trouble for them.

Such cold-blooded self-interest was breathtaking, and he couldn't allow her to do it. That letter was his means of regaining Wexmoor Manor and Aphrodite's Club, others were depending on him, and he would get it from her, one way or another.

"Give me the letter and I'll tell you anything you want to know," he said, leaning threateningly over her, his eyes only inches from hers. Her gaze widened, but try as he might, he could see no fear in her eyes, only a determination to match his own.

"I am tired now," she said in a frosty voice. "Please leave me."

Gabriel remained where he was, making sure she knew how angry he was. "You'll give it to me," he gritted. "That letter is my future."

And hers, too, a voice reminded him.

Still she refused to flinch or turn away. Finally, with a sound of disgust, he left her, striding into the other cabin and slamming the door.

Antoinette slumped back, shaking, trying not to cry. All he cared about was the letter and getting his hands on Wexmoor Manor. That was all he had cared about from the very beginning, only she'd been too stupid to see it.

She had to get away from him. If she could persuade him to put her ashore she would be able to make her way home, somehow. She'd be alone, but it was better than being trapped on the *Sea Witch* with him. She didn't trust him, she'd never trusted him, and she'd been right.

Worse than that, she didn't trust herself when he was around. She was just as likely to throw herself naked into his arms. Antoinette couldn't allow that to happen. She had too much pride for that.

She lay on the bed, the lantern swaying over her, and closed her eyes. Images of the day flitted through her mind, and it wasn't until she reached the one of him standing on the deck with his back to her that she remembered something she could use.

There was a pistol tucked into his belt.

He had a pistol.

If she could get her hands on it she'd be able to force him into obeying her orders for a change. But where was it? Certainly not on him at the moment. Sitting up, she looked about her for his clothing, but he'd taken it with him. Quietly she made a search of the cupboards and drawers, but there were no weapons to be found and certainly no pistol.

He must have it with him then.

Antoinette knew she would have to get close enough to take it from him, and to do that she would have to lull him into believing she was harmless. It would need some thought and planning.

But then, she had all night.

Chapter 25

Gabriel scanned the sky. It was gray. The wind had picked up, too. It looked as if the weather was turning against them. He'd hauled anchor at dawn and they'd made little headway since. At this rate he'd be blown back to where he'd come from. And something else was worrying him.

Antoinette was sick.

When he'd slipped down to the cabin midway through the morning he'd found her groaning in the bed, her face another interesting shade of green. She didn't even have the energy to abuse him when he lifted her head and tipped a few drops of brandy down her throat, although she coughed and spluttered.

"Let me off," she begged him.

"We're miles from the coast."

"I don't care. Set me adrift on a raft."

He bit his lip on a smile. "Try to sleep."

Her reply was a pitiful whimper.

He'd checked on her since, twice, but there'd been

no improvement. If anything, she looked worse. Gabriel sighed. He'd have to go into the next port, and by his calculations it was Arlington-by-Sea. If Antoinette didn't improve, they'd have to make the rest of the journey to London by land.

And then what? Do you hand her cheerfully over to her new protector like some crazed version of a fairy godmother? And then walk away and forget all about her?

No, Gabriel knew he couldn't do that. Not when he wanted her for himself so much that his body ached. And yet he'd known the kind of woman she was from the start; he had no excuses to offer. He couldn't claim he'd been tricked or led astray. No, he'd managed to become entangled with her despite the numerous warnings.

He must be an idiot, because in his heart he still believed she wasn't the woman she made herself out to be. There were too many inconsistencies, too many moments when the real Antoinette just didn't fit with the harlot. And then last night, when they made love, she couldn't have been faking the pleasure she felt, and the way she sighed in his arms and stroked his hair. He meant more to her than she was admitting.

Gabriel felt a burst of optimism. He could try asking her to stay with him. He hadn't really tried that yet. Most of their conversations ended in distraction or an argument, before he had a chance to make his offer. He had to try. Before they reached London he was going to show her just how wrong she was if she thought her future lay as an old man's darling when there was a young man aching to make her *his* darling.

Arlington-by-Sea was a welcome sight when he finally moored the boat just at twilight. The rough weather had slowed them considerably and he'd had to use every ounce of his strength and sailing skills to make the headway they needed to reach safety. It hadn't been pleasant but they were here now.

The harbor was sheltered in nearly all weathers and all winds, apart from one. This one, with the wind blowing strongly from the northeast. Even moored in the harbor, the boat bucked and rolled, and Gabriel knew he needed to get Antoinette to shore and into a warm bed as soon as possible.

He launched the dinghy, throwing in the saddlebags full of his few belongings, and slipped his pistol into his belt. He fetched Antoinette's carpetbag, repacked it, and stowed that, too. Then he returned below for her.

She was sleeping, a frown wrinkling her brow, but she looked washed out and exhausted. Even the brandy hadn't stayed down during the last few hours, and her retching was painful to watch. Gabriel wanted to see her comfortable before he made any further decisions.

He leaned against the doorway and watched her. He must be some sort of monster because in a way he was glad she was sick, if it prevented her from going to her duke. It meant he had more time to convince her to stay with him.

Her eyes opened, dazed, and fixed on him. "Am I dead yet?"

He crouched down beside her, stroking her face, his voice gentle. "No, Antoinette. You won't die of seasickness, although it can feel like it."

She groaned and closed her eyes again. "We're still moving."

"I know. That's why we need to go ashore. Do you think you can manage it, darling?"

"Ashore?" she croaked.

"Yes. Can you manage it?"

She nodded, and then looked down at herself wryly. "I need to get dressed, but first I need a bath."

"We'll deal with that when we get to the inn. A bath and a bed, how does that sound?"

"Heavenly." She sighed.

Gabriel began to gather up the clothing he'd stripped from her last night. She did her best to manage herself, but she was dizzy and weak and obviously still feeling wretched, so it was Gabriel who pulled on her stockings and buttoned her dress and twisted her hair over her shoulder. The cloak helped to cover up any deficiencies.

"Next time we run away can we go by train?" she whispered.

He laughed, and lifted her easily into his arms. "We could make a habit of it. Every year we could run away to a different location using a different means of transport."

She linked her fingers around his neck. "Edinburgh by foot, Cardiff by donkey, and John o' Groat's by elephant."

"You sound as if you're feeling better already," he said, noticing the flush of color in her cheeks.

"It's the thought of getting off your boat."

He made his way carefully to the companionway. Her long skirts tangled around his legs, and he paused to bundle them up out of the way before climbing the narrow stairs and out onto the deck.

The dinghy was bobbing on the water, five or so feet below the deck of the *Sea Witch*. Gabriel lifted her over, holding her as her feet touched the dinghy and she was able to stand in the bottom of the little boat. When she sat down gratefully on the seat in the stern, Gabriel swung his leg over the railing, preparing to join her.

"Oh," she gasped, searching inside one sleeve and then the other.

"What is it?"

She looked up at him, her brown eyes enormous in her wan face. "I've forgotten my handkerchief."

Gabriel raised his eyebrows. "What's one handkerchief? I'll buy you a dozen."

"My—my mother gave it to me," she stammered, and suddenly her eyes were bright with tears. "She died when I was five. I treasure it." She shook her head, putting on a brave face. "But yes, you're right. You've no time to go back for a handkerchief. I'm being silly."

Gabriel sighed, understanding that he had no choice but to fetch her handkerchief. Maybe she'd look more kindly on him. "Very well. I'll only be a moment. Don't rock the boat."

She managed a smile in response, but he saw the way her knuckles were white as she clenched the sides of the dinghy.

He turned back down the companionway and into the cabin. A search among the tousled bed-clothes failed to find the handkerchief, and he was about to give up when he saw a corner of lace poking out from under the mattress. With the handkerchief clutched triumphantly in his hand, Gabriel returned to the deck.

"Here you are—" he said as he moved toward the railing. And stopped, frozen with shock, hardly able to believe his eyes.

The dinghy was moving, making its way across the choppy water toward the shore. And Antoinette was rowing it, inexpertly but strongly, her pale face anxious. When she saw Gabriel she seemed to falter, one oar missing the water altogether, so that the dinghy swung to the side and she had to straighten it.

"What the hell do you think you're doing?" he roared furiously. "Come back here now!"

"No, I won't," she called back, her softer voice faint as it was caught by the wind.

"I can swim, you know," he shouted, climbing up onto the railing to prepare to dive in.

The oars rattled as she set them down inside the boat, and she fumbled for something inside her cloak. His eyes widened in disbelief when he saw she was holding his pistol in her hands, aiming it at him.

"If you come near me I will shoot you!" she declared.

He almost laughed. He didn't want to believe her. But there was a raw look in her wide eyes and her tense, white face that told him he shouldn't take the chance. Antoinette meant what she said, and even if she didn't, a pistol was a very dangerous weapon in the hands of a frightened woman.

"Sparrow . . ." he began, pleading.

"Don't call me that." Her voice shook as if she was crying.

He spread out his arms wide. "Perhaps you should shoot me now because I'll come after you. You know I will."

"Perhaps I should," she retorted. "You deserve it."

"Do you know how to?" he asked curiously.

Her smile was triumphant. "Oh yes. Don't doubt it. Now I am going ashore and you will stay here. This is where we part company."

"Antoinette—"

"There's nothing more to be said."

She picked up the oars again and began to row away. A particularly savage gust of wind blew spray up into her face, and she blinked and shook her head. He watched her, angry and admiring at the same time. His Antoinette was a truly amazing woman.

"I won't say good-bye," he called. "I'll find you."

"This is good-bye!"

He watched her put distance between them. "Don't wager on it," he murmured with a grim smile, leaning over the railing, as if he could bring her back by sheer force of will. "I'll find you, Antoinette, and when I do . . ."

His grin broadened as he imagined what he would do to her. He would find her, he had to. She'd thrown down a challenge, and Gabriel wasn't the sort of man to ignore a challenge.

Antoinette climbed unsteadily out of the dinghy and onto the shore. Luckily there were some fishermen there to help her and to secure the dinghy. She explained she had urgent business ashore and thanked them when they offered to take her to the tavern where she could arrange for transport into the nearest larger town, where there was a railway station.

She glanced over her shoulder only once.

In the fading light she could barely see him, silhouetted on the deck, but she knew he was there. Hating her. Swearing his revenge. He was worse than Appleby when it came to letting her go.

I'll find you.

Antoinette shivered and her heart beat harder. She reminded herself that he would have no way of finding her; he didn't know where she was going. Certainly not to London, as he imagined, but Surrey. She longed for her home, for Cecilia and Miss Bridewell, and all that was dear and familiar. Once she reached them, she would explain what had happened and send Cecilia somewhere safe, away from Appleby's greedy, clutching hands, and then she would travel on to London, alone, and destroy him.

A grim feeling of anticipation helped her to keep going although her knees were wobbly and her arms ached from rowing. Soon it would be over. She could put all this behind her, treat it as if it were a nightmare.

As if to unsettle her, she heard the soft whisper of his voice in her head, saying, *Darling*. Tears stung her eyes, but when one of the fishermen asked her if she was unwell, she told him it was just the salty wind making her cry.

Chapter 26

The rain on the journey home was relentless, but as Antoinette came up the drive toward the house, the rain stopped and the clouds parted and the sun shone. She'd had enough money for the train fare and then a public coach to the end of her drive, but after that she had walked, carrying her carpetbag.

Dupre House rose before her, perfect within its garden setting, the rows of windows glinting in the sun, the elegant facade reminding her that this house was built by a king for his favorite mistress and given to her as a gift.

A gift she threw away for love.

Antoinette's ancestress, the wicked mistress, had captivated King Charles II and given him two children, before she ran off and married another man, abandoning the king, her home, and her children. Charles was naturally upset, and although he allowed the Dupre family to retain the house, there were no titles or other gifts, and he never forgave his errant lady.

Antoinette had always considered her ancestress to have been lacking in foresight. After all, she could have had everything, and instead she ended by vanishing into obscurity. But now, tired and shattered, gazing up at her home, Antoinette found herself with new insight into her wanton ancestress's behavior. It was as if she could understand perfectly well why she might give up material benefit for elusive love, although the abandoning of the children was something else again.

The maid who opened the door was wide-eyed at the sight of her bedraggled mistress and let out a little scream. Antoinette dropped her carpetbag with a relieved sigh.

"It's all right, Hettie. I have been sailing. Can you have a bath drawn for me, and a warm brick placed in my bed? I do believe I am going to sleep for a week."

"M-Miss Dupre, we've been so worried," the girl stammered.

"Thank you, Hettie, but I'm home now and everything will be all right."

Just then she spotted a familiar figure descending the main staircase. "Bridie?"

Miss Bridewell looked up at the sound of her pet name, and gave a shocked cry. "Miss Antoinette?" Her expression spoke volumes as she came hurrying to meet her. "You're wet and . . . and . . ."

"Yes. I was just explaining to Hettie, I've been sailing. Come upstairs with me, Bridie, and I'll tell you everything." She stopped, glanced sideways at the governess. "Well, nearly everything."

"We're so glad you're home," Miss Bridewell declared, giving her a bone-cracking hug.

Antoinette laughed, her face as bright as the beams of sunlight outside. "Where is Cecilia?" she asked, drawing away and looking about, expecting to see her sister appear and come running toward her like the child she still was in many ways.

Instantly Miss Bridewell's face fell and her lips trembled. "You do not know! Then you haven't seen her? Oh, Miss Antoinette, I tried to stop her. I tried my very best. I knew you would not like it if she went, but you know how she is. So headstrong. Once she'd decided to go I could not stop her. I'm afraid she only listens to you and you were not here . . ."

"She's gone to London." Antoinette answered her own question in an oddly calm voice, while inside her emotions were as turbulent as the sea.

Miss Bridewell nodded, watching her and not trusting herself to speak.

Cecilia had always been difficult, but Antoinette knew if she had been there, Cecilia would have listened to her. Well, she was here now. Antoinette drew on her strength, shaking off her tiredness and the terrible fear, and putting aside the thought of a long, warm bath and a dreamless sleep.

"Come upstairs, Bridie, and tell me exactly what has happened."

As they ascended the stairs to the upper floors, she couldn't help but look about her at the house.

So many windows and bright, light colors made this place very different from dark and gloomy Wexmoor Manor.

"It *is* good to be home," she said, with such intense feeling that Miss Bridewell gave her an uneasy stare. Antoinette smiled to reassure her. "I forgot, Bridie, you don't know what has happened since you waved me good-bye. I have a great deal to tell you."

Although, she reminded herself, not everything could be shared with her middle-aged spinster governess; some things were just too shocking for her delicate ears.

Once they were comfortable in Antoinette's sitting room, she insisted that first Miss Bridewell tell her story.

"The letter came a fortnight ago," Bridie said. "In it Lord Appleby invited Miss Cecilia to come and join you both in London."

"But I wasn't even there then!"

"Well, he wrote as if you were. Cecilia would never have gone if—"

"No, of course not. So she went?"

"Yes. I tried to persuade her to let me go, too, but she insisted she would be all right. She said you would be there, and she would be perfectly safe with you, Miss Antoinette."

"Did you tell her about the letter you sent to me? What was contained in it?"

"No," Bridie said miserably. "I didn't feel it was my place, and the contents were so shocking . . . Besides, you said she should not know unless it was absolutely necessary, and I wasn't certain it *was* absolutely necessary."

"I'm not blaming you, Bridie. I'm blaming myself."

Antoinette's need to protect her sister now seemed ridiculously naïve and shortsighted. Surely it would have been better to prepare Cecilia for the worst rather than worry about sullying her ears with shocking tales? She was momentarily overwhelmed by images of Cecilia, a prisoner in Appleby's arms, but she pushed them aside. No time for hysterics now. This situation required prompt action and clear thinking, not a dose of ladylike prostration.

"I have your letter," she said, "but I haven't been able to use it yet. I was watched everywhere I went and then Lord Appleby sent me into Devon, and I was watched there, too. I have only just escaped."

"*Escaped?*" Miss Bridewell echoed faintly. "Oh, my dear, so my fears were well-founded. He planned to do the same to you as he did to . . . ?"

Their eyes met. "Yes, I think he did," Antoinette said quietly.

"Horrible." Miss Bridewell shuddered. "What a truly evil man."

"Bridie, as soon as I have bathed and changed I must set off for London. Cecilia will be staying in Lord Appleby's house in Mayfair, and if luck is with me, then His Lordship will still be in Devon, or on his journey back."

"Lord Appleby was in Devon, too?" Bridie's eyes were starting from her head. "Miss Antoinette, please, please tell me you have not lost the one treasure a lady has to offer her husband to that . . . that cad!"

Antoinette had the urge to giggle, but mastered it. "No, Bridie, Lord Appleby did not molest me . . . Well, not much. He sullied my reputation rather than my body."

Miss Bridewell sighed, relieved. "A reputation can be repaired," she said stoically, "but once a lady's treasure is lost, then it is gone forever."

Antoinette said nothing. She thought Miss Bridewell was too optimistic about her reputation, and how her treasure came to be lost would remain her secret until the day she died.

"The first thing I will do when I get to London is go to Mayfair and try to see Cecilia," she declared. "Then I will get her safely away. After I've done that I'll find the address in your letter, Bridie, and . . . Well, you know what I must do then. Once it is known what sort of man Lord Appleby really is, then he will be ostracized. Ruined. The law will turn its cold eye in his direction and he will be brought to justice and punished."

Miss Bridewell looked relieved. "That sounds like a perfect plan, Miss Antoinette. I am so glad you're here. I felt quite lost without you."

"Never mind, Bridie, everything will work out, I am certain. We will be rid of Lord Appleby once and for all."

"Yes, and we can go back to the way things were before."

Antoinette had been thinking exactly the same

thing, but hearing it spoken aloud didn't make her as relieved as she'd expected. There was a feeling of emptiness deep inside her, of something lacking. Perhaps she had changed more than she realized, and it would take her a while to settle back into her old comfortable life.

Miss Bridewell was watching her anxiously. "Are you quite well, Miss Antoinette? I think you should wait until the morning before you leave for London. Surely a few hours' delay will make no difference?"

"No, I must go at once, Bridie. Lord Appleby may be back in London tomorrow, and I can't risk waiting. I will be all right. As long as I don't have to go sailing."

Miss Bridewell blinked at her questioningly. "Sailing? Why did you go sailing? You never told me."

Antoinette reached forward and clasped her governess's hands, forestalling any more questions. "I'll explain when I return. When everything is comfortable again and Cecilia is safe. I'm sure we will laugh at our adventures then."

Miss Bridewell managed a brave smile. "I hope so, Miss Antoinette, I truly do."

By the time she reached London Antoinette was beyond tired, but she could not think of sleep when there was so much yet to do. After the steam train had chugged into Waterloo Station, she'd taken a hansom cab to Mayfair.

She was tempted to go straight to Lord Appleby's house and knock on the door, but that could be disastrous if she was captured again. It was best, she'd decided, to lurk about in the square and watch the house for a while. With luck she would see Cecilia coming or going, and be able to waylay her.

The cabdriver was amenable to her plan, after she doubled the fare, so she sat and waited. It was almost an hour before she saw a coach draw up outside the house and glimpsed the fair head of her sister beneath one of her newest and most fashionable bonnets.

Cecilia appeared as lovely as ever, and Antoinette's heart ached at the thought of all that sweetness and beauty destroyed by one man's greed.

She had climbed down from the cab and was hurrying forward when someone else stepped from the coach behind Cecilia.

Antoinette recognized him immediately. The well-made jacket and top hat, the cane he used as an affectation, the smirk on his thin lips as he replied to Cecilia's chatter. Lord Appleby was back, and any chance she had of stealing her sister safely away from his house was dashed.

Hastily she turned around and hurried back to the corner, where the cab was waiting. That was where her legs failed her and she had to lean against the railings of a grand Georgian town house and close her eyes until her head stopped spinning.

Her sister was imprisoned in the monster's den, just as in one of the rather terrible fairy tales Antoinette had read as a child. Antoinette knew that she could not save her, not without putting her own freedom at risk. And Antoinette could not be captured again, because if she was there'd be no one left to bring Appleby to justice.

Despite her fears for Cecilia, she would have to carry on, and do what she had come to London to do. She would ask the cabbie to take her to the address in Miss Bridewell's letter, and with any luck the whole nasty business would be over and done with by teatime.

Her decision made, Antoinette opened her eyes and noticed that she was attracting some unwelcome attention from several passersby and a small crossing sweeper. "Tippling at this time o' day!" one gentleman muttered disapprovingly. Antoinette hastily returned to her cab, and after giving the driver the new address, settled back to prepare herself for the coming confrontation.

Perhaps it would help to reread the details?

Reaching with her gloved fingers inside her bodice, Antoinette withdrew the letter. It was creased and stained with salt water, definitely the worse for wear, but it was as precious as cloth of gold to her eyes.

Miss Bridewell's writing was comforting, and Antoinette smiled as she found the relevant paragraph, thinking that soon it would all be over.

They rattled over the Thames and into that seedy area of London known as Lambeth. It took the driver a little time to find the address, and they passed back and forth over rough roads and down lanes so narrow that Antoinette wondered whether they would be stuck. But eventually they came to a halt outside a derelict building.

Antoinette gazed up at it in dismay. "This is it?"

"I'm afraid so, miss."

"The Asylum for Misfortunate Women?"

"Yes, miss."

"But . . . what's happened to it?"

"I dunno. Here, I'll ask. Just hang on." The cabbie jumped down and crossed the lane to a woman with a child on her hip and another at her feet. She gave him a suspicious look but seemed to answer his questions willingly enough. When he came back he knew the whole story.

"Burned down, miss, a year ago. All the patients was moved elsewhere, split up like. I can't rightly tell you where they are now. She don't know. You'd have to find one of those who ran the place and ask them. Did you want to get out here, miss?" he added dubiously, looking about.

It wasn't a pleasant area. Apart from the charcoaled remains of the asylum, there were small cottages and dirty-looking dwellings jammed together and facing the street. Over everything hung a pall of smoke and dust, and the stomach-roiling smell of a glue factory.

"No, I don't think so," Antoinette said firmly. There was no point in wandering around in the ruins. Her bird had long flown.

"Where would you like to go now then, miss?" the friendly cabdriver asked. "Back to Waterloo

Station? You look pretty done in, if you don't mind me sayin' so."

Antoinette thanked him for his concern, hesitating as she made up her mind. There was nothing she would have liked better than to go home and go to bed and sleep for days. But Cecilia was depending on her, and at any moment Appleby might strike. What she needed was help, and the best person to help her was someone who hated Lord Appleby as much as, or more than, she did.

Quite suddenly a name popped into her mind.

"Madame Aphrodite!"

"Beg pardon, miss?"

The woman with the dark flashing eyes who had stormed into Appleby's house and accused him of trying to ruin her. Surely she'd be interested in joining forces with Antoinette? If not . . . well, she could only refuse.

It took a little convincing to persuade the cabbie to take a respectable woman like her to Aphrodite's Club, but once again doubling the fare had the desired effect. Soon they were bowling back over the bridge.

If Aphrodite would help her it would benefit them both, and besides, a high-class brothel was the last place Lord Appleby would look for Antoinette, if he thought she was in London.

It was the perfect solution to her troubles.

Now all she had to do was convince Madame Aphrodite.

Chapter 27

Antoinette didn't know what she expected a brothel to look like but this wasn't it. Aphrodite's Club was a plain-fronted, discreet building that appeared rather like a girl's boarding school than a house of ill-repute. But the cabdriver assured her this was the right address, wished her luck, and left her standing outside.

She hadn't really decided what she would say when she came face-to-face with the courtesan, but there wasn't time to plan. As she climbed the steps to the arched entrance, Antoinette hoped something would occur to her when the moment came. The door was closed, and she reached for the heavy brass knocker, only to snatch back her hand at the last moment, staring in disbelief.

The knocker was shaped like a man's member, complete in each and every detail.

Antoinette hesitated. Was she jumping into more hot water by coming here? But what else could she do? Surely it was worth a chance? Antoinette might find Madame Aphrodite not interested, in which case she would have to think of another plan. But she would not give up. Lord Appleby would not win.

Her mind made up, Antoinette took the object in her hand, closed her eyes, and rapped hard three times on the door.

Gabriel had arrived at Aphrodite's Club the previous day, and he and Madame Aphrodite had spent a great deal of time together in conversation. A couple of times Aphrodite had to cover her mouth to stop herself from laughing too loudly. When he told her about Antoinette stealing his pistol and rowing away from him, for instance, or his disguise as the smelly Coombe. But most of the time she listened in solemn silence.

"It is difficult to advise you, *mon ami*," she said at last.

Gabriel's eyebrows rose. "Advise me? I don't need advice, Madame."

"Oh?" She smiled a wicked little smile. "I thought that you did. You seem to want this girl for yourself, Gabriel. First you are jealous of Lord Appleby and then of this unknown protector, this duke. I can hear it in your voice and I can see it in your eyes."

"You must be joking! She's a lying, manipulative little . . ." But he didn't finish the sentence; he couldn't. "You're right," he admitted dully. "I do want her. And I'm sure she wants me, too, except she won't admit it."

"I wonder . . . perhaps she is as muddled and mistaken as you, Gabriel. You are like cats in the darkness, *oui*? You are attracted to each other, and yet each of you thinks the other is a wild cat that roams the streets when in fact you are both cozy domestic cats, playing at being wild."

"Mmm, I'm not quite sure about that, Madame."

She laughed and waved her hand. "You know what I mean."

"I don't know what to do," he said bleakly. "I thought I wanted Wexmoor Manor, but now I can't see myself being lord and master there if Antoinette isn't by my side. I didn't know what I was missing until she came along, and now I can't stop thinking about her."

"Perhaps," Aphrodite said thoughtfully, "you are in love with her, Gabriel?"

"In love with her?" he scoffed. "Can you fall in love with someone who points a pistol at you and threatens to shoot?"

Aphrodite laughed softly and with a wealth of experience. "Oh yes, Gabriel, you can." And laughed again at his crestfallen expression. *"Mon ami*, it is not so bad. Perhaps she loves you, too, but is afraid to tell you so. How can she commit herself to a man who keeps telling her all he wants is a letter he believes she has in her possession?"

"A letter that her protector gave her to keep safe! And now she plans to use it to 'persuade' Appleby into allowing her to leave him for the duke. She's frightened of Appleby, Madame; I can see it in her eyes."

"And you want to protect her," Aphrodite murmured. "You are on dangerous ground, Gabriel. She could hurt you very badly."

"I don't know how good a shot she is—"

"No, no, I did not mean with a bullet. I meant she could break your heart."

Gabriel opened his mouth to argue, to declare himself completely heartless, to deny such a thing could ever happen to him. And closed it again.

He was more confused than ever. His instincts were telling him one thing about Antoinette and his mind was telling him something else. Suddenly he had a clear image of her rowing away from him, her hair wild, her face white, her eyes big and frightened but determined, too. That was bravery. She was a courageous woman. She had refused to yield when he held up the coach, and although he'd convinced himself that for a woman like that to be threatened with being stripped naked and searched would mean little, he knew it wasn't true. She must have been very frightened, and yet she didn't give him the satisfaction of seeing it, not until right at the end when she'd wept in his arms.

But later, when they came together in the woods, she *had* yielded. She'd given her body to him. Not for any payment or desire to gain something from him, but for the sheer joy and abandonment they found together.

Gabriel groaned and dropped his head into his hands.

"What will I do, Madame?"

"So now you are asking me for advice, Gabriel?" she teased, but gently.

Outside the room there was a loud rapping on the front door and then footsteps hurrying to answer it. Gabriel could hear Jemmy Dobson's deep voice, and then more steps. Someone tapped on the sitting room door, and then it opened a crack and Jemmy stuck his head around the corner.

"Lady to see you, my love," he said quietly. "Put her in your office, will I?"

Aphrodite smiled. "Thank you, Jemmy. I'll be there in a moment."

The door closed again.

Gabriel gave her a quizzical look. "I thought this was a club for gentlemen," he said.

"You'd be surprised how many gentle*women* find their pleasure here," she replied. "There was a very special client I dealt with not long ago, and very happy she is, too. But I must not talk about matters that are confidential."

"You're a very wicked woman, Madame. I always knew it."

Aphrodite laughed. "Perhaps. A little." She rose to her feet, her black silk skirts rustling. "I must see my visitor. You will stay here tonight, Gabriel? I think we should talk again. You know I think of you as the son I never had."

"Of course I will stay." He laughed.

"You are residing in London's most select and famous house of pleasure. You are a very fortunate man indeed." Aphrodite tapped him gently on the shoulder as she left the room.

* * *

Antoinette was standing by the window. When she was first shown into the room she'd sat down in the chair before the desk, but she had felt too much like a new girl waiting for an interview, so she stood up again.

The idea of living such a life made her uncomfortable, and she knew she would be completely unsuited to it. If she'd any doubts that her love affair with the highwayman might have changed her or corrupted her, then she was reassured now. Lying in his arms was special and magical, and no one else could ever make her feel like that.

Anyway, it was over. He was probably sailing away across the sea with Marietta. She could picture them toasting each other with champagne and dancing naked under the stars.

"You wished to see—"

Antoinette jumped, as if the other woman might be able to read her shocking thoughts. Madame Aphrodite had entered the room so quietly she hadn't heard her, and now here she was in her black dress, her graying hair piled loosely upon her head, so much jewelry about her throat and wrists and on her fingers that it made Antoinette blink.

"But I know you," she said with her French accent.

"Yes, we have met before, but we have not been introduced. I am Antoinette Dupre."

Madame Aphrodite closed the door.

"Miss Dupre," she said, curiously. "I remember

you, of course I do. If I seem a little surprised to see you here, then you will understand why. Lord Appleby and I are not the best of friends at the moment."

Antoinette clutched her reticule in front of her and spoke earnestly. "That is why I am here, Madame. I believe your house is the only safe refuge for me in London. I am in dire trouble and I need your help. Will you listen to my story . . . please?"

The courtesan's eyes were as dark and intelligent as Antoinette remembered, and now they held a warmth and compassion that gave her hope and drew her closer. Aphrodite gestured for her to sit down and moved to a chair behind the desk.

"So you have come to me because Lord Appleby is an enemy of mine?" Aphrodite said curiously. "Has he spoken of me?"

"No. But I overheard what he was saying to you, the day you came to see him. I thought you were very brave to stand up to him."

"I hate him," she said, with a glitter in her eyes.

"I think you have heard the gossip about me, Madame. That I am Lord Appleby's mistress?" Antoinette lifted her chin high.

Aphrodite bowed her head in acknowledgment.

Antoinette leaned forward, her gaze on the other's face. "It is a lie. Lord Appleby arranged for certain rumors to be spread about, and then he planned to have us caught in a compromising position. Afterward everybody believed it was true, but I swear to you I was never his mistress. He was a friend of my uncle, and when my uncle died he began to visit me and my sister, pretending sympathy, pretending to be our friend." She spat out the last word bitterly. "He does not know what it means to be someone's friend."

Aphrodite said nothing, watching her face and listening intently.

"He has done such a good job of convincing everyone that now no one believes me," she went on, clearly upset.

"But why would he do such a thing, Miss Dupre? Has he formed a passion for you?"

"He is a wicked man, Madame. He wants my money. He wants me to marry him so that he can take my fortune and use it in his manufacturing business. That is why he has destroyed my reputation, so that I will have no friends to believe me. They will advise me that marriage is the only solution, and Lord Appleby is quite a catch."

Her voice broke and she looked away, steadying herself. This was not a time for tears; Aphrodite needed to hear the facts.

"And yet you came to his house," Aphrodite reminded her.

"He invited me to London from my home in Surrey. He knew I was eager to see the Great Exhibition, and because he had a part in building the Crystal Palace, he said he would be able to bring me to the opening ceremony. I was flattered, and although I had my doubts, I allowed myself to be persuaded. At first all was well, and then I began to hear rumors that he and I were engaged, or in love, or some such nonsense. I felt uncomfortable and approached him about it. That was when he proposed to me."

"And you rejected him?"

"Yes. He seemed to accept it calmly enough, but that was when he must have decided that more direct means were needed if I was to agree. I wanted to go home but he begged me to stay on for his dinner party. He needed my help, he said. That was when he staged the moment when his guests saw us together . . . But it was a trick. He caught hold of me moments before and I was struggling, but he held me so tightly, and . . . Well, I knew then the gossips would ruin me. I demanded he explain and apologize, but he laughed and said now I would have to marry him. And that was when I saw for the first time the real man behind the smile."

Aphrodite stood up and went to ring the bell for a servant. She went to the door, and when there was a soft knock, opened it and spoke quietly for a moment, before returning to her seat.

"I am listening, my dear," she said evenly.

Antoinette tried to read her face but she could see nothing to give her a clue as to what the courtesan was thinking, as she went on with the rest of her story, how she was sent away to Devon.

"Ah, Wexford Manor," Aphrodite said, when she was finished, and smiled. "But then you escaped, I think, Miss Dupre? You are a very resourceful young lady."

"I . . . yes, I did escape."

"On your own?" Aphrodite asked her innocently.

"Ah, no. There was a man." Antoinette covered her face with her hands. "I don't even know his name! He's lied to me ever since we first met and yet . . ." She lowered her hands and her face was pale, determined and honest. "He's the most exciting man I have ever met."

"Cats in the night," Aphrodite murmured cryptically.

"Pardon, Madame?"

Aphrodite smiled knowingly. "This exciting man, Miss Dupre, I think you fell in love with him."

Antoinette's eyes widened. "Of course I didn't," she said sharply. "My life is complicated enough without him in it."

Aphrodite raised her thin eyebrows. "But the heart doesn't always obey as we would want it to. Love is not always tidy, my dear."

But Antoinette shook her head and refused to be drawn. "I was speaking of Lord Appleby."

"Very well, tell me why you have come to me, Miss Dupre."

"Because Lord Appleby is not the wealthy and successful businessman everyone thinks he is. He owes a great deal of money and has borrowed more to complete his contract for the Crystal Palace. He is relying upon my fortune to set things right, otherwise he will be ruined. He is a sham, Madame."

Aphrodite smacked her palm onto the desktop. "He is a monster! A man of such self-importance that he cannot bear to admit to failure, or to be slighted. The smallest insult must be repaid over and over. Do you know why I believe he took my club from me? Because long ago he wanted me in his bed and I turned him down. I was not very flattering in my refusal, but in those days I was young and beautiful and I did not take account of other people's feelings. He never forgot, and when the chance came to revenge himself upon me he took it."

Antoinette nodded. "Yes, that sounds like His Lordship."

"My club is closed. He wants it all and he has decided the way to get it is to force me to sell my share, so he has arranged for complaints to be made. There are some gentlemen in Parliament who like to decide what others should or should not do. He has taken a stick and stirred them about, like a nasty boy an ant's nest, and now he has them dancing to his tune. Can ants dance? Well, it does not matter. My club is to remain closed until it is decided whether or not I am a moral danger to the innocents of London."

"Can they do that?" Antoinette was shocked.

"They have." Aphrodite lifted her hand. "Listen. Do you hear the silence? I do not know how much longer I can bear it."

"I'm sorry, Madame."

"I have a friend who is also in danger of being ruined by Lord Appleby," Aphrodite said, watching her closely.

Antoinette wasn't surprised. Appleby must have hundreds of slights to repay.

So far the courtesan had listened to her politely but she'd said nothing about helping her, and Antoinette could see she had problems of her own. Antoinette wouldn't blame her if she said so in her refreshingly blunt manner.

"You have somewhere to stay here in London?" Madame said.

"No." Antoinette smiled bitterly. "I came to find my sister but he has her, you see. I think the only way I will be able to free her from Appleby is to return to him and agree to marry him. He knows that. He won't let her go. I confess, Madame, that at the moment I am very desperate."

Aphrodite stood up and came around the desk, holding out her hands. Startled, not knowing what to expect next, Antoinette rose and allowed the courtesan to grasp her fingers in her own heavily ringed ones.

"Be assured, Miss Dupre, you have come to the right place. You are safe here. I have sent a servant to prepare a room for you where you can rest and restore yourself."

"Oh." Antoinette blinked rapidly, touched and grateful. "Thank you."

"I am your friend, Miss Dupre, believe me. No

harm will befall you in my house, and when you are rested we will talk again. We will defeat this evil man, and all will be well again."

Antoinette had thought to find an ally in her struggle, but Madame Aphrodite was offering more than that; she was offering her friendship.

"Thank you," Antoinette said again, squeezing her fingers. "I don't have the words to adequately . . ."

"There is no need. You are tired, child."

"Yes, I am tired. I have not slept in . . ." She frowned. "A very long time."

Aphrodite gave a little laugh. "If you cannot remember, then it is far too long. Come with me and I will see you comfortable."

Antoinette followed along in the courtesan's wake.

Chapter 28

Antoinette bought her ticket and entered that triumph of glass and iron, the Crystal Palace. Or to give the event its formal name: the Great Exhibition of the Works of Industry of All Nations. She was as fascinated as she'd been when she was there last time, as a guest of Lord Appleby. Then a choir had sung Handel's Hallelujah chorus, there had been speeches and congratulations, and visitors from all over the world pronounced it a great success.

Now crowds still swept through the grand building, amazed at what was on view, from a working spinning mill to a steamship couch that would float in the event of a marine disaster. There were objects from Britain and its Commonwealth, the United States, France, Germany, and Russia . . . and so many other places that Antoinette lost count.

It was truly a Victorian triumph, and the British people were justly proud of this view of a new world where anything was possible and anyone could aspire to own the objects on display, from

Sevres porcelain to a family photograph to hang in their best sitting room.

As she made her way up the central aisle, the crystal fountain, twenty-seven feet high, grew larger and more amazing with her every step. It was formed of pale pink glass, and water jetted high into the air, creating rainbows from the light that filled the Crystal Palace. Antoinette, among all the other spectators, stood gazing at it, smiling at the splendid sight.

Madame Aphrodite had offered to send a servant with her, or even Jemmy Dobson, but Antoinette had declined. She wanted time alone, and she still chafed at her time as a prisoner in Mayfair and Wexmoor Manor, when she'd been followed everywhere. She was enjoying her independence and looking forward to meeting this person who was going to help her defeat the monster.

"I promise you will thank me for what I am doing. Do you trust me, Miss Dupre?"

Antoinette had known the courtesan for only a short while, but she knew that she did trust her. There was something so compelling in her gaze and the direct way she spoke, rather like Antoinette herself. Whatever this woman was or however she lived her life, Antoinette believed in her. If she had ever been inclined to take the view that a kept woman was far beneath her own social status, she'd learned her lesson. One's position on society's ladder was shaky indeed; that ladder could fall at any time and you would fall with it.

"All will be well," Aphrodite assured her. "Go

to the Indian exhibit and wait there. My friend will find you."

"Can't you give me a name?"

Aphrodite smiled. "Better not, my dear. It is safer for you, and my friend, if you meet as strangers."

"But how will I know who it is?"

"You will know."

Antoinette found her way to the Indian exhibit. This was one of the most beautiful rooms in the Crystal Palace, and everywhere she looked there were sights to make her gasp. Embroidered silks were resplendent with precious jewels and glittering gold. A stuffed elephant stared haughtily at the gawping crowds. In this exhibit, too, was the famous Koh-i-noor diamond, secure in a metal cage hanging from the ceiling.

She stood and waited. People passed through with cries of wonder, and children wore smiles on their faces or grizzled about the heat. Despite the calico coverings on the glass ceilings, the air inside the exhibit was close and Antoinette felt breathless.

It occurred to her that Lord Appleby was quite likely to be about. She knew he enjoyed wandering through the exhibit rooms, being recognized and congratulated by visitors, preening in the light of their admiration. The thought of him seeing her made her edge farther back beside a jewel-encrusted throne, even though she knew she was more or less invisible in her plain gray gown and straw bonnet. She was pretending to be a country girl come to the big city, and Aphrodite had supplied the disguise.

"I have a vast wardrobe. Some of my guests like to dress up. You'd be surprised at what gives them pleasure."

Where was the courtesan's friend?

Antoinette's gaze skittered toward the aisle running by the Indian exhibit, and that was when she saw him.

The highwayman.

For a heartbeat she stared at him as he stood looking about him, taking in the breadth of his shoulders, the color of his hair, that handsome face and strong chin. And as she stared she felt her senses going wild and her heart jumping about in her breast, and the thought formed in her mind that Aphrodite might be right.

She did love him.

Fear caught her by the throat—fear of him and of herself—and she couldn't breathe. The next moment she was moving, unable to stop herself in her blind panic. It didn't matter that he hadn't seen her; she just had to get away from him.

What terrible luck had brought him here today? She couldn't risk falling into his grasp again. And all the time she was zigzagging through the crowd, she was leaving the area where she was supposed to meet Aphrodite's friend. She'd need to double back as soon as possible.

Antoinette sidestepped a couple as they stood gazing around them, expressing their wonder in broad Scots, and glanced back over her shoulder.

He was staring right at her.

There was a puzzled expression on his face, but as their eyes met she saw the flash of recognition. She didn't wait for more. Antoinette sped on, and when she reached a clear space began to run in earnest, telling herself she was running for her life.

She looked back again at the next exhibit, and saw that he was closing in. There was a staircase and she ran up, slipped, only just saving herself by catching on to the railing. She hurried through a stained glass exhibit, the colors like jewels in the light that poured into the building, and then down another staircase. He was closing in; she knew it by the angry exclamations and gasps behind her as he plowed through those who stood in his way.

They were in the central aisle now, and potted plants and ferns and mature trees turned the space into a wonderland of greenery, but to Antoinette it was a blur. She picked up her skirts and petticoats, her bonnet fell back, dangling about her neck by its ribbons. Painted poles and bright banners made her dizzy, and then she saw it.

The way out!

In another moment she was outside in Hyde Park, moving toward the nearest street, telling herself that if she could find a hansom cab or a trolley bus she could escape him.

"Antoinette!" he roared.

With a whimper Antoinette tried to outdistance him, but her tight, heavy clothing was hampering her, and she knew that at any moment he'd be upon her and then all her struggles would have been for nothing. Ahead of her she could see a trolley bus trundling along through the traffic. If she could only get to it, climb on board . . . With a sob she forced her weary body to make a last effort.

His hand closed over her shoulder, spinning her around, and he was wrapping his arms around her, holding her in a grip it was impossible for her to break. She tried to scream but she had no breath left. The fight went out of her then, and she was reduced to gasping and hanging limp in his arms.

He must have known she was beaten. He set her down on her feet, but he kept a strong arm around her shoulders, pinning her to his side so to a casual observer it must have looked like an overly friendly embrace.

"Let me go. I'll scream," she gasped, still trying to breathe.

"Don't be ridiculous," he said, equally breathless.

She tried to pull away from him but his arm was like iron, and then he caught her hands with his free hand and held them, too. "Let me go!" she wailed.

"No," he gritted.

She glanced up at his face. He looked angry and bothered, his hair windblown, his eyes blazing. Her gaze lingered, and she couldn't seem to look away. He caught her watching, and a smile flickered at the corners of his lips.

"Did you think I'd just give up and sail away, sparrow?"

"I didn't think about you at all."

His smile grew. "Are you sure?"

"Very sure."

He laughed, and then suddenly his face went blank. "Of all the cursed luck," he muttered. He was looking over the road, where a coach had stopped, and abruptly he turned her around and headed back the way they'd come. Antoinette fought him, sensing something was very wrong, and when she couldn't escape she craned her neck over her shoulder to see what it was he'd seen.

"Don't look, for God's sake," he growled. "He'll see you."

"He?" She was still trying to see, and suddenly she caught a glimpse of a short man crossing the road with a brisk, confident stride, his hand on his top hat to stop it being caught by the wind, an ivory cane in his other hand.

Lord Appleby.

Shock paralyzed her for the second time. Meanwhile her captor bundled her along, all but carrying her back through Hyde Park and into the Crystal Palace. There was an argument about their tickets—daily ticket holders weren't allowed to leave the building. He muttered something and, propping her against the wall, found enough money in his pocket to purchase two more tickets.

I should run away, she told herself. *But where*

would I go? Lord Appleby was on his way, and suddenly she knew whom she'd rather be with.

"This way," he said. "There's a refreshment room down here."

There was indeed, and when they reached it he found a free table, sat her down in a chair, and drew another close to her, so that he could retain his grip on her hand. It might have been romantic if he wasn't her jailer.

"I suppose you're going to give me over to him now," she said dully, staring at his fingers clasped around hers. "I hope he is paying you well."

"Hardly," he mocked. "I'm not going near him, and neither are you."

She turned her face toward him and blinked. "But . . ."

"You still think I'm his man," he said coldly. "Well, I'm not and never have been. Where's the letter?"

Antoinette groaned. "Not again—"

"Yes, again. And again and again. Until you give it to me."

"I need it," she hissed.

"To give to your new protector—I remember. Where is he, by the way?" And he looked around as if expecting to see someone in ducal robes hovering among the potted plants.

"I only said that because I thought you . . . I thought *Coombe* would be impressed. I wanted him to believe I could give him his racing stable." She tried to wrench her hand free, but still he held it tightly. Her fingers began to go numb.

"Everyone said you were Appleby's mistress." He was watching her intently.

"You shouldn't listen to gossip," she said coldly. "I was never his mistress. He wanted everyone to think I was so I'd be forced to marry him. It may surprise you to know I am quite an heiress."

He shook his head.

"You don't believe me." She tried to keep the tremble out of her voice, telling herself it didn't matter to her whether he believed her. But the truth was it did.

"On the contrary, I do believe you."

He smiled into her startled eyes.

"Come, Antoinette, who do you think Madame Aphrodite sent to meet you? Why did I happen to appear at exactly the right time and in exactly the right place?"

Her face must have shown her sense of betrayal, because he reached out and brushed her cheek with the backs of his fingers.

"No, she didn't give you away. She's on your side. And so am I."

"You can't be." She spoke instinctively.

"Why not?" he retorted, moving in closer still.

Her gaze dropped to his mouth, and she found herself thinking about kissing. Antoinette's eyes flicked back to his, and she saw him pick up on her feelings. There was a sudden tension between them, and this time when she found it difficult to catch her breath, it had nothing to do with exercise.

She realized he was waiting for an answer.

"Because you want the letter, and the only person who would want it besides me is Lord Appleby."

That gave him pause, but he rallied. "You're wrong. That letter belongs to my mother. Appleby used it to take Wexmoor Manor from my father, Sir Adam Langley, and from me. I want it back."

"Then you are . . . ?" she said, dazed.

"Gabriel Langley."

Gabriel, the boy who'd scratched how much he hated sums on his desk. That Gabriel. She'd been close to the truth when she thought he might be Priscilla's son—he was her nephew. There were so many thoughts crowding into her head she struggled to find the right words.

"The letter I am carrying doesn't have anything to do with you or your father."

His eyebrows came down. "I don't believe you."

"Believe me or not, it is the truth. My letter is not your mother's letter."

"Then why did you refuse to give it to me?"

"I thought you were under instructions from Appleby to retrieve it, that he'd learned I had it and he meant to destroy it. And me, too, probably."

He said nothing, watching her, trying to decide whether to believe her. Antoinette knew the signs; she was struggling through the same questions herself.

"How can I believe you?" she whispered.

"Because you know it's true," he said urgently. "Think, Antoinette."

She was thinking. Carefully she relived the last few weeks, seeing it from his side and from hers. Could they have been so mistaken about each other, so stupidly, stubbornly blind? If only they'd trusted each other from the beginning.

"If you'd trusted me," he said, reading her mind, "then this wouldn't have happened."

"Trusted *you*?" she retorted. "The first time I saw you, Mr. Langley, you were holding up my coach with pistols!"

"It was playacting."

"But I didn't know that! Later on I realized—or at least I thought—you'd been sent by Lord Appleby and that everyone at Wexmoor Manor was in league against me. I was completely alone and friendless and in enemy territory."

His eyes narrowed. "Darling, you'll have me sobbing in a moment."

Someone cleared her throat and they both looked up. A waitress had arrived to serve them. Antoinette asked for lemonade and Gabriel requested distilled water—the Crystal Palace supplied water to all who asked, free of charge.

When the waitress was gone he reclaimed Antoinette's hand. She tried to pull away but he wouldn't let go.

"Everyone thinks we're lovers having a tiff," he teased.

"Stop it."

His eyes turned serious as they gazed intently into hers.

"I wanted to tell you the truth. Several times I began to tell you but for some reason it always went wrong. I'm sorry."

"Sorry for forcing your way into my bedchamber?" she retorted, her color high.

His mouth curled up in his wicked smile. "No, not for that."

"You tried to make me tell you where the letter was by . . . by physically assaulting me."

"I wouldn't call it that, darling. Besides, you assaulted me, if I remember correctly." He frowned. "How did you manage that if you're the respectable young lady you claim to be?"

She didn't want to answer him, but she could tell he wouldn't stop until she did. "There were some books in the library."

"Books?"

"You know," she hissed. "*Books*."

"Do you mean the one about the sultan's harem?" There was a glint in his eyes.

"Yes."

"I'm impressed," he said, his gaze dropping to her mouth.

The lemonade and water arrived, and Antoinette made a great production of sipping the cold, sweet liquid.

"So why did you carry on with matters when you weren't the experienced woman I thought you to—"

Her glass thumped down onto the table. "I knew you were going to ask me that! I don't know why. I just . . . it just happened." But she wasn't being honest and she knew it. Not being honest had got them into this mess in the first place.

Her hands tightened around the glass, and she stared fiercely into the pale lemonade. "Lord Appleby had already seen to it that my reputation was ruined and he was going to force me into marrying him. I wanted to fight him, to do something to spoil it for him. I used you, Mr. Langley, to revenge myself upon my abductor. It was as simple as that."

Chapter 29

Gabriel was disappointed, although he hid it well—he was good at masking his feelings. He'd been hoping she'd say she made love with him because she couldn't resist him, although he realized how foolish that was. Antoinette was trapped, frightened, and she must have seen the giving of her body as a way of taking control of the situation. What they did wasn't about love, it was purely a physical attraction.

"I see," he said. "Aphrodite has told me the story you told her, and you've just filled in most of the blank pages. The only question you haven't answered is what you're doing here in London."

She gave him a wary look.

"We seem to be on the same side," he said, watching as she took another sip of her lemonade. "Do you agree?"

"If you mean by being on the same side that we've both been wronged by Lord Appleby, then yes, we're on the same side."

"Then we need to help each other."

"I don't need your help."

It was so patently untrue that he burst out laughing.

"Stop it, people are looking," she said, glancing around. "What if Lord Appleby were to come by?"

"For his glass of lemonade and cream cake? Come, sparrow, let's shake hands and be friends."

She eyed his outstretched hand suspiciously.

"Remember," he said slyly, "I wasn't the only one pointing pistols at people. We've both been at fault. Now let's put it behind us."

She struggled a moment, but in the end her better sense won. She took his hand. Immediately he tightened his grip. Her eyes widened.

"Let me go!"

"I will. Tell me about this letter."

A sideways glance under her lashes, flirtatious and wholly adorable. "If I tell you . . ."

"I can help you, Antoinette."

"Let me go and I'll think about it."

He gave her the time she asked for. As she finished her lemonade he glanced at his fob watch, sighed, and leaned back in his chair, watching the patrons come and go from the refreshment room. The Crystal Palace was truly a wonderful thing, but just now he wanted to be somewhere else.

Preferably in bed with Antoinette.

The image made him smile. He embellished it further, imagining her mouth on his, and the little sounds she made when he was pleasuring her.

"Mr. Langley?"

She was looking at him oddly, and he realized she'd been speaking and he hadn't heard.

"Please, call me Gabriel. We know each other intimately, after all."

Her eyes narrowed.

He waited.

"*Mr. Langley*, I will now show you the letter you have been so keen to possess."

"Possess. I do like that word."

She ignored him, reaching into her sleeve with her fingertips, and drawing out a tube of rolled paper. Carefully she spread it out on the table, before handing it over to him.

Bemused, Gabriel bent his head to read.

It wasn't at all as he expected. The letter was written by a woman called Miss Bridewell, and she was passing on information she had gathered from an acquaintance she'd just visited. She didn't explain what the visit was about but she did give a name and an address.

Mrs. Miller is at 22 Jonah's Lane, Lambeth. She has been a resident there for ten years. There may be restrictions on visiting her, but if you mention the name Orange you will be allowed in.

Gabriel finished reading the words and looked up at her, his eyebrows raised. "What does it mean? Who is this woman and why is her address such a secret?"

Before she answered, Antoinette took the letter back and rolled it up, returning it to her sleeve. "First I will tell you where this information comes from. Miss Bridewell is my governess and my friend. When Lord Appleby first came calling, she remembered the name from an acquaintance she knew from years ago, someone who was once Lord and Lady Appleby's housekeeper, so she wrote to the woman to ask what she knew of him. The woman wrote back warning us against him. She wouldn't say any more, so Miss Bridewell went to see her and persuaded her to tell us what she knew. You see, she was there when Lady Appleby supposedly died, only she didn't."

She looked up at him. "Mrs. Miller is Lady Appleby."

"Lady Appleby . . ." His face grew very grave. "The Lady Appleby who is dead, or supposed to be? Do you mean . . . ?"

"He locked her away once he tired of her. She was an heiress, too. If I can talk to her, prove she is who she is, then his name, his reputation, will be destroyed and my sister and I will be safe."

"Have you been to the address in Lambeth?"

"Yes. The building used to be the Asylum for Misfortunate Women, but it burned down. The patients are scattered elsewhere in London and I don't know where to look."

"I'll find her," he said confidently.

Antoinette gave him a skeptical glance.

"I know someone who is very good at finding people. He's married to my half sister's maid . . . at least she was her maid, once. Marietta speaks of her as a friend these days. I'll go and see him now."

* * *

Antoinette heard only one word. *Marietta.* He'd spoken the name, that name he'd called in the night in his sleep. But Marietta was his half sister. She'd been convinced Marietta was his lover, a rival. Now she saw it was yet another mistaken belief that had kept them apart and suspicious of each other, when one question would have resolved the issue and saved her all that pain . . .

"Antoinette? Wake up, darling. Do you want to stay here, or will I escort you back to Aphrodite's Club?"

Antoinette rose to her feet. "I will come with you."

Gabriel smiled. "Good." He held out his arm, and after a moment she took it.

Antoinette found herself watching him surreptitiously as they sat together in the cab, stopping and starting in the dreadful crush of the London traffic. She couldn't help herself. The shape of his cheek, the curl of his hair, the way his mouth rested in a half smile, even when he wasn't laughing. And his hands, strong and long-fingered. These were the hands that had given her such pleasure in Devon.

She missed the way he made her feel. She'd dreamed about him last night while she slept in Aphrodite's Club. Her body was moving to his touch, heat curling in her belly, and it had been so real that when she woke she truly believed he was there with her. The sense of loss and disappointment she felt when she realized it was nothing but a dream was so painful that she curled up beneath the covers and wept.

She'd accepted then, alone in her bed, that she would never forget him. He would remain with her, a part of her, until she died. Such a realization was a depressing thing for a young woman of twenty years.

And now he was here, beside her, real and in the flesh, and she didn't know what to feel. So she sat stiffly, keeping a firm rein on herself, anxiously avoiding touching him. Because what if she were to give herself away and he guessed just how much she wanted him? What if he laughed in her face, or worse, decided to be kind to her and grant her wish of one more night together?

"We're here."

She looked up, startled. He was watching her. His gaze caressed her face, taking in each feature, and then he sighed and cupped her chin in the palm of his hand.

"Don't look so worried, sparrow," he murmured, and kissed her lips gently, barely a brush of naked flesh, but one she felt to the very tips of her toes.

He turned away and climbed out of the cab, handing her down and ushering her into a building with a brass plaque fastened beside the door which said "Thorne Detective Agency."

Gabriel knew Martin and Lil O'Donnelly well. They ran the Thorne Detective Agency, and were known for their discretion as well as their success rate. As soon as Antoinette had mentioned her need for information, he'd thought of them.

Lil sat Antoinette down, offering refreshments, smiling and friendly, and Gabriel watched her slowly relax and unfurl, like a tightly closed flower that has been afraid to open. Anger simmered inside him at the thought of what she had been through because of Appleby, and his anger included himself. He'd contributed to her distress, even though he'd done so unwittingly.

But he was aware of other emotions swirling around inside him, too. There was relief, because she wasn't Appleby's mistress after all and there was no "duke" waiting to set her up in style. His initial instinct, that she wasn't the woman she'd been portrayed, was correct. He wasn't going out of his mind. And then there was a chance that he might claim her for himself, when this was over.

And Gabriel wanted to. He just didn't quite know how to go about persuading her it was the right thing for them both.

"I'll have the information for you by this evening," Martin's words seeped through his thoughts. "I know someone who knows someone, if you know what I mean, Gabriel."

"I know what you mean." Gabriel smiled. "Thank you."

"Can I ask why you wish to find this patient?"

Gabriel glanced at Antoinette for approval in giving up what was, after all, her secret. She nodded.

"Do you know Lord Appleby, Martin?"

"I know of him."

"He claims to be a widower, but Miss Dupre has discovered his wife is locked away in an asylum."

Martin gave a silent whistle.

"Oh, Gabriel," Lil declared, "does that mean you can get your manor back? And Madame Aphrodite will be able to open her club again?"

"I hope so. At the moment she and Jemmy Dobson sit twiddling their thumbs all evening."

"Oh dear." Lil turned to Antoinette. "And what of you, Miss Dupre? What will Lord Appleby's downfall mean to you?"

Antoinette smiled. "I'll be free to return to Surrey. I have a house there and I am mistress of it, and I live my life very much as I please."

"An independent woman," Gabriel said.

"Yes." She lifted her chin as if preparing for a fight.

"So you spend your days ordering your servants, tallying your accounts, checking that Cook hasn't sold off the best ham?"

"I also visit friends and go riding, I read and write letters, I walk in my garden, I chat with my sister. I am very happy with my life, thank you. And my cook has never sold my ham in her life."

"You haven't mentioned any suitors calling, Miss Dupre. No gentlemen who escort you to church on Sundays or call on a pretext so that they can admire your beautiful eyes?"

She wrinkled her brow at him. "There was one who wrote me very bad poetry. I'm afraid I didn't accept his proposal. I don't think there is a single man of my acquaintance I could think of marrying with any certainty of being happy."

Gabriel caught Martin and Lil exchanging a glance. They were amused by the conversation, but he felt frustrated. He wanted her to admit she missed him, that her life was not complete without him. He wanted some hint that he might win her if he set about it single-mindedly enough.

"I'm sorry to hear that," was all he said.

"And what of you, Gabriel?" Lil asked. "Is there a young lady you plan to make mistress of Wexmoor Manor?"

Gabriel gave his wicked grin, pretending he wasn't feeling lonely and depressed. "I only have one stipulation when it comes to a wife. She must never get seasick."

Martin and Lil laughed, but he noticed Antoinette didn't.

He knew then he must be in a bad way, because even that gave him hope.

Chapter 30

Antoinette announced she had a headache on the journey back to Aphrodite's Club, and they sat in silence among the crush and noise. After supper she retired to her room, pleading tiredness, knowing she was a coward. But she didn't want to sit up with Aphrodite and Gabriel, listening to them laughing and joking and making plans for a future without Lord Appleby. She wanted to be alone.

Not that she blamed Aphrodite for sending Gabriel to meet her; she understood well enough that the two of them were close, nearly related, and Aphrodite wanted the best for Gabriel. It probably seemed very silly to the courtesan that the two of them should have mistaken matters so badly, when one well-chosen word would have ended all the misunderstandings. Looking back, she could see that now, of course she could, but at the time the atmosphere of suspicion and doubt and fear had made it impossible to distinguish friend from foe.

So she stayed in her room, brooding.

Besides, Aphrodite had a way of making her do things she hadn't intended to do, and Antoinette was worried what she might make her do next. She couldn't take much more of Gabriel Langley. One moment he was teasing her, trying to make her angry, and then he was gazing into her eyes as if she was the only woman in his world.

She felt completely bewildered, a unique state for her.

Of course, Antoinette knew that for all her accomplishments and abilities, she was an innocent when it came to men like him. She didn't understand what he wanted from her, and why he couldn't just come out and say it. It might be a little late in the day, but she'd learned honesty was best, and saying what one thought made life a great deal easier. If it wasn't for Cecilia she'd go home right now and leave Gabriel Langley far behind.

She turned over in her bed and stared into the darkness. The room was plain, with none of the ostentation she'd expected—no mirrors on the ceiling or scarlet draperies or lewd paintings. The building itself was echoingly quiet, and, from things the others had said, clearly very different from its usual glittering, frantic pandemonium.

Was that the sort of life Gabriel lived?

He was an adventurer at heart. His reckless behavior in holding up the coach, sailing down the coast single-handed, and making love to her in the woods in a thunderstorm, made that clear enough. He was wild and unpredictable and . . . completely, heartbreakingly captivating.

Antoinette found herself smiling into her pillow and straightened her mouth. It wasn't a laughing matter. When she was with him she acted in a very uncharacteristic way, a way that would deeply shock those who knew her well.

She still didn't know the answer to the question she'd asked herself at Wexmoor Manor. Had the real Antoinette Dupre, some wicked throwback to her wicked ancestress, been hiding all these years, just waiting to get out? Did Gabriel encourage her naughty side? Well, it couldn't go on. Cecilia needed stability, a sister who would provide sensible advice, not someone who ran through mazes shedding her clothes, used a pistol to escape in a rowboat, and made love to a masked highwayman.

In time those brief, wild days would be nothing more than a fuzzy memory. What a relief that would be!

Antoinette lay wide-eyed in the darkness, and wondered why, if she was doing the right thing, she felt so utterly bereft.

Someone was shaking him. Hard. Reluctantly, Gabriel opened one eye. Jemmy's battered face was looming over him, worry in his gray eyes.

"Wake up," he said in a quiet, urgent voice. "Appleby is downstairs with the police. He knows you're here. You must get up and leave. *Now.*"

The words brought him instantly to full wakefulness. He sat up, shocked. "How?" he spluttered.

Jemmy sighed. "You're not that innocent, are you, lad? There are always those who're looking for a few easy sovereigns. Could have been one of the servants, although Aphrodite won't believe that, or one of the boys who fetch the cabs and hold the horses, or even a passerby who noticed you and Miss Dupre coming and going. Right now 'who' isn't important. What matters is you have to get away before you're arrested."

Of course he was right. But Gabriel wasn't going anywhere without Antoinette.

"Is Miss Dupre awake?"

Jemmy's grim mouth twitched. "One of the girls is just doing that now."

Jemmy left and Gabriel dressed, running his fingers through his hair in lieu of a comb, and went out into the corridor. Jemmy was waiting for him. A moment later Antoinette peeped out of her own door, and seeing the two men, came to join them.

Her eyes were wide and worried, and he wanted to hold her, comfort her, tell her it would be all right.

He contented himself with a gruff "Don't worry, he can't stop us now."

"He must be desperate, to come here like this," Jemmy added. "A good sign, I reckon. You have him on the run."

"Let's hope so," Antoinette murmured.

They went toward the gallery. Gabriel could see Madame Aphrodite and several of her household huddled in the foyer. Suddenly there was a violent pounding on the front door. Everything seemed to shake; even the glass in the chandelier tinkled.

"Police! Let us in!" shouted a voice from outside. "Let us in or we'll break the door down!"

Aphrodite looked up at Jemmy and smiled. Her eyes glittered, her cheeks were flushed, and she looked as if she was enjoying herself, her boredom quite gone. "I will," she called out, making her voice high and slightly hysterical, "when I find the key. Please wait."

Jemmy grinned back at her and then led the way into a room at the side of the house. He went to a wardrobe against the far wall, and when he opened the door Gabriel saw there was a hidden staircase built inside the wall, twisting down into darkness.

"Just in case our guests want to make a hasty exit," he explained, as the other two peered over his shoulder. "Now, I'll go first, then Miss Dupre, then you, Gabriel. Remember to close the door behind you."

The narrow stairs required their full attention, and no one spoke until they reached the small and dingy room at the bottom. Jemmy searched about on the wall above his head and gave a grunt of satisfaction. Another door clicked open, and he pushed it carefully ajar, peering out.

They were looking out onto the narrow alley that ran down this side of the club. It was barely wide enough for a man to walk along, and a shrub was planted strategically between the door and the street, to hide any comings and goings.

Gabriel had been aware of the noise from the police as they hammered at the front door, but now there was a splintering crash and a scream, followed by Aphrodite's voice, rising in fury. "My door! You fools, you imbeciles, I told you to wait until I found the key!" The sounds faded as the two parties moved farther inside the club. Gabriel knew they didn't have long. Soon the police would realize their quarry had flown and begin to search outward from the perimeter.

Jemmy beckoned them along the alley to the street, pressing himself to the wall and peering around the corner. He jumped back, holding up a warning hand. Gabriel had been right behind him, and he'd caught a glimpse of what startled him. There was a man in a top hat standing, smoking, under the portico outside the front door. Even in that brief moment Gabriel had recognized him by his stance and the inevitable cane gripped in his hand.

It was Lord Appleby.

Gabriel made a sound, and Antoinette stretched out her hand to grasp his. He squeezed her fingers, thinking she was afraid, but she whispered, "Don't do anything reckless, *please*," and he understood she was holding his hand to stop his misbehaving rather than for comfort for herself. They waited and Jemmy glanced around the corner again. He gave a grunt of relief. Appleby had finished his cigar and followed the police inside.

"We must hurry," Jemmy said, and led the way out to the street and around the next corner. There

was an area here where hansom cabs and hack-
neys waited for trade. They'd had a slim time of it
since Aphrodite's Club closed, and when they saw
three possible customers coming toward them,
some of the drivers began to call out excitedly, offering reduced fares.

Jemmy chose a hackney and bustled them into
it, glancing nervously behind. "Take care," he
said, banging on the door to signal to the driver
to proceed.

The hackney lurched forward and rattled
away. As it moved out into the street they'd just
left, Gabriel peered out of the window and could
see Aphrodite's Club, with its door smashed and
leaning drunkenly to one side. Light spilled onto
the front steps, but there was no sign of the police
or Appleby.

He leaned back with a chuckle.

"You're enjoying this, aren't you?" Antoinette
said accusingly.

"Of course. Aren't you?"

"No, I don't enjoy running for my life every few
days, being pursued by people who want to lock
me up or take my money, never knowing what to
expect next."

He searched her profile, wondering if she was
serious. "Doesn't the excitement of it make you
feel alive?" he ventured.

"No."

"When I chased you from the schoolroom and
caught you, you seemed excited, darling. Very excited. Don't you remember?"

She bit her lip.

Gabriel leaned closer and whispered in her ear, making her jump. "I think you're fibbing to yourself. You love living on a knife edge. If I kissed you now you'd be in my arms like a shot."

Even in the dim light of the hackney lantern he could see that her color was high. "If you think that, then you don't know me at all."

"Don't I, darling?"

She was as rigid as a lamppost, and he wondered whether he should stop, just leave her alone, but he also knew she wasn't being truthful with him.

He pressed his lips to her cheek, enjoying her soft skin and the scent of woman. *His woman.* He trailed the kiss across her skin to the corner of her mouth, taking his time. She made a sound that could have meant anything. He worked on her lower lip, running the tip of his tongue back and forth. She made another sound, and this time there was no mistaking her meaning.

Miss Dupre liked what he was doing.

He kissed her properly now, parting her lips and sliding his tongue against hers. His hand cupped the back of her head, and he made the most of her response. Very soon she was beyond thought, caught up in the heat of their passion.

Satisfied he'd proved his point, Gabriel sat back in his corner of the hackney and waited. After a moment she opened her eyes, and the dreamy expression cleared from her face. "I hope you're satisfied," she hissed, and patted her hair, refusing to look at him.

"You know I'm not," he replied with a sigh. "I'm extremely unsatisfied."

The hackney slowed, and for the first time she seemed to notice they were over on the other side of the river, in Lambeth.

"Where are we going?" she said sharply.

Gabriel smiled. "We're going to visit Lady Appleby."

"Martin O'Donnelly sent word after you'd gone up to bed," Gabriel explained. "It seems that when the asylum burned down she was moved into a smaller establishment, beside the river, but still in Lambeth."

A moment later the hackney set them down. A single gas lamp fought a losing battle with the shadows. Antoinette could smell the dankness of the river, although it was hidden from view by fog. Gabriel pointed out the house that was their destination, and Antoinette saw a narrow brick frontage, a bare garden, and the flicker of light behind the curtain in an upstairs window.

"Someone is about." Gabriel led the way to the front door. "Are you ready for this, sparrow?"

"Of course I'm ready," she said, as if there was never any doubt.

He rapped on the door.

Footsteps and muttering, and the sound of a bolt being drawn. The door opened and a wizened face peered out, so wrinkled and discolored it reminded Antoinette of an apple that had been in storage all winter. "What you want?" it demanded rudely. "We don't take parish cases. This is a private establishment."

"I wish to see one of your patients," Gabriel announced pompously. "I am Dr. Long and I have here the sister of Mrs. Miller. Open up, my good chap, and let us in."

Antoinette was so astonished by his ability to playact that she nearly missed the wary reply.

"I don't know whether we 'as anyone of that name here."

"Now listen to me, my good man." Gabriel's voice turned belligerent. "I don't have time to stand out here in this blasted fog. When I ask—"

But Antoinette had remembered something in Miss Bridewell's letter. "Orange," she burst out.

The wizened face turned to her, and then it grinned toothlessly and was withdrawn. They heard more bolts and locks being turned, and the next moment the door swung wide open.

"Come in, come in," it invited them jovially. "Welcome to River View Asylum."

Chapter 31

The little old creature was a man, Antoinette saw now, attired in a nightgown and slippers, and with a nightcap on his head. Bizarrely, he reminded her of the boy from the nursery rhyme Wee Willie Winkie, except he wasn't a child.

"She's asleep. You're going to wake her up," he complained as he stomped up the stairs. "Takes us hours to get her to sleep sometimes."

"Can't be helped," Gabriel retorted. "This is an urgent matter. I may have to move her from here. For her own safety, you understand. His Lordship is fully aware of the situation."

The old man nodded his understanding. "His Lordship's been rumbled, 'as he?" Slyly he tapped the side of his nose. "Been good to us, His Lordship has. Wouldn't want anything to 'appen to him."

"I'll bet," Antoinette murmured darkly, as she followed.

They passed along a dingy corridor with closed doors. There was a smell of illness and the lingering odor of cooking, but try as she might, Antoinette couldn't see any dirt. The corridor was scrubbed clean.

The old man paused by one of the doors, giving them a hard look. "Maybe I should send word to His Lordship, just to be sure? He's very partic'lar about Mrs. Miller."

Gabriel was dismissive of the threat. "Please yourself. Are you aware how much His Lordship enjoys being woken in the middle of the night?"

The old man thought about that a moment, gave a grudging nod, and then proceeded to open the door. Inside, the room was dimly lit by a lamp. There was barely any furniture, the narrow bed was placed in the center, and a child with raggedly cropped fair hair, and wearing a petticoat and chemise, was lying on the covers. It was only as Antoinette ventured closer that she realized this was not a child but a small woman, and then she saw, to her horror, that the woman's arms and legs were tied down with straps.

She was a prisoner.

The old man sensed disapproval in their silence and became defensive. "She 'as to be restrained. Tries to run off, she does. Even managed it once, and she got as far as the river before we caught her. Can't be doing with all that fuss."

"Mrs. Miller" was gaunt, her face all eyes and cheekbones as she turned to stare at them. Her mouth opened as if she was about to say something, and then her gaze slid past Antoinette to the old man and she closed her lips hard. Antoinette watched as her hands clenched into fists, the leather bindings cutting into her pale flesh where there were already old bruises.

"Gabriel," Antoinette whispered, her voice tight with emotion.

It wasn't until she felt his fingers tight around hers that she knew she'd reached out to him, and he'd responded. He gave her a little shake, a reminder that they had a long way to go yet, before they were out of danger.

The man was watching her, his wizened face suspicious. "Who'd you say this lady was?"

"Mrs. Miller's sister," Gabriel replied evenly. "She has agreed to take your patient home with her."

He shook his head so vigorously his nightcap wobbled. "No, Doctor, I can't let you do that. His Lordship wouldn't like it."

"It was His Lordship who sent me. Now, release her," Gabriel commanded. "You know it'll be the worse for you if you don't."

Antoinette moved closer to the bed, placing her hand on the woman's shoulder. She could feel the bones beneath her skin. "I've come to take you home, sister," she said, staring into those frightened, watchful eyes, and silently begging her not to give away the lie.

"Home?" she said, and Antoinette tried not to gasp. Out of that thin, mistreated body had come the most melodious voice she had ever heard—the voice of an educated and refined lady. "I have no home," Lady Appleby declared bleakly.

"Hush, sister. Have you forgotten?" Antoinette insisted. She leaned closer and whispered the name of the Applebys' housekeeper.

Lady Appleby's eyes darkened and closed briefly, and then she nodded. "Now," she said, "I do remember."

"Doctor, can we go?" Antoinette glanced urgently at Gabriel.

Lady Appleby turned her attention to her jailer. "These straps are far too tight, Horace. And I'm cold. I want to leave."

But Horace wasn't happy, and he looked as if he was regretting letting them into his domain.

"Come, come, man," Gabriel spoke impatiently. "I'm sure His Lordship will be pleased to hear you are cautious when it comes to releasing your patients, but you know he won't appreciate being kept waiting."

The mention of His Lordship seemed to do the trick, and Horace scuttled forward and released the straps. Lady Appleby sat up and rubbed her wrists, shivering in her thin chemise. After Antoinette helped her to her feet, Gabriel pulled the cover from the bed and wrapped it around her shoulders. She snuggled into it, making a face.

"Your blankets are too thin, Horace. The blankets at Misfortunate Women were of a far better quality. Surely you can afford some new ones; my husband must pay you enough. Lord Appleby is very rich, you know."

Horace's eyes swiveled in their sockets. "Shhh! You know you're not s'posed to say his *name*."

"Lord Appleby, Lord Appleby, Lord Appleby," she said loudly and precisely, and gave a broad smile.

Antoinette shot Gabriel an anxious look, and they began to hurry their patient toward the door.

"You're a wicked woman," Horace hissed. "I don't know why I've put up with you for so long."

"Well, now you won't have to, will you? I'm leaving. Your service leaves a lot to be desired. I won't be recommending you to my friends, you may be sure of that."

Gabriel groaned softly as they reached the top of the stairs. Horace was padding along behind them in his slippers, agitated and angry. Lady Appleby, who had managed very well until now, was clearly in considerable pain as she lowered herself down each step. Her face was even more gaunt, her lips pressed together in a white line, but she didn't make a sound.

Antoinette was impressed by her courage. She wasn't sure what she'd expected, and to her shame she'd probably seen Lady Appleby as a means to an end and a fate to avoid, rather than a living, breathing person. Now this formidable woman who, after ten years of imprisonment, was still too proud to show her pain, brought tears to her eyes.

They reached the door and Horace opened it.

"Good night, Horace," Lady Appleby said grandly. "And good-bye."

"Good riddance," Horace muttered behind them, and the door closed with a solid thunk, followed by the resetting of the locks and bolts.

The hackney was waiting, and after Gabriel helped Lady Appleby inside, he turned to Antoinette. "All right, sparrow?"

She met his watchful gaze. "I can't help thinking that I might have ended up just like—like . . ." she stammered.

He leaned closer, his size and warmth giving her a welcome sense of protection. "You're safe, Antoinette, never doubt it."

Before she could answer he stepped back, ushering her into the cab. Lady Appleby was trembling beside her, and Antoinette removed her cloak, placing it around the older woman, and drawing the hood over her cropped fair hair.

"You are his latest, are you?" Lady Appleby said, catching Antoinette's hand and holding on.

"How did you know?" Antoinette whispered.

Lady Appleby gave a wan smile. "I don't have a sixth sense. My old housekeeper came all the way from the country to visit me. She wondered if she had done the right thing in giving up my whereabouts, and she felt guilty she'd kept the secret for so long. She wept, so I suppose that was something." She sighed and leaned back. "I was an heiress, too. He took my fortune and my youth, and locked me in a madhouse. My husband is a cruel man."

On Antoinette's other side, Gabriel leaned forward to see into the pale face under the hood. "So you will help us?" he said. "To see him punished for what he's done?"

She looked white-faced and exhausted, but there was fire in her eyes. "Oh dear me, yes, it will be my pleasure, Doctor."

As the hackney reached the end of the street, a river of fog swirling about the wheels, another vehicle drifted past them, going in the opposite direction, so for a brief moment they were side by side.

Lady Appleby gave a little scream. Antoinette looked up, and with a frisson of shock, she saw Lord Appleby sitting inside the other vehicle. He was still wearing his top hat, but beneath it his face looked drawn and tired, lit by the coach lamps. He'd been looking down, but when the hackney rattled past he raised his head. Recognition of Antoinette snapped his brows together, and then his gaze slid to the huddled figure at her side. He lurched forward, palms pressed to the glass window.

But it was already too late. They'd moved on.

Gabriel thumped his fist on the roof and shouted for the driver to hurry up. "That was close," he added, his pale eyes sparkling, as if this was just another game to him.

Antoinette, her arm about Lady Appleby's slight form, sent him a look of disgust. "He'll come after us. He'll catch us."

"He'll try. And then he'll rally his cronies

around him and try and hide behind their might and power. That's why we have to act now. At once."

"Gabriel, why can't you answer me without making a riddle of it?"

"I think, Antoinette, we should go straight to the very top."

"Gabriel, please—"

He grinned at her. "The palace, darling. We're going to Buckingham Palace."

Chapter 32

I t took them time to gain access to Prince Albert, the royal consort. Gabriel explained once and then again, and still they were refused. Prince Albert was in bed, they were told, and besides, he did not see anyone without an appointment, especially at this time of night. But gradually, as Gabriel explained the situation over and over, emphasizing that this was going to cause an enormous scandal—and did the palace really want them to take Lady Appleby to the offices of one of the more rabid newspapers?—he wore them down.

"You really should have let me dress for the occasion," Lady Appleby said, as they made their way into an anteroom, surrounded by disapproving servants.

"You are perfect, my lady."

She chuckled. "I imagine I am, if you want a fright."

Gabriel pulled forward a chair and made her comfortable. She was remarkably composed, considering what she had been through. He didn't know what he'd expected when he entered the asylum, but Lady Appleby was a revelation, a remarkable woman whose strength of character had brought her through ten years of shocking deprivation.

She reminded him of Antoinette. She, too, had fought for her independence and freedom, despite Appleby's threats and cruelty. She was a wonderful woman, brave and beautiful, generous and kind, and with a budding sensuality he wanted to make it his lifelong mission to expand and explore.

Life with Antoinette would never be dull. They were very different as people, but he liked that. She could pull him into line when he needed it, and he could give her a taste of that wild edge she had been missing. It was as if they'd been fashioned exclusively for each other.

He watched her as she stood in the middle of the room, a pocket Venus with tendrils of her hair coming out of its pins and her spectacles slipping down her nose. There were shadows under her eyes and her skin was pale with weariness, but she was still . . . perfect.

As if suddenly aware of his eyes, she turned her head and found him. He wondered what she saw in his face to make her look so long and so hard. She trusted him, he knew that much, but enough to stay with him when this was over? Or would her comfortable, predictable life in Surrey draw her back?

Gabriel smiled, and immediately her mouth curled in response, as if they were the only people in the room. He didn't even notice that the prince had arrived.

"Mr. Langley?" Albert spoke in his usual brisk manner.

"Your Majesty." He bowed, while Antoinette curtsied.

"You have frightened my staff into letting you inside my home at a most inconvenient hour. I do hope you are not wasting my time."

"My apologies, sir. I assure you I am not wasting your time. Have you met Miss Dupre?"

The prince looked at him oddly before turning to Antoinette and nodding. "I have indeed. Miss Dupre."

"And this lady"—Gabriel gestured toward the woman still seated—"is Lady Appleby."

"Lady Appleby is dead," Albert replied, but his eyes were watchful. He had already been told the story conveyed to his servants by Gabriel.

"As you see, I am very much alive." Lady Appleby was struggling to rise. "A little battered, perhaps, but still breathing."

After a moment of shocked stillness, Albert crossed the distance between them and pressed his hand upon her shoulder. "No, please, Lady Appleby, stay seated. I am sorry if I insulted you. It is a fantastical story. Do you wish for refreshments while we talk? I will send for coffee."

"If you send for anything, sir, let it be Scotch whisky," Lady Appleby said firmly.

His mouth twitched, and he turned to gesture to one of his servants. There was a pause while the whisky was fetched, and he took the glass and placed it in her hands himself.

"My prison did not run to good whisky," she said, and sipped. "Ah, my friend single malt," she sighed with pleasure, "how I have missed you."

Prince Albert smiled. "Only the best, eh, Lady Appleby?" As quickly as it came his smile vanished. "I feel I should apologize. Lord Appleby visited me often and I believed he was a good man, a hardworking man, and someone this country could be proud of."

"Lord Appleby has a way of gaining our trust, sir," Antoinette spoke at last. Gabriel watched her gathering her words, ready to lay before him the humiliation she'd been subjected to. "He gained my uncle's trust. It is my belief that when my uncle spoke of my sister and me, and our fortune, he planned to take it. And that was why he ingratiated himself into my family."

She continued to speak, quietly, firmly, telling her story and damning Lord Appleby with every sentence. Once or twice Lady Appleby made a murmur of disgust.

"He had run out of my money, it seems," Lady Appleby said. "He needed another heiress and he chose you, Miss Dupre."

"My sister, Cecilia, is staying at his house in Mayfair." Antoinette glanced to Gabriel and back to the prince. "I'm worried he may harm her."

"Of course, of course. I will send word to the chief of the Metropolitan Police that he is to find Lord Appleby and arrest him."

Antoinette swayed with relief. "Thank you, Sir."

"Sit down, please, Miss Dupre." The prince sounded concerned.

"Sir, I'm well; it was just knowing it was all over. I—I am very relieved."

"My brave darling," Gabriel murmured.

Antoinette flicked him a startled glance and he felt her pull away, putting distance between them. "I am not brave. It is Lady Appleby who is the heroine here."

"Sir?" One of the servants came running, his face a study in shocked amazement. "Lord Appleby is here and asking to speak with you. Should I . . . ?"

"The man's arrogance is breathtaking!" Prince Albert cried angrily. "Does he still believe he will convince me of his innocence?"

"Sir, perhaps he doesn't know we are here," Gabriel said urgently. "If you were to allow him in, we may force him to admit what he has done."

Prince Albert hesitated, his thoughtful gaze traveling from Lady Appleby to Antoinette, and then he nodded at the servant. "Very well, I think we would all like to hear what Lord Appleby has to say."

Antoinette stood stiff and straight beside Lady Appleby's chair. She didn't want this. A moment ago Gabriel had called her his "brave darling," but she didn't feel brave. She just wanted to go home and forget this had ever happened. Pretend it was a nightmare and wake up in the morning at Dupre House with the sun shining and the birds singing and her books of accounts to tally.

But it was too late.

Already the door was opening and she could hear Lord Appleby's voice approaching, sounding jovial and confident as he chatted with one of Prince Albert's secretaries. It wasn't until he entered the chamber and saw the reception that awaited him that he understood his predicament. A wary expression came over his face.

"Miss Dupre?" he said with a startled laugh. "I hardly thought to have the pleasure of seeing you again, and now here, of all places."

"Lord Appleby," she spoke quietly, with dignity. "Do you remember Mr. Langley? And of course . . . your wife."

On cue, Lady Appleby lifted her hands and pushed back the hood of her cloak, disclosing her gaunt face and boyish fair hair. Her smile was ghastly. "My dear husband," she greeted him, "I've been waiting for this moment for so very long."

As Appleby stared into her face, all color drained from his own. He shook his head and turned to the Prince, but whatever he saw in the other man's eyes was enough to stop any excuses he was about to make.

"My lord, I find it difficult to reconcile the beauty you created in the Crystal Palace with what I have learned of you tonight."

"Sir, I beg you—"

"You never visited me once, Rudyard," Lady Appleby interrupted, her voice so much bigger than her person.

"Visited you?" Lord Appleby stared at her in amazement. "How could I have visited you?"

"Why not? I know you paid for my little holiday in the asylum. The least you could have done was call now and again."

He gritted his teeth. "I couldn't visit you because you were supposed to be dead, you stupid woman!"

Lady Appleby went off into peals of laughter, and Antoinette wondered if the whisky had gone to her head. "Did I have a nice funeral? I always wanted white lilies, you know. Nothing but white."

"I don't remember," he said stiffly. "The undertaker made the arrangements."

Lady Appleby smiled. "Dear me, Rudyard, still with a heart of stone?"

The viciousness in his voice seemed to stun even his wife. "You are nothing but a crazy old woman. No one wants to listen to you."

"I am listening," Prince Albert informed him in a very stern voice. "I have sent for the police, my lord."

Appleby shook his head in apparent disbelief. "Sir, you know how important my manufacturing business is! I couldn't allow it to falter. I couldn't let that happen. You must see that? You told me yourself how proud you were of men like me, men who were self-made. Don't you agree it would be in everyone's interest—*Britain's* interest—if we pretended this hadn't happened? I could find my wife a house in the country, make her an allowance, and no one need ever know."

He believed it, Antoinette thought. He truly believed he could slide out from under the weight of his crimes and merrily carry on. She knew she shouldn't have been surprised; she'd heard him on the subject of his own importance many times. But still his arrogant self-interest stunned her.

"I'm afraid I do not approve of criminals, my lord," the prince answered, and now his eyes were as cold as his voice.

But Lord Appleby didn't believe it. He tried again, his words tumbling over one another as he made his case. When he saw the negative expressions on his audience's faces, he grew frustrated and began to curse his wife once more, heaping blame on her for his predicament.

"Why couldn't you just accept you were of no use anymore?" he ranted. "Wives were put aside in days gone by. It was expected."

Disconcertingly, Lady Appleby was enjoying herself hugely. She began to laugh, and the more he ranted, the more she laughed, until finally Appleby could take no more and lurched toward her, intent on violence. Prince Albert gave a sharp order, and his servants restrained Appleby. But he shook them off, panting, his graying hair tousled, glaring wildly about him.

"The letter, Appleby."

It was Gabriel, wanting to know, needing to

know. He confronted the man who'd stolen his dreams.

"Where is my mother's letter?"

Appleby focused his gaze on Gabriel. "Young Langley," he sneered.

"So, are you saying I am Adam's son, after all?" Gabriel pretended his heart wasn't pounding as he waited for an answer.

Appleby's mouth tightened. "You're no blood of mine, boy. I still bear the scars from your assault on me."

"You took what didn't belong to you, Appleby."

"I took because I could. Your mother lied to me and your father was too weak to deal with it. If he was a stronger man, a better man, I wouldn't have been able to take anything from him. He's taken two women from me, and I wanted him to suffer for it, no matter how long it took."

"My father is worth a dozen of you." Gabriel took a step toward him. "He gave you Wexmoor Manor because he was protecting my mother. Something you wouldn't understand. How could you understand, when you care for no one but yourself? You're a cad, Appleby. A lying, thieving rogue who deserves to be locked up forever. You call yourself a self-made man? You're nothing but a disgrace."

Appleby gave a roar. He was holding his cane, gripped in white hands, and when he suddenly lifted it Antoinette thought he meant to strike Gabriel with it. Instead, suddenly, he pulled on the handle and the stalk of the cane came away, and to her horror she saw it was a rapier, thin and deadly. Before Gabriel could get out of his way, Appleby struck, his arm jerking in and out.

Antoinette screamed, and then everything turned to chaos. Prince Albert's servants ran to restrain Appleby, wrenching the rapier from him, forcing him to his knees.

"Gabriel . . ." Antoinette was beside him, her hands shaking as she touched the spreading crimson stain on his side, as if seeking for a way to stop it. "Please, please, don't die."

Reckless adventurer he might be, but he didn't deserve this. Antoinette knew she wouldn't be able to bear it if he died and left her.

"Darling," he whispered, "hold me."

So she did, while around her people rushed and spoke in panicked tones, until a doctor came. Antoinette was led to a separate room and given sympathy and tea, but she felt disassociated from those around her. All she could picture, over and over again, was the image of her beloved, his face white, his body limp, lying on the rich royal carpet and bleeding his life away.

Chapter 33

Cecilia Dupre hugged her sister close, bending her golden head so that she could rest it on the shorter Antoinette's shoulder. "When you weren't at Lord Appleby's house I was so worried. I asked him, but all he'd say was that you'd gone to stay with friends. He was lying, and I couldn't find you."

"It's over now," Antoinette soothed. "I'm here and you're safe."

Cecilia stepped back. "Would he really have married you and locked you up, Nette? Just for your money?"

"Yes, he would have, Cecy."

"I'm never going to marry!" Cecilia declared.

Antoinette reached out to hug her and stroke her hair. "You will. Not many men are like Lord Appleby. Most of them are fine and good. I promise you, Cecy, you'll find a man to love."

Cecilia lifted her face, tears staining her cheeks. "And you, Nette? What about you?"

Antoinette forced herself to smile. "Never mind me, Cecy. I have Dupre House and you to look after. When would I have the time to marry? Hush, don't cry, everything is back to normal now, and that's the way it's going to stay."

Sir Adam Langley held the letter in his hands, staring at his wife in disbelief. "They found it?"

"At his bank, my love. Aphrodite arranged for it to be given back to us. She has a great many friends, it seems."

His wife had never been jealous of Aphrodite; that was one of the things he loved about her. She knew Adam loved her and it was enough; his past was just that. And until recently her past had been a secret, too.

"Do you want to read it again?"

Adam shook his head. "No, I don't want to read it again. I want to know why you wrote it. I believed everything between you and Appleby was over long ago."

"It *is* over."

Adam hung his head. He looked ill; the last few months had taken their toll. "Is it?"

She reached out and took his hand, holding it tightly. "Adam, how can you doubt me?"

"Have I been a proper husband to you and a good father to our children?"

"Yes! I've never regretted marrying you, never. I was so proud of you and our children, foolishly so perhaps, because when I saw Rudyard's name in the newspapers, I wanted him to know it. I'm sorry. I never thought he'd do such a thing, or believe Gabriel was his son. Rudyard's changed, Adam."

Adam's mouth twisted in a faint smile. "You always did believe the best in people."

"I believe the best in you," she whispered, her eyes full of tears. "You know Gabriel is your son, don't you? In your heart you must know?"

He sighed. "Yes, I think so. But it has been difficult to conquer the doubt. When he was young, I tried to believe, I really did, but . . . My father saw my difficulty and stepped in, giving Gabriel the childhood I should have done."

"Because he loved you. We all love you, Adam." She shook her head. "Do you really think Gabriel would have done what he did if he was Appleby's son? He is a Langley through and through, brave and strong and loyal."

Adam reached out to the letter on the table in front of him.

"Adam?" his wife whispered.

"I'm sorry," he groaned, "so sorry. I've been a selfish fool. When Appleby showed me that letter, I thought you must have written it because you regretted leaving him. I—"

"Hush." Again she put her hand over his. "Adam, marrying you was the best thing I ever did. I can never regret it."

He lifted her hand to his and pressed his lips fervently to her fingers.

"Now," his wife said firmly, "are you going to burn that wretched thing before it gets us into any more trouble?"

"Yes."

They watched the pages catch alight in the

hearth, curling and turning to ash. Soon there was nothing left to see. Sir Adam Langley and his wife sat and stared contentedly into the flames.

"You look rather well for someone who was supposed to be at death's door."

Gabriel opened his eyes and smiled. "Marietta."

"The same." His half sister sat down beside him on the garden seat, her fair hair dazzling in the sunshine. She was a beautiful woman, and a happy marriage had only enhanced her looks.

"Thank you," she said now, "for saving the club. Aphrodite would be lost without it."

"I don't think I did anything much," he said wryly, "except make a fool of myself."

"Nonsense. By all accounts you were extremely brave. They're even saying you stepped in front of Prince Albert to receive the wound meant for him."

Gabriel raised his eyebrows. "Good heavens, are they? I almost feel sorry for Appleby. He probably imagined he'd garner some sympathy, and now he's a would-be assassin."

"Sorry for Appleby!"

"I said 'almost.' "

"I suppose you'll be returning to Wexmoor Manor in darkest Devon, will you? I'm surprised to find you still in London."

"Madame has been very kind to me while I recovered from my wound."

"She's overjoyed to have the club reopening

again. She says the refurbishments will be finished by the end of the week. I think"—and she twinkled at Gabriel—"she's planning a little thank-you supper for you and your friend Miss Dupre."

Gabriel groaned and closed his eyes. "Not matchmaking."

"Why not? I heard you were fond of her."

"If there's wooing to be done, I'll do my own."

Marietta searched his face, suddenly serious. "Has Miss Dupre been back to see you since she returned to Surrey?"

"No. She did wait until the doctors declared me out of danger before she left. She wrote to me, however. A brief, one-page letter wishing me well. It sounded like a good-bye to me."

"And you're not going to accept that, are you, Gabriel?" Marietta said with a smile.

"Certainly not. I am planning to marry her."

And for once Marietta was speechless.

Chapter 34

The invitation had arrived last week, engraved in gold print with intricate curls about the borders. Antoinette opened it at the breakfast table and sat staring at the wording for so long that her sister grew tired of asking her what it said, and eventually came and stood behind her and read it for herself.

Madame Aphrodite requests Miss Antoinette Dupre attend an exclusive supper to celebrate the reopening of Aphrodite's Club.

There was also a note with it from Aphrodite, assuring her that the select gathering would be for friends only, and none of her girls would be present. It was a thank-you gift from Aphrodite to her friends, and she counted Antoinette as one of her very best friends.

"Are you going?" Cecilia asked. "You should go, Nette."

"I don't know."

Gabriel would be there. She had stayed away from him once she knew he was going to be all right, after Lord Appleby's attack. She hadn't wanted to go, but he had his family about him and he didn't need her. Best to cut herself off, she'd decided, and to return to her own life. There would be nothing worse than hanging about him and wearing out her welcome.

But now it seemed churlish to deny Aphrodite, who had been such a good friend to her. And surely there'd be plenty of other guests there. She could mingle in the crowd and stay well away from Gabriel. A quick hello and a smile and then it would be over.

He'd probably forgotten her anyway.

For Cecilia's benefit she forced a smile. She seemed to be forcing herself to smile a great deal these days. "I don't know if I need to go, Cecy."

"Yes, Nette, you do. You must go. I will be perfectly all right. You mustn't worry about me."

"Of course I don't worry about you."

But she did, and Cecilia knew it.

"Please go, Nette. I'll never forgive myself if you don't. We will all be waiting for you when you come back; it's not as if anything will change here. Nothing *ever* changes," she added, with a dissatisfied grimace.

"Do you miss Mayfair then?" Antoinette teased.

"No. Yes. I suppose I do, in a way. Sometimes it is very quiet here, Nette."

Cecilia was growing up. Soon she would want to fly the nest, meet people, live her own life. Antoinette would be alone, her life constant and unchanging. Now why did that depress her?

"I will go," she said, making a sudden decision. And once she said she would, there was no turning back.

London hadn't changed; it was just as noisy and busy and smelly as ever. She took a room at one of the finer hotels and arrived at Aphrodite's Club the afternoon of the supper, as requested.

Aphrodite met her at the door and hugged her.

"I am so happy to see you, Antoinette! Look, you see we have made changes."

Antoinette laughed and hugged her back. "I see you have a new door, Madame. The last time I was here it was hanging by a thread."

"Huh, Lord Appleby has much to answer for. Well, he is locked away now."

"And Lady Appleby? I have not heard much of what happened after . . . afterward."

"Didn't Gabriel tell you all the news, my dear?"

"I have not seen him, Madame. I have been at home in Surrey."

"Lady Appleby was living in the Mayfair house but she will probably have to sell it, to pay her husband's debts. Life is unfair, *oui*?"

"Very unfair. Love is unfair, Madame." Antoinette wondered where that had come from; it seemed Aphrodite was having her usual effect.

The courtesan sighed and shook her head at Antoinette, as if she were a hundred and Antoinette still a child. Perhaps, to a woman of her experience, that was how it seemed.

"Antoinette, does love frighten you? That is no way to be. You must seize life and hold on to it tightly, not hide away from it."

"Well, I have seized it, and I am here." Antoinette changed the subject before she could be further lectured to. "You asked for me to come early. What was it you wanted me to do, Madame?"

Aphrodite laughed. "Come, you will see."

"I don't like surprises," Antoinette said quickly.

"You will like this one," Aphrodite assured her, slipping her arm through Antoinette's, and leading her across the foyer.

Antoinette was beginning to wonder whether she had stepped into a dream. There was a modiste named Elena, whom Aphrodite called her oldest friend, and the two of them fussed about her and circled her, studying her figure and discussing her as if she wasn't there.

Antoinette shopped in London when she could, but most of her clothes were made by a seamstress in the village. She was happy with the arrangement, but Aphrodite was unimpressed by such provincial ways.

"A woman of your looks, Antoinette, should have only the best fabrics and styles."

"I don't know what you mean," Antoinette said, bewildered.

"You will see," the courtesan promised.

Elena was a little woman with a stern face and gray hair. "Yes, you are right, as always, Aphrodite," she said, ignoring Antoinette for the moment. "We will dress her in the white gown."

It was spoken so reverently, as if in capital letters. The White Gown.

"I don't understand." Antoinette looked between the two of them. She had the suddenly frightening thought that if she allowed them to dress her and change her, then she would be entering a glittering sensual world, a dangerous world, and there could be no going back. Nothing would ever be the same again.

As if she'd read her mind, Aphrodite touched her cheek and smiled. "Come, what can it hurt? It is one night, that is all. Indulge me, please. After, you can go back to your little house in the countryside."

"Do you always get your own way, Madame?" Antoinette asked wryly.

"Always!"

That was when Elena produced the white gown, and Antoinette understood their reverence.

Of the finest silk, it was low-cut at the bodice, tight at the waist, and flared out into soft folds and flounces over the hips. It was a dress for a fairy tale, and fairy tales frightened Antoinette.

She backed away. "No, really, I can't wear something like that. I—I would feel too—too exposed . . ."

"Psht, my dear. We are your friends. Why should you not show yourself off a little? I promise you will look beautiful. Gabriel will be speechless."

Gabriel, the one name she'd sworn not to think

of. She opened her mouth again to refuse, but instead found herself reaching out to touch the white gown with her fingertips. So soft, so smooth, so beautiful. It glowed like moonlight. What would *he* think of her in such a dress? Would he regret, even for a moment, that he had let her go so easily?

"Try it on," Elena tempted her, "and if you don't like it you need not wear it."

Antoinette didn't remember saying yes, but the next moment her clothing was being removed from her despite her protests and the white gown was drawn carefully over her head. The miles and miles of silk floated about her, slipping into place with such breathtaking ease that it was as if the dress had been made for her and her alone.

At last the two women stood back to inspect her, and their faces lit up with smiles. "Perfect," Aphrodite said. "Absolutely perfect."

"This is too generous of you, Madame. I can't—"

"Nonsense. I am bored and this is a diversion."

"Aphrodite, let the child look at herself," Elena scolded, and, taking Antoinette's hand, led her toward the end of the room, where a standing mirror had been turned to the wall. Elena pivoted it toward them with a flourish, and suddenly there Antoinette was, reflected and revealed.

She didn't think it was another woman; she wasn't that simple. It was definitely Antoinette Dupre. But it was the new Antoinette, the one she had heard in her head but had never actually seen before in the flesh. The silk clung to her curves, draped low on her rounded bosom, and complimented her little waist, before caressing the flare of her hips. And with so many folds and gathers, the silk, fine as it was, was not transparent.

Well, not quite. There was a flash here and there of naked flesh, but Antoinette hoped no one would notice in the dimly lit salon.

The two older women began to remove the pins from her hair, arranging it loosely about her shoulders. "There, you see," Elena murmured. "The natural look suits you. A wreath of flowers, perhaps. You are the goddess of the woods, Miss Dupre."

Nothing could have been better designed to win her over. Antoinette met the women's eyes in the mirror, and suddenly she knew this was what she wanted to do. She *had* changed, only she'd been afraid to acknowledge it until now. Gabriel and the events of her recent past had altered her and molded her, and the dress was the symbol of that change. She must wear it, just once, and Gabriel must see her in it.

"Enjoy yourself," Aphrodite murmured, as if she read her mind, and smiled. "I wish you well, my dear."

Gabriel stood in the famous salon and looked about him. The room was dazzling, with candles reflected in endless mirrors and elegant furnishings placed about the room; no doubt in normal circumstances it would have been occupied by el-

egant guests. A table held food, hot and cold suc-
culent treats, while champagne was chilling on
ice and waiting in sparkling glasses.

Gabriel took a sip of the champagne and sur-
veyed the food. He was hungry, and if Antoinette
didn't join him soon, he'd have to start without
her. His heart sank. Perhaps she wouldn't come.
Perhaps after all she'd been through she preferred
to stay away . . .

At that moment the doors opened behind him.
He turned, the champagne glass in his hand, and
beheld an ethereal vision of sensual beauty.

She was wearing white silk, the cloth draped
about her and clinging to all those wonderful
curves. Her glossy brown hair was loose about
her shoulders, framing her face, echoing the
glow of her eyes. As she moved toward him, the
gown flowed about her like mist, and he could
see her naked skin. Or was that just his hopeful
imagination?

"Champagne?" he offered, his eyes warm on
hers as he held out his glass.

Antoinette came toward him and he tried not
to groan aloud. She took the glass from him, her
fingers brushing his. After she sipped, she ran the
tip of her tongue over her lower lip, and Gabriel
knew he was lost.

"Antoinette, you are gorgeous."

She smiled. "So are you."

Gabriel was wearing black evening wear with
a crisp white shirt. He knew the austere look
suited him, made him appear more of a gentle-

man than she was probably used to after his roles as the highwayman and Coombe. Or was she flirting with him? As usual she made him feel off balance.

He cleared his throat. "Are you hungry, sparrow?"

"I am."

He filled a plate with morsels for her, before loading his own. They sat on one of the elegant couches and nibbled their food and drank their champagne. "I thought this was a party?" Antoinette said, glancing about at the splendor of the salon.

"It is. A party for two."

She looked surprised and then resigned. "Oh."

"Aphrodite's treat," he added, wondering if she was disappointed.

"Will there be music?" she said.

"Do you want to dance?" At once he was on his feet. "Will you dance with me, Miss Dupre?"

Antoinette hesitated, and then, as if making up her mind about something, she set down her plate and glass. "Yes, Mr. Langley, I will dance with you."

He gathered her in his arms and began to waltz her around the salon. Antoinette clung to him, feet flying, the room spinning. This was perfection. Why couldn't it have been like this the first time they met? Antoinette imagined dancing with a man and falling in love with him.

Her steps faltered.

The problem was that for her everything had happened the wrong way around. She'd given Gabriel her treasure, as Bridie called it, and then she'd fallen in love.

Gabriel's lips brushed her temple. They were barely moving now, swaying back and forth to imaginary music. His hand was warm and firm on the small of her back, and he drew her against his body so that she could feel every muscle with her soft curves.

"Look at me," he whispered.

She looked up, startled by the intensity in his voice.

"I love you," he said. "I want you with me always. I can't be without you, Antoinette."

Emotion welled up within her as she remembered the weeks she'd spent with him, the excitement and fear, the highs and lows. It felt like someone else. Life had returned to normal now, the days planned, her tasks set out like the columns and figures in her books, away into a future that was smooth and calm as a windless sea.

But she wanted a return to the turbulence, even if it made her a little seasick.

Her eyes stung and she blinked furiously. It wasn't fair. She had longed to get back to her home, and now she couldn't stop thinking about the past. And him. And just when she'd convinced herself they weren't meant to be, here he was, telling her he loved her.

His fingers brushed her cheek. He rested his brow against her hair and breathed in her scent with a sigh.

"Antoinette," he murmured, "my darling. I've missed you so much. Please tell me you've missed me, too, or I don't know what I'll do. I might have to abduct you and take you back to Devon with me."

Tears spilled down her cheeks. She tried to laugh but made a snuffly sound instead. "I've missed you, too, Gabriel."

"Ah, that's good." He nuzzled her cheek, lightly brushing his lips against her skin. She turned her face blindly, and their mouths touched and clung. Her arms slipped about his neck, and he drew her in against him, holding her body pressed to his.

"I know, before, we were at cross purposes," he went on, lifting his lips from hers. "I couldn't understand why I always knew you weren't the sort of woman to abide a man like Appleby."

"And I couldn't understand why I wanted to be with you despite knowing you were a highwayman."

"I do love you, Antoinette," he murmured. "Can we start again, this time without any secrets?"

She laughed and held him close. "I love you, too. And yes, please," she said.

"Then I think we should get married."

Epilogue

The *History of the Langleys of Devon* was not the sort of book Antoinette would normally pick up. She wasn't sure why she'd done so today.

She glanced at the clock on the mantel. Twenty more minutes until her assignation in the maze with her husband. Her mouth went dry at the thought of it, and him. Antoinette opened the book at random, the words a blur, to pass the time.

Antoinette and Gabriel were very happy. Every day was a wondrous adventure, and every day she thanked whatever unlikely chance had brought them together. Although there were times when he drove her to distraction, and no doubt she him, she wouldn't change a thing.

She blinked. There were names in the book, written in Sir John's neat hand, and for a moment Antoinette thought she was seeing things. *Dupre?* She adjusted her spectacles.

"Eleanor Dupre married to Robert Langley." The date was during the reign of King Charles II and the wedding had been celebrated here, at Wexmoor Manor.

Her wicked ancestress was called Eleanor Dupre. The woman for whom the king built Dupre House, the woman who ran away and married for love and vanished into the shadows of history.

Eleanor Langley.

Antoinette laughed; she couldn't help it.

"Talking to yourself, sparrow?" a warm voice said behind her, and a pair of strong arms slid around her.

"Gabriel, you've finished?" She turned to look up.

Gabriel took the opportunity to kiss her long and well. "Yes, I'm finished with the army of restoration experts," he said at last. "Or just about. I want Wexmoor Manor to be a crown fit for my precious jewel of a wife."

Gabriel said such delightful things.

"I thought we were going to have a tryst," she spoke softly, smiling into his eyes.

"We are. Why do you think I'm here?"

He took her hand and led her toward the door. Antoinette glanced back at the open book on the table.

"What is it?"

But Antoinette only smiled. "I'll tell you when we reach the heart of the maze," she promised, her fingers entwined with his.

It would be appropriate. She knew Gabriel would be amused and amazed, just as she was, that their meeting hadn't been chance after all. Their love was predestined, and if their ancestors had anything to do with it, so was their happiness.

Next month, don't miss these exciting new
love stories only from
Avon Books

Never Dare a Duke by Gayle Callen

Christopher Cabot is the perfect duke. His family's penchant for
scandal has proven to him the need to suppress his recklessness
and instead focus on leading an exemplary life. But the
unexpected appearance of a meddlesome yet beautiful woman at
his house party may undo all his hard work—especially if she
succeeds in uncovering his one secret.

Bedtime for Bonsai by Elaine Fox

An Avon Contemporary Romance

Pottery artist Dylan is starting a new life when he opens up his
own shop across the street from Penelope's store. While the
chemistry between them may be heating up, neither has any
illusions about the other: They are from different worlds. Until
Mr. Darcy, Penelope's mischievous dog, suddenly forges an
unbreakable connection between them.

The Abduction of Julia by Karen Hawkins

An Avon Romance

Julia Frant has secretly loved Alec MacLean, the wild Viscount
Hunterston, from afar. So when he accidentally snatches her
instead of her lovely, scheming cousin for an elopement to
Gretna Green, Julia leaps at the chance to make her passionate
dreams come true.

A Bride for His Convenience by Edith Layton

An Avon Romance

Lord Ian Sutcombe has no choice but to seek a marriage of
convenience and sets his sights on Hannah Leeds, a newly
wealthy merchant's daughter. They wed, and soon learn that
passion and desire and a commonality of interests force them to
know each other, yet their pride may prevent them from
discovering a once-in-a-lifetime love.

Avon Romances

the best in

exceptional authors and unforgettable novels!

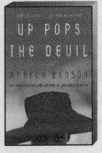